WHAT TO DO ABOUT EMMA

A New Zealand Mystery

Ilene Birkwood

ISBN: 1492988294
ISBN 13: 9781492988298

BUT WHAT TO DO ABOUT EMMA?   Ilene Birkwood

Other books by Ilene Birkwood:

Fiction:	Suddenly Silence
	Deadly Deception
Non-fiction:	The Second Torpedo
	Stress for Success

Prologue

*O*n Monday he decided to kill his wife.

Divorce was out of the question. The crazy divorce laws meant she would end up with half his hard-earned income. Half! The courts had too much discretion. They could award her a lump sum, maintenance for life, and even part of his pension. Outrageous! He had worked his guts out while she just sat around the house.

Things could change if she remarried, but fat chance of that. She'd just stay at home and feel sorry for herself. She would look so pathetic in court; sad little face, tears running down her cheeks, sagging shoulders, defeated air. The judge would glower at him and award her a huge settlement.

By Thursday, he had the perfect plan in place.

After he had perfected the plan, he sat lost in thought for a few minutes. She thought she had been a good wife. So he decided her life should end on a high note without any pain. As he wrote that objective, he smiled, his body relaxed. After all, what more could a woman want?

CHAPTER ONE

She'd made it! Dammit, she'd made it!

As Nicole sank into the overstuffed chair, a smile flickered across her face. Sunlight streamed through the open window and a light breeze carried the scent of camellias, daphne, and new-mown grass. She tilted her head into the cushioned comfort and looked up at the sturdy beams of the 100-year-old thatched cottage. The smile turned into a broad grin.

Two years ago, dumbfounded friends had waved goodbye to her at New Zealand's Auckland airport. Viewing with ill-concealed skepticism her plan to live in a small English village and become a Miss Marple – an improbable ambition for a recently widowed, 30-year-old, software consultant. It had been hard trading New Zealand's sun swept beaches for gray London sidewalks, but she had to get away. The other side of the world seemed a suitable solution.

With clothes whirring in the dryer and the house looking unnaturally tidy, she decided her aching bones deserved a cup of coffee. Leaving for work at 7:30 every morning and getting home at 7:00 pm left no time for chores in the week.

She jumped as the heavy knocker thudded on the door. "Yoo hoo, Nicki, it's just me." Her irrepressible neighbor's voice trilled through the open window. Nicole sprang up to open the door, brushing a damp errant curl from her forehead on the way.

Iris burst through the door. "Heard your Hoover going hours ago. Decided it was coffee break time. I've just baked some fresh scones, and the coffee's ready, so come on over." Without waiting for a response, she turned tail and led the way across the lawn and through the small gate that divided their properties.

An enthusiastic retriever greeted Nicole with lolling tongue and delighted eyes. She bent over and scratched behind his ears. He leaned against her leg, ecstatic, then bounded off after Iris. Once through the gate he was joined by a barking Jack Russell, and two exuberant pugs. A large white bulldog with a brown patch over one eye glanced in her direction and went back to sleep.

The smell of fresh baked scones and excellent coffee almost overwhelmed the smell of wet dog. The dog in question, a statuesque white poodle, looked disgusted with its damp state, and an orange tabby cat on the windowsill opened distrustful eyes that dared her to steal the silverware.

"Take a pew," Iris said, pouring coffee into two large ceramic mugs. She took a sip of coffee, deemed it too hot, set it down again and launched into a long explanation of the facilities available in the village, richly embellished by tidbits of scandal. As Nicole swallowed the last piece of a deliciously crumbly scone and wondered how soon she could get away, the doorbell rang.

Iris hopped up and opened the door. "Come on in, Emma. I've just made a cup of coffee. I'll pop those plants down here for the time. Thanks a bunch, I need some more flowers."

A small woman with doe-like eyes and wisps of hair escaping from her swept back brown hair came in but stopped in her tracks at the sight of Nicole. Pink suffused her face as she stammered, "But you've got company." She turned ready to bolt.

Iris blocked her way. "No stay and have a coffee. I want you to meet my new neighbor, Nicki."

"But, I'm all messy. I can't." She glanced down at her jeans, which had small earth smudges, and suddenly seemed to remember she held the tray of plants. She looked around frantically.

Nicole leapt to her feet and took it from her. "Hello, Emma. Pleased to meet you. Do come in – I was just leaving. I'm in the middle of my housework."

Emma's face, a picture of gratitude, looked up at Nicole. For the first time in her life, at 5'4", Nicole felt tall. "Thank you, Nicki. Please don't leave on my account. I just popped by with these. I'm all dirty. I can't stay. Please enjoy your coffee." She turned imploring eyes on Iris.

"Nonsense," boomed Iris. "Come and sit down the pair of you, there's plenty of room." She pushed the retriever and two pugs out of the way.

Noticing Emma looking down at hands smudged with earth, she added, "Go wash your hands in the bathroom and have a cup of coffee." Emma scuttled off to do as she was told. She returned a few moments later with freshly combed hair and sat on the edge of a chair.

Tiny waves of coffee broke over the edge of Emma's coffee cup as she clutched the saucer. She listened attentively to the conversation but said little. When Iris or Nicole made a joke, her brow furrowed. But the moment the other one laughed, she joined in. Eager to please.

"What time do you leave Monday, Emma?" Iris asked.

"Three thirty from Heathrow."

"Where are you going?" Nicole asked. "Off on holiday somewhere nice?"

"Bermuda."

"Wow! Great. How long will you be gone?"

Nicole's eyes widened when Emma said, "About six months."

"Her husband's a technical hotshot and compiles data for the seminars he gives in the States," Iris added. "He decided he can work just as easily in Bermuda as here during the winter."

"That's great," Nicole said.

"In fact," Iris interjected, "she's giving a farewell tea party tomorrow."

"It's not much of a party," Emma insisted. "I just used up all my baking supplies – they'd be wasted otherwise – and the women at the WI came up with the idea of a party."

Iris laughed. "The WI is the Women's Institute. They always bully Emma into doing things."

"They don't. I like to help," Emma protested.

"Anyway, do come," Iris insisted, quite oblivious to the fact that she was not the hostess. "Emma is the most incredible cook – yummy fruit cake."

Color suffused Emma's face and crept down her neck. "W-would you like to?"

She seemed surprised when Nicole agreed.

Nicole pulled on her jacket and ran out to Iris's car. Ten minutes later they drew up beside imposing stone pillars. The iron gates swung slowly open to reveal a pebble driveway leading to the solid complacency of a Georgian house. Iris tapped four times in quick succession on the solid oak door and trilled, "Hello, Emma, it's Iris."

A few minutes later a flushed Emma opened the door and beamed in genuine delight when she saw Nicole. "I'm so glad you came. Do come in and get out of the cold."

Emma ushered them into a living room where a fire blazed in the grate. Flustered, she touched the sofa. "Please sit down. I'll just pop into the kitchen and make tea."

A table placed in front of the conservatory was laid with a sparkling white linen tablecloth and covered with a full-scale afternoon tea. A large round fruit cake held pride of place surrounded by sausage rolls, cheese sticks, fruit tarts, a Swiss roll, chocolate fancies, and wafer thin sandwiches cut into small oblongs.

Nicole followed Emma out to the kitchen to help carry in the tea things. The kitchen was cozy with flowery drapes, and fresh herbs on the window sill. As Emma began to pour hot water into the teapot, the doorbell rang. She looked startled, but Iris's reassuring voice shouted, "Don't worry Emma, I'll let them in."

By the time the tea was prepared, several women had arrived and the level of voices grew. While everybody talked at the top of their voices and had a good time, Emma fluttered around non-stop making sure everyone had full tea cups and enough to eat.

At the end of the party, they all bundled out into the chilly early evening air amid a chorus of "Thanks Emma," "Have a good trip," "Great cake," "Thanks for coming." A dark blue BMW drew up and a tall, handsome man in a tailored suit stepped out. He stopped a moment, surveyed the unruly gathering, and then with a wide charming smile swooped over and kissed them all on the cheek leaving delighted blushes behind him.

Nicole watched from the front seat of the car as Iris revved up, gave him an airy wave, and then accelerated out of the driveway ahead of the crush. "Who was he?"

"That's Adrian. Emma's husband."

"Oh!" Nicole's eyebrows shot up.

Iris, swinging around a tight bend, laughed. "Yes. He is a bit of a surprise."

"How on earth does that marriage work?"

"They married very young before he was successful. Now she's too scared to entertain his business associates, poor dear. Wonder he doesn't trade her in for a younger model like they all do these days."

Outraged, Nicole exclaimed, "For heaven's sakes, he wouldn't dump poor little Emma would he?"

"No way. He still loves Emma to bits. You should see them together. He's very protective."

The car wandered over the center line as Iris talked. An oncoming car flashed its lights and honked. "Road hog!" Iris yelled.

CHAPTER 2

*H*e watched her car disappear around the corner, then checked each room to make sure the cleaner had left.

In the stillness of the empty house, he went to his office and pulled out a file marked 'Forward Planning'. A pleasant bubble of amusement warmed him. No way would she be interested in his business files. Her disinterest always annoyed him, but this time it would be her undoing.

Plan in hand, he headed for the living room, settled in an easy chair, and began to read. For two whole weeks he had fought the temptation to reread the plan. Experience had taught him, you need fresh eyes to catch the flaws.

Two deep lines above his nose marred his handsome features as he narrowed his eyes to read. He knew he should wear his glasses, but even in private they made him feel old. He scanned the document. It looked good. Difficult to find anything that would point the finger of suspicion in his direction. He walked into the kitchen and poured himself a glass of wine. With a satisfied sip, he carried it back to the living room, sat down and read the plan again. No question it was a winner. The perfect murder. No clues. No one would know what had happened to her. The smug smile waned. He took a healthy sip of wine, swallowed and reflected.

His role as the devoted husband must be flawless. So far, it had gone well, but he needed to be more careful. The husband was always the police's prime suspect.

He'd take an interest in her garden. Surprise her with an unexpected lavish lunch rather than work around the clock. Buy her expensive gifts. What's more he needed to pay attention to her bimbo friends. He sighed. Making conversation with those stay-at-homes whose major achievements in life seemed confined to a quilt they had made or the number of pounds they had lost since Christmas was difficult. But charm them he would. When the police talked to them, they all had to recoil in disbelief at the thought that he could be involved.

CHAPTER 3

Nicole picked up a wicker basket and took the short walk to the village shopping center; a narrow street, anchored at each end by a pub. One, a rather up market modernized building, sported an impressive sign *The Angry Boar* and a row of colorful flower-filled tubs out front. The other, whose faded, barely discernible sign announced *The Kings Head*, had a roof that sagged under the weight of the centuries, creaky boards and mismatched wooden seats around scratched tables. This one was packed to the gills.

She wandered along, stopped to buy fresh fruit and vegetables, and looked in the photographer's window. The photos of self-conscious brides and terrified grooms stared back at her, and a furtive little card in the corner of the window said, "Passport photos". In the newsagents where she picked up a weekend copy of the Telegraph, two small boys, knuckles white around their pocket money, surveyed the magnificent array of candies in a fidget of indecision.

Getting past the hardware store, which spilled its contents out onto the sidewalk, was a fascination rather than a challenge. Each week it displayed a bin of sale goods extraordinary in their uselessness. Clothes pegs in a wild variety of colors, flip flops in January, strange Chinese-made toys that barked or quacked, spanners, and an assortment of cleaning devices that defied the imagination. Moving on past bustling shoppers, she reached her favorite bakery. Squaring her shoulders, and remembering Oscar Wilde's "I can resist anything but temptation", she purchased a crunchy brown loaf, two Eccles cakes and two apple turnovers, their flaky pastry oozing apple and cream.

Arms full of groceries, she pushed the garden gate open with her rear end, and headed for the front door. She only made it half way along the garden path.

"Hello Nicki. Finished your shopping?" Iris's head popped up from behind the laurels that separated their properties.

"Yes. Just going to put them away and have a cuppa."

"Take your time. But how about a walk on the heath in an hour? Might rain later."

"Okay, sounds good." Nicole put down the groceries, unlocked the door, called, "See you at two, Iris" and shot inside before Iris started a long conversation.

Forty minutes later, Nicole, Iris and the golden retriever, strode down the Roman road on the way to the heath. A canopy of trees diffused the light and the impenetrable thicket of hawthorn lining the road deadened the sound of traffic. In the cathedral hush and half-light they walked in silence, relishing the feel of treading where sandal- clad legions had marched before.

At the end of the road, they turned along a little path that led across the heath. The sandy yellow path wound its way through the heather, brambles, tall grasses and occasional trees. The wind, carrying the smell of mud and stinging nettles, whipped their cheeks, and small white clouds scudded across a clear blue sky.

"So where's Martin today?" Iris and Martin walked together most Saturday mornings.

"He's staying at our pied-a-terre in London."

"So why aren't you up there having a wild weekend on the town?"

"No chance. He's dealing with a messy divorce case; a broker got a bit too chummy with his French secretary. Told his wife he needed to go to Paris to clinch a deal once too often. So she's divorcing him and is going to end up with a very lucrative settlement. At least, she will if Martin lives up to his reputation."

As they negotiated their way past a low-lying boggy patch, the retriever – up until this point a model of good behavior – flung himself into a large muddy puddle and wallowed gleefully.

Iris laughed. "Bath for you as soon as you get home."

Still puzzled by Martin's stay in London, Nicole persisted, "But why does Martin have to stay on the weekend?"

"The divorcee could only get away to see him on Friday and Martin likes to compile all the information immediately. Can't stand having me around. Says I distract him. Even when I go out shopping all day, he says I come home in the evening and clatter around getting him dinner. He likes to get his head down and put the whole case together the minute he has the information. He lives on takeaways."

"So he'll be back tonight?"

"Doubt it. He called just now and said it looks particularly sticky so he'll probably stay over."

They labored up a hill and were rewarded by the sight of the entire heath spread out before them. Wild and open to the elements, criss-crossed by meandering yellow paths, it conjured up memories of Tess of the D'Urbervilles and other tragic heroines. Looking at the muted winter colors, Nicole longed for the spring blaze of yellow gorse and purple heather.

She stood wondering why Martin needed to be alone to work. Why would it bother him having Iris there at night? Seemed strange.

Exhilarated after the walk, Nicole felt ready to tackle the mail. Standing at the kitchen table, she flipped through, tossing adverts in the bin and putting bills on a small table in the corner. Delighted, she came across a postcard from her mother. The picture on the front showed her small mother, wreathed in smiles, sitting on a truculent camel beside a bewildered-looking guide. In the background the pyramids loomed. The brief message, written in an immaculate hand, said they were having a blast in Egypt, had sailed down the Nile, visited two pyramids and slept out under the stars. Nicole laughed and shook her head. Where would that crazy mother of hers go next?

After thirty five years of marriage, she had deserted Nicole's father and run off with a man not much older than her daughter. Since then, she had traveled constantly. Stlll chuckling, Nicole remembered how outraged she had been initially – angry at her mother's ridiculous behavior, but mainly saddened for her confused father. However, after the first bewildered shock had passed, his reaction amazed her. He calmly stated he was going to move to Tauranga and live in their beachside cabin. He intended to live on the beach, and spend his time fishing and painting. She had a sneaking suspicion that was something he had always wanted to do.

Thinking of her father reminded her she hadn't checked for phone messages. She hit the play button to be greeted by Jan's voice. Jan had been her friend since high school. On their first day at the new school, Jan, gawky, with knobbly knees protruding below her skirt, and Nicole, overweight and painfully shy, bonded. Faced with the over-confident girls from St. Heliers with their turned up noses, it was a simple question of survival.

Jan's voice, as always filled with laughter, said, "How about coming to Seattle for a couple of weeks in March? Cliff and I can take some time off. It would be a blast. Give me a call."

Nicole felt a pang of guilt. Jan had been bugging her to visit their new home in Seattle for almost a year. She sighed. If I do, it will all start again - that constant campaign to get me to remarry.

But Jan had been such a good friend, she must do it. Somehow she just had to put the past behind her. Squaring her shoulders and clenching her jaw, she decided to go.

She hadn't had a vacation for over two years. Somehow all the tempting trips to Paris, Lake Como and the Austrian Alps had no appeal without Jay. Having fun with Jan and Cliff might just be a good idea.

CHAPTER 4

"**G**ODDAMIT!" Adrian flung his phone down on the cream leather sofa. An alarmed lizard scurried up the wall.

Emma's cookery book thudded to the floor. "What is it dear?"

Adrian stomped over to the window, grasped the sandstone sill with white knuckles, and looked sightlessly at Bermuda's azure blue sky. He wheeled around, his face red. "It's Tyler." He ran a hand through his hair in a fast, furious gesture. "He wants me to start the tour in three weeks. THREE WEEKS!" he screamed and headed for the study.

Arms wide across the doorway, he stopped. His eyes moved from stack to stack of piled documents that lined two walls. Each one a column of reports at the bottom, followed by an untidy mix of bound and unbound reference papers, then neat pages of typed notes. All anchored by hefty reference tomes.

Nine stacks in all. As his gaze traveled slowly from one to the other an icy lump of cold dread extinguished the fury of his earlier outburst. His shoulders slumped and he shook his head fighting back tears. It was impossible. He couldn't do it.

Behind him, Emma fluttered. "Come and have a cup of tea, Adrian, it will make you feel better." The magic cup of tea. From death to major disaster, tea was the antidote. Biting his lip, he managed a weak smile. "Okay, I'll be right there."

He followed her to the living room and flopped down in a chair. Emma placed a small maple table shining with polish close to his elbow and carried a cup of tea to the strategically placed coaster. His stomach lurched at the sight of the proffered homemade shortbreads. They drank in silence for several minutes and he knew from Emma's worried glances that he should explain but he felt too gutted to even try. She'd never understood what he did, and he just couldn't face trying to explain the problem now. What a useless wife she'd turned out to be. He sighed.

After he refused more tea, she ventured, "Does this mean we'll only have another three weeks in Bermuda?"

"Yes," he grunted through clenched teeth.

He strode over to the hall stand and picked up his keys. "I'm going to see Clay." Clay would be a good sounding board and more importantly a companion while he had a stiff drink. Battling the mixture of fury and despair that engulfed him, he took a deep breath, returned to the living room and placed a soft kiss on Emma's forehead. "That tea's made me feel much better." Making his way to the door, he added, "As soon as I've worked out what to do, I'll let you know the dates so that you can book a flight home."

"I'm sure you'll work it out in no time." She smiled encouragingly.

Outside the warm air, carrying the heady smell of jasmine and hibiscus, buffeted his cheeks as he mounted his scooter. He skidded out of the driveway and headed for town. In spite of the restriction of one car per family, the narrow road was crowded. Someone in the oncoming traffic waved but he ignored them, eyes on the road.

Steve, in the hotel bar, polished black face grinning over a startlingly white shirt, greeted him. "What will it be?"

Adrian glanced out the window and saw Clay sitting in his usual corner of the terrace. "Two Tom Collins, Steve." He handed over his Visa. "Might as well set up a tab."

"Okay, I'll bring them right out."

Adrian made his way through small tables, shaded by red-striped umbrellas. Edged by tubs of bright geraniums, the terrace overlooked a perfect semi-circle of pink sand lapped by translucent blue water. Toward the horizon long Atlantic rollers fragmented themselves into shards of white spray as they beat against the reef.

"Hello, Adrian old son. Who let you out of your cage this early?"

"Just the need for a good strong drink."

Clay's eyes flickered over Adrian's face. "Take a pew. Life will look better through the bottom of a glass." He looked up. "And here comes Steve, right on cue. He's got an uncanny knack, that lad, of knowing when a drink is really needed."

Steve set down a dish of nuts, napkins, and two tall frosted glasses. Bobbling on top of each glass were ice cubes, a cherry and orange slices. Wordless, Adrian picked up his drink, clicked Clay's glass and took a long deep pull. The delicious lemony gin slid down his throat.

Clay polished off his gin and tonic, then sipped the Tom Collins. "Mm, good." He pushed back his chair. "So what's the problem? Emma giving you a hassle?"

"No. It's that bloody Tyler. The idiot who sets up the lecture tour. He's just told me I have to be ready to go in three weeks."

"Three weeks! You're joking. You've got another three months here haven't you?"

"That's what I planned. I reckoned I'd have the pitch completed in a month, then have a couple of months scuba diving and fishing."

"This is serious. Your handicap will go to blazes if you don't get in a bunch of games soon. All this work's going to reduce you to the point where even I can beat you." He nibbled a handful of nuts and took a reflective sip of his drink. "Why the sudden rush?"

"It's the darned economy."

"What's that got to do with it?"

"Tyler's getting resistance from companies. They don't want to be seen sending executives on expensive boondoggles." He paused and ran his finger around the frosted glass leaving a small wet trail. "His brilliant idea is to do the tour in two pieces. One right away and a follow-up in six months or so. That way they'll have a cheaper tab to pick up. But in two pieces they'll probably end up paying more in the long run."

"Clever. Less outlay initially keeps the shareholders happy. Then another installment later in the year that no one will notice."

Adrian exhaled in disgust. "But I have to completely rethink my game plan." He aimed a kick at the empty chair next to him. "And all at the speed of light."

Clay's brow furrowed. "Maybe it's not so tough." He paused and watched a couple walk along the beach. The woman appealingly clad in a skimpy bikini that revealed a perfectly toned body covered by an even tan. His smile took ten years off his age. "Another fine product of the hotel gym."

Glancing at Adrian's almost empty glass, he whirled a finger in Steve's direction and the ever-vigilant bartender emerged five minutes later with a tray bearing two more Tom Collins.

Clay pulled a pen out of his shirt pocket, spread a napkin on the table and asked, "So what are the issues?"

"I prepare a presentation that gives execs a potted version of all the latest technologies. This takes several months and I still need another six weeks to polish it off. Then I'd normally take a break since I've been going flat out for weeks."

"So?"

"That damn Tyler wants a shorter version in three weeks and the rest toward the end of the year."

Clay paused a moment, pen poised. "So issue number one is how do you break it into two and have it make sense." He scribbled for a moment, and then asked, "Do you have everything summarized?"

"Yes, all the major technologies – not ready for presentation, but all the info distilled. However, I still have to hit the issue of the emerging areas. These are the technologies that pop up and bite a CEO in the bum if he's not up to speed."

"I think you just solved your first problem. Give them the stuff you have ready, and tell them just what you told me about the emerging stuff. That should have them running back for the next one."

Adrian heaved a huge sigh of relief. Good old Clay – he used to be the industry's darling until he made so much money he decided it was more fun to pickle his brain in alcohol. They sat together for another hour sipping and working as the sun dropped towards the ocean, suffusing the sky with a pink that matched the crescent of sand in the cove.

Adrian looked at his watch. "Heck, it's past dinner time. I'd better get home before I ruin Emma's meal."

Clay downed the last of his drink. "Okay, old son. I'll get us a taxi while you park your scooter out of the way. I'll drop you off on the way home."

As Clay dozed on the way home, Adrian began to feel good. With an approach to the problem mapped out, he felt confident he could have his pitch ready in time. Of course, it would mean working round the clock for the next three weeks but hard work had never bothered him. He relaxed back against the leather seat and smiled. When he hit New York he'd give Caleb and Cindy a call, a couple he'd met in the hotel. They'd had a really good time together over the Christmas holiday, and they'd urged him to call next time he was in New York. A night out with them would set him up for the tour. Caleb was good fun and that Cindy was something else.

CHAPTER 5

Adrian checked himself in the full-length hotel bedroom mirror, picked a speck of lint off his navy blue suit and adjusted his tie. Smoothing back his hair, he practiced a confident smile and then launched into the first few lines of his presentation.

He rode down in an elevator that smelled of burger and fries and strode across to the huge auditorium. He ran up the steps to the stage and smiled in acknowledgement of the light applause that followed his introduction.

"Good afternoon, ladies and gentlemen. I am going to give you a swift overview of the latest technologies. I'll try not to bore you too much. I remember well the speaker who continued with his over-long presentation as one by one the audience drifted out of the door until only one man was left sitting in the front row. Bemused, the speaker asked 'Sir, I can't help noticing you are the only person left. Why have you stayed?'

"I'm the next speaker.'"

The audience tittered and relaxed, and Adrian launched into his pitch. It went well and after fielding twenty minutes of questions, he was asked to make way for the next speaker.

On his way out, he bumped into a consultant he knew from last year's circuit. "Adrian! How about dinner tonight at Michael's? It's just along the road from the hotel, and a bunch of us are going. Seven thirty suit you?"

"Yes, sure. That'd be great." Dinner with a group of the regulars on the circuit was always good fun. With their pitches out of the way, they were all ready for a few drinks and a lot of laughs.

He wound his way through the tables in the crowded seafood restaurant. Taking one of the few empty chairs at the reserved table, he looked across the table at a hugely overweight man. Belly pressed against the table, the man extended his hand. "Peter Helger."

Hand crushed by the other man's giant fist, Adrian knew the name. A leading authority on computer forensic science. Good, he could pump him for information. Adrian smiled over his extended hand and introduced himself. As he leaned across the table, he saw with a start Cindy smiling at him from several places farther down. What on earth is she doing here? When he had tried calling Caleb in New York, they had been away.

After dinner, he discovered she had given a presentation earlier. Apparently, she was an expert on how to retain your best contributors. As she said over a nightcap in the hotel bar, "The real hotshots are prima donnas and everyone is out to poach them. So how do you keep them happy?" She laughed as she downed the last sip of her Chardonnay. "It's always worth the effort. . . well managed prima donnas make you look awfully good."

Dressed in a conservative white sheath dress with a simple pendant that probably cost as much as his car, she looked terrific. He found her fascinating. In Bermuda, wearing casual clothes, he had taken her for a trophy wife. Now here she is the complete professional. They sat for over an hour laughing about Christmas in Bermuda and discussing the audiences they had just faced. She checked her watch. "I really must go to bed now or I'll be a wreck in the morning. I need to catch the 6:30 a.m. flight to Atlanta."

"Really!" Adrian tried to suppress his delight. "You mean you're doing the tour?"

"Yes, indeed." She planted a light kiss on his cheek. "Now I must be off to my room to talk to Caleb before he turns in."

Ouch! A none too subtle reminder. She's married.

❖

Arriving home on Friday evening, sticky and tired, Nicole stripped off her suit and changed into jeans and T- shirt. After checking the mail, she looked at the naked refrigerator shelves, checked the freezer, shrugged her shoulders and flopped into her favorite chair. A glance at the old grandfather clock that ticked comfortingly in the corner told her it was six thirty. She leaned back pondering what delicacy she could whip up from the isolated items in the freezer - frozen spinach and peas. She rested her head back and closed her eyes.

Half an hour later, Emma rang. "Would you like to join me for a dinner Nicki? I always cook too much for myself, and I'd love some company."

"That's great. Thanks. I'll be right over." Emma, back from Bermuda, frequently asked her over. She found the shy little woman a wonderfully relaxing companion. Emma fussed around, feeding her and asking her how the week had gone. She wondered why on earth Adrian didn't take her along on his seminar tour. With all the travel and nervous energy of major presentations, Emma's soothing presence would have made sense. But Adrian worried about her sitting in strange cities in a hotel room every day. Nicole had to admit he had a point. Emma didn't seem the type who could cope with busy foreign cities.

After dinner, Emma hauled out her photograph album and showed Nicole the delightful little villa she rented in Bermuda. Then, growing a little pink, she showed shots of Adrian playing golf, in scuba diving gear, and holding up a massive fish. He looked just as handsome in casual clothes as he had when she had seen him as Iris drove away from Emma's house. Even in that fleeting glance he had looked vaguely familiar, but as Emma showed even more photos she became convinced she had seen him before. But where?

"Emma, don't you find it lonely in Bermuda? It sounds as if Adrian is either stuck in the study, or dashing off fishing and golfing when he's finished working."

"Oh, no. I enjoy puttering around the house, cooking and growing things. I can't do any gardening there – that's all taken care of by the gardeners – but I have some wonderful pot plants." She looked wistful. "I hope someone's looking after them now I'm gone."

When Emma showed her a photo of Adrian addressing a huge audience in Amsterdam, Nicole suddenly remembered where she had seen him before.

"There were two thousand people in the audience," Emma said, her voice full of pride. "An international meeting on something or other. Doesn't he look handsome?"

"Wow. What an audience. Yes, he's a handsome man." But as she said it, Nicole had a nasty feeling in her stomach. At a conference in Los Angeles, when she had delivered a package of information backstage she overheard a speaker giving a tongue lashing to some poor, unfortunate woman. She couldn't hear what was being said but the woman cringed away from him, and Nicole caught sight of his reddened face, and heard words coming from between thin lips. Not wanting to add to the woman's embarrassment, she had slipped away unseen by Adrian.

Ten minutes later she had seen him walk onto the stage, beam benevolently at the audience and launch into his pitch. She was soon laughing at his witticisms and hanging on his words like every other member of the audience. Had she been seeing things earlier? She shrugged it off as pre-speaking nerves. Now, listening to Emma gush about her clever husband, she was worried.

She rose reluctantly from the comfy sofa. "It's time I was going. I have an early start tomorrow." As she put on her coat, she added, "Thanks for a great meal. Your casseroles are something else."

Emma blushed slightly and murmured, "I'll have to cook something special next time."

"I almost forgot to tell you," Nicole said, "I'm off to Seattle in a couple of weeks to visit my Kiwi buddies. My project is wrapping up, so I'm going to take a break before they rope me into something else."

Emma gave her a warm hug. "Take care of yourself. Time you had a break. Don't forget to send a postcard."

CHAPTER 6

Adrian walked along the soulless hotel corridor, found his room, pushed back the drapes and looked over the roof tops to the shining expanse of ocean. Methodically checked his presentation materials to make sure nothing had disappeared in mid-flight and headed for the shower. The hot water pounding on his shoulders loosened his tight muscles and washed away the grubby travel feeling, but did nothing to lift his depression.

He felt like a kid at the end of summer vacation. He should be flying high. Only one more presentation and he would be going home for a well-earned vacation. He knew he needed one; cutting short his Bermuda trip had meant nothing but non-stop work for over six-months. With no idea where to go and what to do, it didn't help at all. Why? He pushed the thought away, knowing he must keep his head clear before his presentation.

A few minutes later he was buttoning a shirt still crisp from the dry cleaners' packaging. He decided on the gray suit for his talk. With its faint silver stripe echoed in his burgundy tie, it gave him the right look. He surveyed his reflection in the mirror, smoothed back his hair, and adjusted his tie.

After a swift email check, he sat down to relax for half an hour before going to the auditorium. Two minutes later he was on his feet, walking around the hotel room, looking out at the view and checking the breakfast menu. He tried sitting down again. Picked up his book, read a few pages without registering what he was reading, then wandered around the room once more. Looked in the mini bar, riffled through the What to Do in San Diego booklet, then sat down. Finally, he just gave in and paced up and down.

Twenty minutes later, he strode out of the elevator, and heels clicking on the marble surface of the lobby, made his way to the auditorium.Surrounded by a gratifying number of people after his presentation, Adrian fielded questions -giving each person his full attention, and all the women an engaging smile. Listening to an extraordinary looking man who sported small wire-rimmed glasses and a moustache like Adolf Hitler, he caught sight of Cindy sweeping through the reception area deep in conversation with a tall man in an immaculate suit. A thunderbolt struck him. That's why he had that end of vacation feeling. He wouldn't be seeing Cindy anymore.

They'd shared several dinners together with the other pre-senters and frequently lingered afterwards over a cup of coffee. Their conversations ranged far and wide over the business scene, and when he had explained the problems he anticipated with follow-on presentations, she made two excellent suggestions. How different from Em who couldn't understand what he did, and showed little inclination to learn.

He shook his head and laughed at himself. I'm starting to think like one of those ridiculous men who chat women up with the line "My wife doesn't understand me." With a heartfelt sigh he realized time spent with Cindy made him understand what he was missing.

Almost every evening they'd had dinner with the other pre-senters, but on one memorable night in New Orleans they snuck away and hit all the bars listening to some incredible jazz. It had felt like playing hooky from school. They'd soaked up the jazz and giggled like school kids.

But Cindy would probably be flying out on the red eye later tonight. He would not see her again. Dragging his attention back to the earnest man who was expounding his theory on where the industry was going, he managed to agree with a reassuring smile.

After a few more questions he made his escape and decided to find a quiet spot somewhere to make a few phone calls.

In the far corner of the restaurant, he ordered a hot tea and a slice of carrot cake. That should hold him until dinner time. His flight didn't leave until tomorrow so he might as well eat with a client. He dug in his pocket for the card some electronics CEO had given him but pulling it out, he stopped and stared at it deep in thought. On an impulse he called Cindy's number. Maybe she wasn't leaving until very late and they could grab a quick drink together before she left. The phone rang and moved to her voice mail.

"Cindy, it's Adrian. I was hoping we could get together for a quick drink before you head home." He paused, watched the waitress taking an order four tables away, then added, "Any chance you could make dinner? I know a dynamite place on the seafront. The fish dishes are superb."

Feeling like an anxious teenager, he pocketed his phone, dangled his tea bag in the not-hot-enough water and looked up to see Tyler, the tour organizer, heading in his direction.

When he returned to his room at seven o'clock, the light beside his bed was blinking. He hit the messages button and was delighted to hear Cindy say, "Eight o'clock suit you? I'll meet you in the lobby near reception."

Humming, he stripped off his clothes and headed for the bathroom. After a quick shower and a careful shave, he slapped a discreet amount of Polo aftershave on his chin. Donning casual slacks, open-necked shirt, and a zip-up sweater, he admired himself in the mirror. Okay, dinner time.

He headed for the lobby and selected a deep leather chair beside a massive display of flowers. Cindy arrived ten minutes later. Right on time – something else he liked about her. No being late and making a dramatic entrance. She laughed when she saw him. He grinned back and said, "Snap." She, too, was in casual clothes. Cream slacks and a gray silk shirt. He had seen her earlier in a hip hugging black dress. Laughing, arm-in-arm, they headed for the restaurant opting to walk along the seafront. It felt good to be out in the open after the long day in an air-conditioned building full of people.

It was a mild night with the gently moving air full of salt. Lights bobbed on the harbor and far out by the harbor mouth a blast on a ship's siren sounded. A faint smell of drying seaweed flavored the air. Within ten minutes they arrived at a small restaurant with oars and spars around the walls and a long bar decorated with ships' wheels. Above their heads, a wooden ship's figurehead in the shape of Helen of Troy loomed – undoubtedly a fake, but impressive.

She ate a green salad while he enjoyed Oysters Rockefeller, and they both opted for lobster thermidor to follow. Sipping a decent bottle of chilled white wine they spent the evening laughing over the day's presentations, and talking about nothing and everything. Declining dessert, they drank espressos.

"Well, this is it. Tour's over."

"What will you do now?" Cindy asked.

"My flight leaves about noon. Then it's a few days at home to clear up bits and pieces. After that some vacation time – probably three weeks or so – before I start research for my next round of talks." He rolled the stem of his glass between thumb and first finger and looked over at her. "I'm going to miss our chats."

Cindy avoided his eyes and studied the pattern on her coffee cup. "I've a bunch of things to do when I get back to New York. Caleb wants to entertain some clients so I'm going to have to get the house shipshape and organize some functions . . ." Her voice trailed off.

Around them, waiters were clearing tables and the last of the diners were leaving. "I think we'd better head back to the hotel before they start sweeping under our feet," Adrian said.

Cindy looked around, smiled, turned back to him to give a retort and caught his eye. She picked up her purse, Adrian signed the tab, and wordless they walked out of the restaurant.

Outside the air was still balmy and puddles of orange light illuminated the seafront. They walked back to the hotel, their pace faster than their earlier walk. The hotel lobby was quiet. Most of the guests had signed out, or were in their rooms preparing for an early departure. They walked into the elevator and Cindy punched the button for the fourth floor. Adrian stood beside her. Two other men, deep in conversation, joined them and hit the eighth floor button. As the elevator pinged to a standstill on the fourth floor, Cindy stepped out and Adrian followed. "My mother always told me a gentleman should see his lady friend safely home."

Cindy merely looked at him. When she reached room 422, she inserted her plastic key, the little green light winked, and she entered, holding the door open for him. He followed, she turned toward him and they came together in a simultaneous moment. Scattering clothes behind them they made for the bedroom.

Adrian woke up in tangled, sweaty sheets as the bedside clock flashed 3:20 am, rolled over and saw Cindy lying there. Mussed hair, smeared makeup, she still looked beautiful. He lightly brushed a strand of hair from her eyes, lay back with a contented sigh, and fell into a dead sleep.

Light seeped in around the blinds when he next awoke. With a start he took a quick look at the clock and then rolled over. Cindy might have an early flight. He had until noon so he could enjoy a leisurely breakfast. Man, he felt hungry. But the bed was empty and the sheets cold. He smiled indulgently; she'd beaten him to the shower.

Arms behind his head, he lay back and waited for her to emerge. The minutes ticked by. No water running. Oh well, women take ages in the bathroom. She must be putting on her makeup. Fifteen minutes passed. Curious, he climbed out of bed and listened at the bathroom door. Complete silence. He pushed and the door opened, revealing an empty bathroom. Empty of all signs of toiletries. Nothing in the bedroom other than his clothes neatly folded on a chair. Worried, he rushed to the closet. Empty. She had left. He looked around the desk and the bedside table. No note. Nothing. She'd gone.

CHAPTER 7

Adrian's legs hurt, his head pounded, and he could feel a massive blister on his right foot. He looked around. Where on earth was he? A quick glance at his watch told him it was three hours since he left the hotel. He screwed up his eyes against the throbbing headache and looked around for a coffee shop. Not a coffee shop in sight – only neat suburban houses with no signs of life.

About ten minutes later, a well-dressed woman in her seventies came round the corner dragging a dachshund in a ridiculous tartan jacket in her wake. Relieved, he put on his most engaging smile. "Good morning. Lovely day." Thought to himself what a damn silly thing to say in California. "Is there a coffee shop anywhere nearby? I'm staying at the Marriott and seem to be lost."

Her eyebrows shot up. "The Marriott! You've come a long way. *Herman, stop that.*" Herman, nose pressed into Adrian's pant leg, glowered as a sharp tug on the leash pulled him away. "Walk up to the corner, turn left and then keep going straight, you'll come to the shops. It's only ten minutes from here."

Thanking her, Adrian limped away as Herman received another sharp tug on the leash to stop him doing anything embarrassing in front of a stranger. It seemed a very long ten minutes as the blister burst and his shoe rubbed his raw skin. As he contemplated taking off his shoe to relieve the pressure on his heel, he finally saw a traffic light and shops.

A blast of cold air, an overpowering smell of coffee and a hubbub of voices greeted him in the crowded restaurant, but he found a booth in a quiet corner and ordered coffee. Without breakfast or even a cup of coffee before his walk, the thought of food still repelled him. He'd really thought a brisk walk would dispel the depression brought on by that gut-wrenching moment when he discovered Cindy had left without as much as a farewell note. Leaving him believing he'd been nothing but someone to amuse her while she was on the speakers' circuit - probably one of a long succession of gullible men.

He'd felt shattered. Then bewildered. Why did he feel so upset? Surely, this was the perfect solution. They'd had a great time together, culminating in a memorable night, and now she was gone leaving no dangling problems. Perfect. With no sticky situation to resolve he could return home.

Home to Emma. Oh god! He ran his fingers through his hair. Picked up the menu and studied it. Looked out of the window at the parking lot. Three hours and he was no nearer to figuring out what he wanted than when he started. He was married to a good woman, but he had never felt more alive than when he was with Cindy. It wasn't just how attractive she was. The waitress filled his coffee cup and he stirred in some cream, stirring far longer than necessary. Cindy's gorgeous, and last night was fantastic, but it was more than that. Over the last ten days, they'd talked up a storm. He shared all his hopes with her, thrashed out the problems in his upcoming talks, discussed politics and they'd laughed helplessly at the same jokes. What had he been missing all these years? Now that he knew how life could be, the thought of another twenty years with Emma – fixated on her domestic world and with no interest in his – was insufferable.

On his second cup of coffee the two irritating women at the next table left. Their long discussion of their weight problems – as they downed two massive bear claws – and last night's TV did nothing to help his pounding head. But in the blessed quiet of their departure, his mind began to clear and rational thought replaced the confusion. After his third cup of coffee, he paid the check and set off for the hotel with a determined stride, sore heel forgotten. The swirling dilemma settled, he knew exactly what to do. No way could he let Cindy go. He squared his shoulders. What kind of a wimp was he, giving up this easily?

He just needed to talk to her; women wanted to be persuaded. It might take a little time but she'd come around. Only one problem, he didn't have Cindy's number. After finding a park with a handy bench dedicated to *Will Johnson, Bird Lover,* he sat down and dialed Caleb's office. He let out an inaudible sigh of relief as a woman answered. He'd guessed right, Caleb was way too important to answer his own phone.

"Good afternoon, I'm the organizer of the seminar that Cindy Wright has just given in San Diego. I need to contact Mrs. Wright" he rushed on, "she left some papers behind and I need to get them to her. Could you give me her number please?"

"I'm sorry I can't do that. Why don't you just mail them here and I'll see they get to her."

With his voice barely above a whisper, Adrian said, "I'm afraid that wouldn't work. L-look this is terribly embarrassing. You see, I'm new at this job and I was supposed to make sure Mrs. Wright had all her papers packed ready to go when she left yesterday." He took a deep breath. "But I forgot to give these to her. I took a quick peek in the hope they were just handouts or something, but it's just awful." He let the silence hang.

"Why?"

Good, she was hooked, not impatient. "They're very important and they're sort of confidential. She's organizing a surprise party for her husband. I'm sure she doesn't want him to see these papers. And to tell you the truth," his voice gathered speed, "I was really hoping to get a job with your company some time soon. If Mr. Wright finds out what an idiot I am, that will be the end of my chances."

"That's true. He doesn't suffer fools gladly. Also," and her voice had a note of finality, "he generally checks the mail before I do. He gets into the office at five thirty in the morning." She paused letting him think on that for a moment. "But I still can't give you her number."

"Look. Please do. She's such a nice lady. She saw how nervous I was on the first day and has been very kind to me. I'm sure if I could have a word with her, she'd let me send them to her."

"I grant you she's a sweetie. Okay." She let out a sigh. "I'll give it to you. But promise me you'll just use it once. Or my head will be on the block."

"I swear. In fact, I'll eat it after I've talked to her."

She laughed and gave him the number.

Adrian contacted the airline and switched his flight to New York, then called Emma and told her he would be a couple of days late as he had to go to a meeting.

After checking in at the St. Regis in New York, he called Cindy, his heart thumping and the hand gripping his phone slippery with sweat. "Cindy? This is Adrian."

"Adrian! What are you doing calling me here?" Her voice a furious whisper.

"I have to see you. We can't leave it like this."

"Absolutely not." A voice in the background said something he could not hear. "*No one dear. Just a loose end from the conference.*"

A loose end from the conference. His heart sank. "Cindy, please. Just ten minutes of your time. Meet me for a coffee and then I'll be on my way."

"*I'm coming Caleb. Really. Okay, okay.* Look I have to go. Where are you staying?"

"St. Regis."

"I'll meet you in the hotel bar ten tomorrow morning. Then that's it. I don't want to hear another word from you." The click of her phone ended the conversation.

Adrian let out a contented sigh. Spirits rising, he went down to the hotel restaurant in search of food.

◈

Sitting in a quiet corner of the bar with an untouched Bloody Mary in front of him, he checked his watch for the tenth time. Nine forty five. Another fifteen minutes to go. He straightened the table mat, checked his tie to make sure it was straight, looked at both entrances to the bar and checked his watch again. Maybe she wouldn't show up. He felt as nervous as he had on his first date. He tried breathing in on the count of eight, and out slowly on the count of fifteen. After three breaths, he still felt as nervous as when he started. He looked at his watch again.

Dressed in a silk shirt, skin tight pants and high boots, she swept into the bar looking devastating. Even casually dressed, she was undoubtedly the complete New Yorker. She walked straight over to him and sat down without saying anything.

"Mimosa?" He motioned to the waiter.

"No, a Perrier with a slice of lime." She gave the order directly to the waiter. "This has to be quick, Adrian. I only have ten minutes."

"Cindy, we can't leave it like this." He managed to keep the pleading tone out of his voice but could tell from her expression it wasn't working. "I'm sorry about yesterday. It was a mistake. I can't bear the thought of not seeing you again. Can't we just be friends? These last ten days have been the most enjoyable of my life."

"Spare me the melodramatics. This has to end. I am married. You are married. I've never done anything like this before, and I hate how I feel. Let's just say goodbye now and forget it ever happened." She began to stand up.

An impressive act, but her eyes betrayed her.

He put out a hand to stop her. She shied away from him. "Don't touch me." Hand withdrawn, he leaned forward. "Cindy. You have no idea how much being with you means to me. Can't we just meet from time to time? You must go away on business regularly. Caleb doesn't need to know."

"Don't be naïve. Of course, Caleb would know. I am an integral part of Caleb's empire. I spend my days organizing dinners for his business associates, accompanying him to functions and fending off people he doesn't want to meet. You name it. I have a full-time job with him." She leaned back in her chair and took a sip of her drink. "What you don't understand is how precious those lecture tours are to me. For two whole weeks I get to be my own person. I call the shots and my free time is my own. It's heaven."

Adrian sat back startled. He'd viewed her as a successful business woman in her own right, not someone running around for her husband. He'd imagined personal assistants did all the supporting. On the other hand, she would be a tremendous asset in charming Caleb's business acquaintances.

Now her eyes filled with compassion. "I'm sorry Adrian. If we'd met before I married Caleb and you'd been free, this could have had a very different ending."

He couldn't believe it. She felt the same way he did. This is wonderful. His eyes shone. "Cindy, we could be so happy together."

"No, Adrian. You are married. I will not be party to making another woman miserable." She stood up. "I'm going. I don't want to hear from you again."

He put out his hand to stop her. *"Don't touch me."* The waiter started to move toward them. She almost ran to the hotel door. As he watched her disappear, he felt as if Sonny Liston had hit him in the solar plexus. His over-loud exhaled breath caused raised eyebrows from the waiter and a hasty retreat from the bar. Signing the check, he made for the elevators and the privacy of his room.

By the time he reached his room, shoulders drooping, he'd made the decision to go home. He started to dial the airline to get the next available flight to London but stopped halfway through. Home. Back to married bliss with Emma.

Emma. Such a sweet little soul but oh, so out of her depth in his world. They'd met at college. A group of six friends, all from quiet country areas who drifted together. Adrian, having gone to an unexceptional country school felt intimidated by the large campus full of loud, confident young men from private schools. He strongly suspected the other five felt the same way but, of course, none of them were about to admit it. Instead, they joked about their surroundings, studied hard, determined to excel and had a great deal of fun together on the weekends. He first noticed Emma because even in this group she seemed shy and ill at ease. But she had a pretty face and nice legs, so he spent time trying to bring her out of her shell.

Emma and Marge, one of the other students, left after they gained their BAs and shared a flat not too far from the campus. Emma worked as an editorial assistant to a publisher of a trade magazine and Marge in a travel agency. After a while, the two girls invited Adrian and another friend to their flat for a meal. The girls' flat after Adrian's untidy and rather stark student accommodation was a haven of warmth and comfort. Warmed by a gas fire fed by a meter and by the marvelous meals the girls produced in their tiny kitchen, Adrian and his friend relaxed and accepted a second invitation with alacrity.

When he graduated, he moved to Plymouth to work for an aviation company. His accommodation there was a drafty flat above a shop which specialized in cheese. With the few sticks of IKEA furniture he could afford and the smell of cheese, which no amount of air fresheners covered, it was dreary and cheerless. All his workmates lived out in the country, and although he went out to dinner with them occasionally, he found he was spending too many nights on his own. He slipped into the habit of catching the express to London on the weekend and spending time with his friends from student days. As the friends got married and moved out to the suburbs, he was left with just Emma. She listened with rapt attention as he told her about his new job and fussed over him whenever he went back to her flat for afternoon tea and the occasional dinner. Realizing he missed her when he was in Plymouth, he decided it would be nice to have a wife to come home to, particularly one who would have dinner ready.

For the first few years they were happy and lived a quiet, contented life. However, as he grew successful in his job, he needed to entertain other managers and clients. Knowing what a good cook Emma was, he invited a client to their house for dinner. It was a total disaster. Emma was so nervous that she overcooked the meat, spilled gravy on the table cloth and knocked over a glass of wine – white fortunately – that landed in the client's lap. Emma mopped him with a clean napkin and he laughed it off. Emma sobbed helplessly after he left.

He tried taking her to company functions and including her in restaurant invitations, but she worried so much about making a good impression that she was a nervous wreck by the time the evening came around and so painfully shy she was an embarrassment. So they began to drift apart.

Why had he been in such a hurry to marry? Why hadn't be waited until someone like Cindy came along who fitted perfectly into his world.

What was the matter with him? Why was he giving up so easily? He knew without the slightest doubt Cindy felt the way he did.

To heck with it! No way was he going to give up this chance of a blissful life. Cindy would crumple if he persisted. Once he'd divorced Emma and she'd done the same with Caleb, they could have a great life. Divorce? With a jolt, he remembered Martin telling him that women always get half in a divorce case. Half of everything he'd work so hard for while she'd sat around the house doing nothing. No. He'd have to find a way round that. With quiet confidence he sat back and began to plan.

CHAPTER 8

"*Please return to your seats and fasten your seat belts. We'll be landing in Seattle in about twenty minutes.*"

Nicole pulled off her airline socks and fished under the seat for her shoes. Wriggling her feet into the slip-ons that felt two sizes smaller than when she boarded, she settled back in her seat and gazed vacantly at the clouds. As the plane lost altitude, patches of mountain appeared, but little else. Her mind wandered.

A bubble of excitement rose at the thought of seeing Jan and Cliff again. When Jay had been alive, the foursome had spent some fantastic vacations together: trekking in New Zealand's South Island, fishing in Northland, and doing serious research into the vineyards and wine industry wherever they went.

She frowned out of the window as the plane circled. Guilt replaced excitement. She should have visited them sooner. They had been so great when Jay had been killed in an accident. They spent time with her to dispel the gaping loneliness, and took care of the seemingly never-ending paperwork involved in an untimely demise. But as the months rolled by the campaign began. Time for her to move on. "That was then, and now is now," Cliff insisted. "You're young. You must start getting out." He didn't understand. All she wanted to do was curl up in a chair in the evenings and remember the wonderful times with Jay.

When they invited her to a concert or out to dinner, they brought along a "friend" who just happened to be the same age as Nicole - invariably good looking and lots of fun. Time and time again, tightlipped, she had explained she did not want to start dating. They listened patiently. Held off for a week or two, and then repeated the formula. Running away to London had been the only way to escape the constant barrage.

Tantalizing patches of mountains appeared through the clouds. She realized how little she knew about Seattle . . . rain, Frasier, Microsoft, Starbucks and *Sleepless in Seattle* about summed it up. As the clouds cleared, she stared. Everyone talked about the rain, but no one mentioned the beauty. With its backdrop of snow-capped mountains, innumerable lakes and evergreens, Seattle looked more like an Alpine resort than a city.

She followed the crowd to immigration, shuffled along in the irritatingly slow line, and had her passport inspected by a stone-faced official. After customs had swiftly okayed her bags, she dumped them back on the conveyor belt and took the train to the baggage hall. Here she was greeted by Jan and Cliff with massive hugs, tumbled greetings and a large cup of coffee.

An hour later they were in her friends' apartment being greeted by a frantic pug that sniffed Nicole's shoes in approval then ran in excited circles around the living room. Jan laughed. "You seem to have made another hit."

"I probably smell of food and god knows what else from the plane - always an aphrodisiac to a dog. Talking of which I'd love a shower."

"Come right this way." Jan showed her to her room: a queen-sized bed with a comforter she recognized from Auckland days, a shelf of books and a desk in a corner with a port set up for her lap top. The bathroom's large square shower, its rail packed with warm towels, looked wonderfully inviting.

"As soon as you've showered, come on out and we'll have a glass of wine and do some catching up." Jan gave her another involuntary hug. "Jeez, it's good to see you. It's been way too long."

≪≫

The next ten days passed in a whirl of sightseeing. Cliff acted as chauffeur and Jan as a non-stop chattering guide. They bought flowers and fresh fruit in Pike's Place Market and watched a fish-monger pick up a massive salmon from a display slab and toss it across the counter for filleting.

A twenty minute drive into the mountains brought them to Snoqualmie Falls, a waterfall one hundred feet higher than Niagara. The Snoqualmie Indians believe the mists rising from the falls connect Heaven to Earth. Enveloped in the mist, the falls thundering down, Nicole could share their belief – until the wind changed and the mist saturated her, shattering the awesome moment. Laughing, they hurried to the coffee shop for a restorative latte.

As they prepared to go out for dinner one evening, Jan said, "We've invited Jerry along. You'll like him."

Nicole tightened her lips but could not control the involuntary frown. "Look, I've told you, and told you. I don't want to be set up with a date. I'm perfectly happy as I am."

"It *isn't* a date," Jan argued, her tone rising in response to Nicole's angry face.

"Whoa, hold your horses the pair of you." Cliff walked over and put his arm around Nicole's stiff shoulders. "Come and sit down a minute and let me explain." Glancing across at his wife, he said heavily, "As we should have done in the first place."

Nicole forced a smile and sat on the sofa trying hard to squash a rising anger. Dammit, they were at it again.

"Jerry's moving to London at the end of the month. They've offered him a major promotion to make the move, but he's very leery of the whole thing. Knows no one in the English office and doesn't like the idea of London. He's one of these outdoor types and not really into city life."

Jan leaned forward in her seat itching to butt in. Clive cast a meaningful look in her direction, and continued, "He's also very down these days. About three months ago, his wife up and left him." He shook his head. "Strangest thing. They seemed happy together. In fact, she doted on him. She's one of these homemakers who live for their husband." A wistful expression passed across his face.

Jan, looking troubled, added, "It came as a real shock. She just took off saying she was going back to the East Coast to find herself, and that's the last he's heard of her."

"Must have read one of those damn silly books that tell women to become their own person. Discover the hidden you. Crapola!" Cliff frowned, his lips pursed.

"Yes, but she should have contacted him and let him know how she's doing," Jan said. "I think it's odd. She didn't seem the type to do anything that extreme."

"You never know. Maybe some friend persuaded her." Nicole suggested.

"She always looked happy and he was a good husband," Cliff said. "She did call Jerry the other day." He looked apologetically in Jan's direction. "I meant to tell you about it. Apparently she's met up with some old high school friends and is starting to get out and about."

"Anyway," he continued, "he's been really depressed so we're glad he's going to London. He needs a change of scene but he's still dragging his heels about the move. We just thought chatting with you might make him feel more comfortable about the whole thing. You made a major move and seem to have adjusted to life among the Poms."

Nicole grinned. "Well, it does help that they speak approximately the same language."

"So do you mind if he comes along?" Cliff asked quietly. "I think it would help him."

"That's fine," Nicole agreed, and muffled a sigh. A wild night out with a depressed outdoorsman.

◈

They had just settled down in the Palisade restaurant at a table overlooking the marina, when Jerry arrived. Tall, broad-shouldered, slim-hipped with wavy brown hair and an easy smile, he came over to the table, kissed Jan on the cheek and shook hands with Nicole.

"How are you enjoying Seattle? Have they given you the tour?"The conversation flowed easily. His "outdoorsmanship" turned out to be cycling, hiking, kayaking and fishing. Not the camouflaged hunter- creeping-around- in the woods- shooting- Bambi- type, she was expecting.

She answered a series of practical questions about getting set up with an apartment in London, and assured him that although London was an expensive city it offered a wealth of free museums and art galleries. It also had plenty of open space for running and cycling, and kayaking on the Thames would be fun. She didn't mention any of the clubs. She felt sure his co-workers would educate him in that direction, although some-how she doubted he would enjoy the club scene. Before they left the restaurant, she gave him her card and promised to help with any relocation problems. She felt sure his new company would arrange everything and that would be the last she would hear of him.

A few days before she was due to fly home, she emerged from her bedroom after catching up on her emails. Jan brandished the cof-fee pot. "Good idea?"

"Perfect timing." Nicole flopped into an easy chair.

As Jan poured, she said, "Sorry but I have to go back to work. Crisis down in the Bay Area. I'll have to hop on a plane. Just an overnighter. Back by Thursday evening." She took two cups over to the coffee table and joined Nicole. "I feel bad leaving you on your own. We knew Cliff would have to bail out and go to Beijing but I thought that was great. We'd have a few days on our own. I had a wild day out at a spa in mind!"

"Don't worry. I can keep myself amused for a couple of days." Exhausted by the constant round of sightseeing, she relished the thought of wandering around the bookstores.

"Okay, you can loaf around tomorrow. However," Jan's eyes sparkled, "I've set you up with a treat for Thursday."

"Why do I have the feeling I'm going to be surprised?"

"Before you left home, you used to witter on about settling down in a little village in England and being a Miss Marple."

"Yes," Nicole said warily.

"So I've enrolled you in a Private Investigators Seminar."

"Wow! That sounds like fun. But I can't go – I've zero qualification, and even less intention of being a private eye."

"No problem. I explained the whole situation to them and they are more than happy to have you come along. No qualifications required." She laughed. "They probably think they can convert you."

"Move over, Mata Hari, here I come."

CHAPTER 9

Nicole squished herself into the last available seat – a close call. On her left, a woman in an orange sweater and massive square glasses occupied a seat and a quarter, and on the other side a muscle-bound giant in a T-shirt tried to make more room for her. His solid bulk destroyed a gallant attempt. He smelled of soap and Polo aftershave. It could have been worse.

Positioning the "Private Investigation Seminar" binder on the table in front of her, she pulled out a pen to appear ready for business, and then gave in to her curiosity. Not expecting to see trench coats or Hercule Poirot look-alikes, she was still surprised – none of them looked like investigators. They came in all shapes and sizes: an ancient hippie in worn jeans, check shirt and a straggly pony tail; an earnest young woman in heavy-rimmed glasses with librarian written all over her; several casually dressed men in their thirties; a tired looking middle-aged man with a defeated air; an extremely attractive young woman in an expensive suit, and a clean-cut, earnest youngster in a crisp shirt.

The instructor, fiftyish, strolled in, greeted a few students by name and favored the rest of the class with a warm smile. With amused eyes, he warned them that movies, television and books portray the life of a private investigator as wildly exciting. In reality, the PI spends hours anchored to a computer, trudging to libraries, and sitting, cold and bored, waiting for something to happen during surveillance. Research is often tedious, and agitated clients, anxious for results, a constant bugbear.

"However," he continued "if you enjoy research, have patience and a capacity for hard work, it's a fascinating career. The thrill of digging out the elusive truth is a never-ending source of satisfaction." He stopped, smiled and shook his head. "The look on a parent's face when you reunite them with a lost child makes everything worthwhile."

During coffee break, the ex-librarian, in a faintly officious tone said, "I'm here to take the exam. I think most people are."

In response to Nicole's puzzled expression, her muscle-bound neighbor explained, in a soft cultured voice, anyone after taking the seminar could work as an investigator under the eye of a qualified PI, but to set up on your own you needed to pass an examination. "I've been a PI for a couple of years now." He gave a rueful grin. "Time to take the exam."

When the next session started, she sat, eyes glued on the instructor, as he outlined the legal bounds of a PI. "It is okay to take photos of a person under observation from all angles but you must never cross their property line. Climbing up trees in the park next door to take photos is alright; hopping over their fence is not. A photo taken within their property is illegal."

Her mind reeled at the number of things an investigator needed to know; a PI was liable for prosecution if they infringed any city, county, state or federal regulation.

Looking serious, the instructor added, "Even worse, attorneys and insurance companies shun investigators who are prosecuted." His face relaxed, "The last thing an insurance agent or attorney needs is attention drawn to his nefarious activities."

Nicole thought private eyes gained most of their business from wives or husbands investigating erring spouses, but learned insurance companies and attorneys are a far richer source. The subject of insurance fraud sparked a flurry of questions and innumerable funny stories. Defrauding insurance companies had developed into an underground economy. Investigators had photographed people claiming back injuries, playing golf, lifting weights, and digging gardens.

Tracing missing persons, runaway children, and disappearing spouses turned out to be another lucrative source. The police investigate dutifully, solve many cases, but cut back their efforts if the first month or two fails to produce results. The unsolved cases are left open but the police turn to more pressing issues. Hence the need for private investigators.

She found missing heirs a far more interesting topic. The division of spoils of a large estate is held up until the last beneficiary is traced. Agitated relatives, anxious to gain their booty, rush to gain the help of a PI in finding the missing family member. This caused her to pause, brow wrinkled. Was there any chance some far off branch of her family had lost track of her after her parents moved to New Zealand? Perhaps a vast fortune was following her around the world. With a small sigh of reality, she returned her attention to the instructor.

While the instructor gave tips on surveillance techniques, he mentioned to the surprising number of women in the class they should be careful if the person under investigation goes into a bar. "I don't advise a woman on her own to follow the subject into a bar. A lone woman is conspicuous. Your target is going to notice you – so your cover is blown. However, if you go in with a man, chances are you'll not be noticed."

The attractive dark-haired woman raised her hand. "Yes, I've had that happen on a couple of occasions. I slipped into the bar quietly expecting to escape notice but the man I was following looked straight at me." She looked troubled.

Nicole had a hard time keeping a straight face. Didn't she realize with a figure like hers and lush dark hair she would attract attention anywhere?

The earnest youngster asked why private investigators were called private eyes in detective stories. "Ah, that's all down to the Pinkerton Agency," the instructor replied. "The logo of the Pinkerton Agency was a big eye, indicating the investigators never slept and were always watching."

"Who was Pinkerton?" Nicole asked. "I know his agents pop up in all the old Westerns but why was he so prominent?"

"He was a canny Scots immigrant who set up the business in 1850 and managed to make it the best known agency in the country. Most of his fame came when the government employed his agency to chase train robbers." Students began to stir, ready to ask more questions.

The instructor came right back to business. "Fascinating as this is, we have lots of material to cover, so let's move on to interviewing witnesses and how to gain their co-operation."

During the breaks, Nicole spent time getting to know her fellow students and asking them why they wanted to be a PI. Most had been doing research for private investigation firms or attorneys when they made the decision. In doing the desk-bound, tedious part of the investigation they developed the urge to complete the whole job and to be a fully-qualified PI. One stoop-shouldered little man, who resembled a bassett hound, said, "I tried to get in the police force but couldn't pass the physical. Ridiculous requirements if you ask me." He winked. "Fooled them though. Became a PI."

The pony-tailed ex-hippie stuck out his jaw. "I spent a fortune on a PI to find my wife who took off without a word about a year ago. He finally found her. Problem was when I went to see her, she told me to get lost." His smile was forced. "I was so ticked off about the amount of money I'd spent, I decided I might as well become a PI to recoup my losses."

The idea of having a shot at the examination crossed Nicole's mind. She had zero intention of becoming a PI, but it would be a real kick to get an official certificate stating her qualifications. Displayed prominently on her office wall back in England, it would be a huge joke for her project team and clients, and she hoped a cause for consternation for a priggish software architect with a Cambridge degree and an insufferable attitude. No way could he match a PI professional qualification.

When the seminar finished, she decided to go for it, and head down, read rapidly through the key areas in the information-packed binder. She was amazed when two hours later she was driving back to her friend's home as a fully fledged private investigator.

When she entered the condominium, she was delighted to see Jan. Jan greeted her with a hug. "Ah, there you are! I managed to catch an early flight."

They spent a pleasant hour over a glass of wine and a long account of the seminar, then dug in the refrigerator for some pasta and shrimp that Nicole had bought the day before. Half way through the pasta and all the way through her second glass of wine, Jan said, "Okay lady, now you're a fully qualified Miss Marple, when are you going to set up shop?" With a wicked glint in her eye, she added, "Your village sounds the perfect fit."

"You're right! I'd almost forgotten" Nicole pulled out a strand of hair and surveyed it critically. "Humph, not gray, but I found one yesterday. I'm all set."

Jan gave in to her suppressed laughter as Nicole continued, "Only one problem. That darn village is so peaceful, the chances of anything intriguing happening are somewhere below zero."

CHAPTER 10

*H*e stood in the doorway and watched his wife back her car out of the garage, swing around and set off down the drive. After her car disappeared around the corner, a small smile crept across his face.

Closing the front door with soft deliberation, he set the lock. After a quick tour of the empty house satisfied him there would be no prying eyes, he went into his office. The warm wood tones and soft leather chairs exuded a pleasing masculinity. Fishing his keys out of his pocket, he unlocked the maple-fronted filing cabinet and humming a mite tunelessly under his breath, he flipped through the file folders. All labeled in cryptic code: PTF 14, 15, 16, which stood for Printer Technology Future – years 2014, 2015 and 2016.

About a dozen crammed files with the same type of label stretched to the back of the cabinet. When he reached one labeled PPST, he pulled it out and carried it to his favorite chair – a maroon lounger of soft Italian leather – and settled the pages of his Personal Planning Strategy and Tactics on his knee.

With quiet pride he read the steps he had laid out with such care several weeks ago. He spent a moment gazing out of the window, then sighed in satisfaction. Everything going according to plan.

The long slow process of laying the foundation. Playing the perfect husband. Giving his wife all the attention she had craved while he was working his butt off amassing enough money to ensure a long and fun filled retirement. With a rueful grimace, he acknowledged he'd spent little time with her. The only way to succeed in the dog-eat-dog technology world was to give it your all. Work, work,

work. Keep your priorities straight; focus on your job first, your job second, third and fourth. Wife and family a distant last.

It suited him. He enjoyed his work and after the first few years of marriage, talking technology with his peers was a damn sight more interesting than discussing her shallow, colorless life. Although she seemed to enjoy them, all her interests bored him rigid. Their worlds drifted apart. Although drifted didn't quite describe it. More like him zipping along, full tilt, in a catamaran while she floated along in a canoe, one manicured hand trailing in the water.

An irritating refrain had kept invading his world. "I hardly ever see you. You're always away on business trips, and when you're home all you do is work."

With a healthy seven figure investment portfolio amassed, he began to think about retiring while he was still young enough to enjoy it. Realization came like a thunder bolt – he would be spending all his time with his wife. The thought appalled him.

He needed to get rid of her and find a new partner. Someone who would fit in his world and enjoy the things he enjoyed. Divorce was the obvious answer, or was until he realized the consequences. She'd get more than half his hard-earned money. Money he'd worked his tail off to make while she skittered around in her pleasant, leisurely little world. It was damned unfair. Fat chance of the judge seeing it his way – especially now loads of them were women.

So he had developed the plan. He smoothed the sheet of neatly written type.

STEP 1: Play the loving, dutiful husband. Make her feel good.

STEP 2: Take a long vacation together.

STEP 3: Eliminate the flaw in his long term plan. Make sure she didn't get the lion's share of his cash.

As he wrote that step, he remembered experiencing a few misgivings. Could he really carry out the elimination part? Thinking about it was one thing. He wiped the sheen of sweat from his upper lip. Actually killing someone appalled him.

He strode over to the window. Watched a squirrel run up a tall birch, venture out too far on a flimsy branch, and then as the branch bent too far over, leap to safety. But what alternative did he have? His attorney told him he'd lose the house and boat, at least half the cash and securities, and have to pay her more than 200K a year maintenance. When he protested the maintenance fee, the attorney explained patiently that this was the style to which she was accustomed. It was so unfair. She hadn't started out with that style of living – that was all his doing. He was being penalized for all his hard work. There was no damn justice in the world.

Okay, he would do it. The law left him no alternative. He stood up, walked to the window and slapped his open hand on the glass. Of course he could. She wouldn't feel a thing.

Suppressing his euphoria, he sat down again and forced himself to read the next step.

STEP 4: Convince everyone that she is still alive.

He exhaled a long, slow breath. The last step was the crucial piece.

CHAPTER 11

Vacation over, she drove to work delighting in the small country roads, their hedgerows lined with pale yellow primroses, and a small wood carpeted with bluebells.

Co-workers greeted her with, "Did you have a good sleep in Seattle?" or, "How was the rain – any wetter than ours?" Since they all vacationed in the sunny climes of Spain or the Bahamas, her trip to Seattle was regarded with mild bewilderment.

She settled down at her desk to deal with urgent emails before she tackled the pile of reports that seemed to have spawned in her in-tray during her absence. After only three emails, the CEO's personal assistant came by.

"Welcome back. Did you have a good time?" She gave an abstracted smile in response to Nicole's effusive reply, and then continued, "His nibs wants you in Conference Room 3 at 10:30 a.m."

"Uh-oh, what's up?"

"Don't know, but he's got a brow of thunder. Better put on your flak jacket."

Four people were already waiting in the conference room when Nicole arrived: a shirtsleeved engineering manager with the obligatory two pens clipped in his top pocket, the VP of sales in a tailored dark gray suit, the manager of systems engineering fidgeting with a notebook, and a sales rep looking as if he wanted to be anywhere other than in Conference Room 3. Everyone said hello, and the VP of Sales mouthed a, "Welcome back", and gave her a re-assuring smile. Good. She wasn't the one on the carpet.

A moment later, the CEO, a small man with forgettable features and receding hair, arrived. "Morning all." Pale gray eyes paused on each of them. "I received a call from Richter in Geneva a couple of hours ago. Tells me he is planning to pull the account."

She let out an inaudible "Whoa!" Richter was the Chief Operating Officer of Genève-Blanc, a major international player. Trylon systems were in all their information technology departments across Europe and the Far East. If the account went, so would a third of Trylon's business.

"They can't be serious!" Deep worry lines creased the VP's face.

"It sounds horribly as if they are. What's going on? As I understand it, it's just down to a problem in their IT department." The CEO frowned.

The systems engineering manager, looking grim, said, "Apparently some ego-maniac in IT refuses to acknowledge the problem lies in their application design and not in our system."

"I don't give a toss who's responsible. Get over there and fix it. We can't lose this account." The CEO's quiet voice, full of authority, belied his small stature.

"Of course, I'll take a flight this afternoon." The systems engineering manager pocketed his notebook.

"Want me to go along?" The sales VP asked.

"No." The CEO glowered at the sales rep. "You need to be on top of this, Ryan. Don't just leave it to the software types. Get over there and get it sorted."

The sales rep, robbed of his usual bluster, said meekly, "Of course, I'll go right away." He looked ready to bolt.

The sales VP, his voice soft and conciliatory, said, "Why don't you take Nicole along? She can take a fresh look at the situation and may be able to help."

At eleven thirty, she found herself driving home to pick up her bag, and a few hours later looking out the plane window at the staggering beauty of the Alps.

<>

From her seat with a view of the sparkling blue water of Lake Geneva backed by the craggy grandeur of the Alps, Nicole surveyed Genève-Blanc's management dining room with quiet amusement. The hushed room full of delectable aromas was a far cry from Trylon's cafeteria with its plastic tables and chairs, clatter of crockery and the pervading smell of sausage, egg and chips. Waiters in crisp, cropped white jackets moved among the elegant linen and silverware of the tables. Her wiener schnitzel arrived in a covered silver dish removed by the waiter with the quiet aplomb of a 3-star Michelin restaurant. By the time the coffee had been served from a silver pot into her bone china cup, she felt she could get used to this life in a hurry.

Her aspirations crashed on the second day. The software problem turned out to be no more than the IT applications programmer and Trylon's systems engineer, both with massive egos, refusing to believe their software could be at fault. Having listened to both sides of the story, she suggested a simple workaround. The two men rounded on her with derision. They both agreed it would never work. However, if they put their heads together they would solve this in no time. She sat back suppressing a grin; her work was done.

Anxious to return home, her hopes were dashed by a call from Trylon's VP of sales. "Congratulations, Nicki. You've done a great job. Now. As you know, the reward for work well done is more work. So I want you on a train to Munich tomorrow with the systems engineering manager. You two need to hit all their major offices."

"You've got to be kidding."

"No. We've got to show Genève-Blanc we mean business, I want them raving about our customer support."

The next weeks were a blur of hotels, rental cars, flights and hasty meals. With the weekends spent traveling, it was more than three weeks before she sank thankfully into her seat on the last leg to London and home. She closed her eyes and fantasized about sitting in her peaceful little cottage with nothing to worry about.

Wonder if there will be any postcards from mum? Last one had been from The Forbidden City in Beijing. Said they were having a wonderful time and not to forget to call Dad. She dumps poor old dad after thirty years then reminds *me* keep in touch with him. Nicole's laugh caused the man next to her to edge away and become avidly interested in the view from the window.

CHAPTER 12

Nicole took a deep breath of fresh country air – nectar after the air-conditioned plane – and hurried up the path in anticipation of a shower. Before she had time to open the door, Iris bounded over, earth smudged face and trowel in hand. "About time you came back. What have you been up to? Last I heard you were just going to Switzerland for a couple of days." She pushed her hair back from her face with the back of her hand. Her wide smile exposed a crooked front tooth. "Did you find a nice Swiss millionaire?"

"I should get so lucky," Nicole said.

Smile gone, Iris looked at her closely, "You look worn out. Just pop your bag inside your door and come over for a cup of coffee and cake. It'll be ready in two shakes of a tail. It'll give you the energy to unpack."

Seated in Iris's sunroom, Nicole leaned back in the wicker armchair with its well-worn cushions covered in dog hair. The filtered sunlight on the lawn outside was occasionally shadowed by a passing cloud. On a small table between the two women sat a tray with a coffee pot, milk and a homemade fruit cake. A black Labrador and a springer spaniel sat to attention in front of the two women, ears pricked and eyes glued to the fruit cake.

"Will you quit it, you two," Nicole said to the dogs. She turned to Iris. "Mmm, great cake. How's Emma doing? I tried calling her from Hamburg but just got the answer phone. Surely she's not still in Bermuda."

Iris slapped her forehead. "Good heavens, I forgot to tell you. Of course, you were away when it happened."

"What happened? Is Emma okay?"

"Yes, she's fine now, I think. Poor little soul came back from Bermuda while Adrian was on his lecture tour. She'd just settled in and bought three tray loads of plants to spruce up her garden – she's always trying to make it better – when Adrian came home."

"So why poor little Emma?"

"Barely four weeks after she arrived here, Adrian comes barreling home and tells her to pack her bag, they're off to New Zealand. She was in a right tiz. Took me three cups of tea to calm her down."

"Why on earth New Zealand? And why so soon after the Bermuda trip?"

"Because he reckoned he'd not had any vacation. You know he had to rush to complete his pitch and give it in the States right away. Emma tried to explain it to me but she always gets it muddled up."

"That's right. She told me about it. They wanted him to do a shorter version of his lecture tour immediately. I gather it made him angry. He missed out on his planned vacation." She paused, thought about it for a moment. "Of course, he did all the preparation for the tour and was expecting some time off before he went to the States." She sipped her coffee. "Hang on a minute, though. Why New Zealand? Why not just go back to Bermuda?"

"We had them over to dinner before they left. He was really gung ho about it. Thought it was time to explore somewhere different. Apparently, he'd managed to find a great property way out in the boonies. He showed it to us on the internet. Looked gorgeous."

"Makes sense. If you get away from Auckland, you can find some fantastic bargains."

"Bargain or no, I worry about Emma. I wonder how she's doing in a strange country with no one to talk to while Adrian is off fishing and golfing."

Nicole swallowed a mouthful of cake and tried to ignore the reproachful gaze of the two dogs. "I wonder why he chose New Zealand. Do you think Emma told him that's where I come from?"

"I doubt it. She never seems to tell him anything."

"Do you know where they are?"

"Emma sent a postcard but damned if I can remember. It was one of those weird Maori names they have over there."

"Not Wellington, Hamilton, Christchurch, Dunedin or Cambridge then?" Nicole said with a huge grin.

Iris broke off two small pieces of cake from the slice on her plate and threw them to the dogs, then took a vigorous sip of coffee. "Enough about Emma. Tell me about your trip. Why did it take so long?"

Nicole told her about her assignment and after answering a further volley of questions, managed to extricate herself so she could tackle the waiting backlog of chores.

She had just finished loading the washer, when the phone rang. "Hi Nicole, this is Jerry."

Jerry, who the heck is he? American accent. Oh yes, the guy I had dinner with when I stayed with Jan and Cliff in Seattle. "Hello, how are you doing? Managing to cope with the Poms?"

"Yes, I love it here." He hesitated. "I promised myself I wouldn't bother you." Another pause. "I really need some advice."

"Sure, what's the problem?" She hoped he'd be quick. She needed to buy groceries and take some stuff to the dry cleaners.

"I went apartment hunting as soon as I arrived. It was a pain. I looked at a bunch of rentals but they were pretty gruesome. The ones in central London are fabulous although they cost an arm and a leg. They told me I could get a really good one if I go out a bit farther but I can't stand the thought of riding the subway every day."

"It isn't that bad and there are some great areas like Hampstead or Chelsea."

"Sure. But to cut a long story short, I ended up buying one on the Thames."

"Fabulous. So what's the problem?" She glanced at her watch – she needed to get to the post office before it closed.

"I bought this great looking place. But once the owners took their furniture away it didn't look anywhere near as good a buy." He paused. "And, yes, I have bought furniture but it just doesn't look right."

"So what can I do for you?" She tapped an irritated foot.

"I want the place to look comfortable so that when Madison, my wife, decides to come back to me, it looks like home. I think we'd have a ball here. I don't want her itching to go back to the States."

"Okay, so get an interior designer on the job."

"No way. They'll have me looking up market and elegant. I want it to look like *home*."

"Then get someone from your office to help. Must be women there."

"Sure. Problem is they all look fourteen and spend their spare time clubbing." She could almost see him shudder. "Hate to think what they'd do to it."

Nicole laughed. Working among young software types herself, she could see his problem. "Could you possibly come up to London for the day and take a look. You're the only grown up I know in England and something tells me you have taste."

"At least you didn't say you were convinced I was homely." Now it was his turn to laugh. "Remember I come from the background of the people that believe you can fix anything with a piece of 8" wire – you could be sorry."

"I'll take my chances, and I hate to resort to bribery but how about I buy you dinner in the Savoy grill?"

"Make it lunch at Fortnum & Masons and you're on." A day trip to London on Sunday after all her work sounded like a great idea.

"I'll meet you at Waterloo. Or does that sound too much like Wellington inviting Napoleon?"

"Another atrocious joke like that and I'll change my mind. Okay, 11 a.m. by the Information center. Tomorrow do you? Empty trains and low day trip rates on a Sunday."

"Perfect. I'll wear a red carnation. You've probably forgotten what I look like by now."

"This is a one-off offer by the way. I'll stroke my chin, look wise, and make suggestions. Then you are on your own. I'm too fond of my little corner of the world to trek to London again."

CHAPTER 13

Jerry unlocked the door of his apartment on the seventh floor and stood back to let her in. The smell of new furniture mixed with a faint aroma of carpet shampoo reminded her of show homes in upscale neighborhoods.

The view instantly dispelled the impression. A panoramic view of the Thames, Tower Bridge and the Gherkin spread out before her. Directly below, the London traffic crawled and beeped its way through central London; the sound muted by the double glazed windows. She turned back to Jerry. "What a fantastic view! Must be beautiful at night, with the lights of the city and the boats on the river."

"Yep – and as dawn creeps over the city."

"How did you manage to get it? Views like this must be like hen's teeth."

"Sheer luck. Belonged to a broker who'd lost his job – needed cash in a hurry. I had money sitting in the bank."

She just managed to suppress a whew – about $2 million. Where did all that money come from? "You must have been all his dreams come true. No chain of sales and no mortgage to clear."

"Like I said, he grabbed it." He moved toward the kitchen. "Like a cup of coffee?"

"No, thanks." Suddenly remembering why she was there, she stood with her back to the window and surveyed the room: expensive leather futon and chairs, modern Swedish wood table. Berber carpet. Masculine. Sparse. Looked too much like an up market hotel suite.

He watched her closely. "I can see you share my opinion. Doesn't work, does it?"

"Nooo," she intoned, then added quickly, "Where are your books?"

Visibly surprised, he responded, "'I've a few in the closet. Gave the rest away before I left home."

"You need bookshelves and a bunch of books to fill them. A couple of rugs on the floor, and some paintings." She pointed to the cream walls devoid of everything save discrete, elegant light fittings. "Nice, warm colorful ones."

His eyes widened. "You're right where do I buy it all?"

"Bookshelves from the outfit where you bought the furniture. Paintings. Cheapies on the railings at Hyde Park on the weekends, or oodles of galleries off Bond Street. Better yet go to some county towns, you can pick up great buys there. Or hop on an express to Glasgow – there's a hotbed of artists there who sell at the right prices."

He made notes on a pad by the phone. "Books?"

"Oh, for goodness sakes! Bookstores everywhere in London. Just look on the Web or take a walk. Everything from W.H.Smith to rare first editions at Harrington's in Chelsea."

"Jeez . . ."

"C'mon, you'll have a ball looking for all this."

"You going to help? Could be fun."

"As much fun as it sounds – I've done my bit." She plonked down on the sofa and grinned. "Okay, time for my pound of flesh. We can walk to Fortnum and Masons along the Thames path from here."

His lopsided grin answered hers. "You're right. Let's get going. I'm starving."

"After lunch, we can walk up Bond Street and look at some galleries – just to get you started."

CHAPTER 14

With a disgusted shoulder slump, Nicole surveyed the room. Three weekends toil after her return from Europe and still it needed more spit and polish. How do housewives put up with it - no sooner do you clean the place than the spiders festoon the beams with cobwebs, and the brass ornaments grow green before your eyes? With martyred resignation she went in search of the metal polish.

"Guess who dropped by last night?" She turned to the window and saw Iris's beaming face.

Hallelujah! Saved by the bell. Iris, not expecting a response, continued, "Adrian."

"Adrian! Great, I'll give Emma a call. I'd love to hear her impressions of New Zealand."

"Not just yet you won't."

"Why not? Think she's too busy to see me?"

"No. Come on over for a cup of coffee and I'll tell you all about it."

With her audience comfortably seated, coffee in hand, plate of hot scones at the ready and two adoring pugs in attendance, Iris deigned to answer Nicole's question. "Emma's not back yet. Adrian came on ahead. Says she'll be coming in about three weeks."

Nicole's eyebrows shot up. "What on earth is she doing?"

Iris beamed with delight. "She's apparently gone off to South Island on a photographic expedition. That place where they filmed "Lord of the Rings." She stopped and laughed. "What am I doing explaining South Island to you?"

"Emma. On her own?" Nicole had a hard time believing shy little Emma would take off on a trip with strangers.

"I think it's marvelous! Sounds as if she's finally come out of her shell. Time she had a life of her own instead of just running around after Adrian."

"But who's she with? And where's she going?"

"Seems she joined a photography group in that funny little place she was staying, and they persuaded her to come on some trip they'd organized a couple of months before. She was probably so flattered she didn't dare say no."

"But why on earth didn't Adrian wait until she got back from the trip to come home?"

"You obviously don't know him. When he has something planned, he doesn't deviate. No way would he change his airline ticket."

"So she'll be back in three weeks?"

"Yes. Adrian changed her ticket and brought her big suitcase home with him so she doesn't have to cope with too much luggage." She paused a moment, cup suspended half way to her lips, then added, "She'll have just enough clothes for jumping around on mountains or whatever they're going to do. She won't need anymore because she'll come straight back after the trip."

Iris prattled on for the next ten minutes about the woman on the corner whose husband was in Afghanistan. Seems she had a frequent male visitor. Nicole didn't bother to point out that it might be her brother or cousin. There was no point. Iris much preferred to be outraged at the scandal. She was only listening with half an ear anyway. How on earth had timid little Emma plucked up the courage to take off on a trip with new friends? It seemed way out of character.

A dull thud from the hallway caused Iris to leap to her feet. "Mail's here."

Glad of an excuse to escape more scandal, Nicole said, "Good. I'll go check mine. Thanks for the scone. Delicious."

<>

That evening, deep in an armchair with a Louise Penny mystery, she was interrupted by the phone. She looked at the caller ID: Jerry. Should she just let it switch to her voice mail? Her conscience got the better of her. "Hi, Jerry. How are you? Bought all your books and paintings yet?"

"That m'dear is the problem."

"Why are you always calling me with problems? Why not just send a letter to an agony aunt?"

"Because *you* caused the problem."

"How? I haven't done a thing."

"Oh, yes you have. That painting we saw in the gallery near Bond Street. I looked at it again and couldn't resist it; what's more, the silver-tongued assistant talked me into another that went beautifully with it. They look fabulous on my wall but now I am penniless."

"Sorry, I don't give loans to footloose Americans."

"No, I don't need a loan. Just want you to buy me lunch tomorrow. Thought I'd come down on the train. You could take me out on one of those great walks you were talking about and then buy me lunch in an olde worlde pub."

"Sorry, but I'm all tied up tomorrow."

"Oh, no you're not. You're afraid I want to jump your bones."

Not sure whether to laugh or be angry, she hesitated and he continued calmly, "Look, lady, I'm married and the last thing I need is to get entangled with anyone before Madison makes up her mind to come back to me. And," this with heavy emphasis, "you've made it crystal clear you don't want a relationship. So why don't we just be buddies? I had a great time with you last Sunday."

"Okay." Her voice mirrored her reservations. With a reluctant sigh she acknowledged, but not out loud, he would be good company on a long hike.

"I'll catch a train about nine o'clock. Which station do I ask for?"

"Get a day return to Poole. I'll pick you up there. Don't blink too much after you pass Southampton or you may miss it."

The small station boasted two solitary railway lines, the platforms connected by an overbridge. The handful of Sunday travelers looked expectantly up the line, or sat on one of the wooden benches reading the newspaper. Within minutes, the sleepy Sunday silence was shattered by the arrival of the express. Doors swung open, and passengers rushed to the exit. Jerry, wearing hiking boots, a light jacket and a broad smile, jumped off. He grabbed her arm. "Lead on, lady, take me to your trail."

She grinned back and guided him out of the entrance across to the small parking lot. After she negotiated her way through the quiet Sunday streets, they arrived at the beginning of the Coastal Trail. "I'm glad you had the forethought to wear hiking boots. The trail is 630 miles long."

"What!"

"No kidding. It starts at Poole goes all the way along the south coast– that's through three counties Dorset, Devon and Cornwall – right to Land's End then goes back along the northern coast of Cornwall and Devon to Somerset."

In response to his puzzled look, she added, "That's down around the South West corner of England."

"The bit that sticks out like a spare leg?"

"Right, and unlike your enchanting description, it has spectacular scenery and takes you past Agatha Christie's house, the moor where the Hound of the Baskervilles roamed, and Tintagel where

King Arthur's court convened." Reflecting, she said, "Tintagel is quite something. Just rugged coastal rocks, but when you stand there you're convinced the Knights of the Round Table are going to loom up out of the mist at any moment. Were I not talking to an ignorant techie, I would say it's awesome."

She pulled into a parking lot, and they set off along the path which wound across the downs close to the rocky coast. The gusting sea air carried swirls of fog. With the taste of salt on her lips and the strong breeze filling her lungs, Nicole bounded along on the short springy turf. Jerry stepped out, his long legs eating up the ground, eyes sparkling.

On their left, the incoming tide washed restlessly against the chalk cliffs. Gulls squawked and screamed above the vertical cliffs, and to the right, the downs swept upward in a clean sweep as far as the eye could see.

They soon reached Old Harry Rocks, pillars of white chalk sitting off shore still wearing caps of green turf that matched the grass-covered cliffs. The sea, with a light gray/green chop, looked benign and innocent of the stormy temper that created the rock formations. Knowing the rocks marked the beginning of the Jurassic Coast World Heritage Site, she decided to reserve her commentary until later and just enjoy the pleasure of the unfolding scenery.

Other than an occasional, "Jeez, that's spectacular." Jerry was a pleasantly silent walking companion.

After two hours of brisk hiking, Jerry said, "I vote we don't do the whole 630 miles in one go. How about that lunch you owe me?"

Nicole, having trouble matching his long stride, was happy to oblige. A short deviation from the path brought them to a small village with an ancient pub. Inside, a pleasant babble of voices, the smell of ale, heavy overhead beams, flagstone floor and an enormous fireplace greeted them. They found a dark wood table and chairs in a quiet corner away from a well patronized bar. Most drinkers appeared to be locals: some churchgoers in formal clothes but most in casual Sunday wear. A few with cheeks glowing after a walk along the coast, others with newsprint fingers and a few errant toast crumbs on their shirts.

As Nicole studied the menu, Jerry headed for the bar. "What would you like to drink? I've been told by my buddies at work to ask for a pint of their best bitter in country pubs. They say there are some good local brews."

"I'd like a shandy. Why don't you hang on a minute and look at the menu. We can order the meal at the same time as we get our drinks."

They spent a moment on the menu then looked up and noticed the blackboard specials.

"The duck a l'orange is for me."

"I'm going to go native and have a cottage pie," Jerry said, catching the eye of the bar maid and placing the order. An unbidden memory of life with Jay popped up. Strange how tall, good-looking men always catch the eye of a bar maid no matter how busy the bar.

"I'll just open up a tab. That way we can decide on dessert and coffee later."

The food was superb, and the large dish of vegetables set between them fresh and gently cooked. After Jerry's dessert of apple pie and hers of sticky toffee pudding, both covered in creamy custard, they sat back and exhaled. "I don't know about you, but I'm way too full to walk back. Would we be wimps if we caught a bus?" Jerry joked.

"Better idea. Let's order coffee and move over to the fireplace. We can study the horse brasses and pretend we're watching an ox roast. I swear it's big enough to do it."

The rather unnecessary fire crackled and cast a warm glow over the room. They settled down in comfortable leather chairs, and as they sipped coffee and talked an hour slipped by.

In answer to Nicole's questions about his job, Jerry explained how his small company expanded to the point where one of the big guys swallowed him up. Their offer of a cash settlement, and stock options if he would work for them for a year, was too good to turn down.

"And," he said, "I really like the company. I tell you, it's a big relief not having to worry about whether I could meet the payroll each month in my own company." He leaned back, stretched out his long legs, and studied his hiking boots. "There's a lot to be said for designing while someone else worries about the details."

After getting them a second cup of coffee, he asked why on earth she lived in a little village instead of in London. She told him how much she enjoyed the relaxed atmosphere and the fabulous walks. "I tell you these Brits have done a great job of preserving trails right across the countryside."

"Tell me about some of them."

"Let's see now. You can walk right across Sussex – that's in the South East – on the South Down Way, or the Isle of Wight that's just across the water from here, has a 21-mile walk. That's the total length of the Island, on top of the downs with spectacular ocean and rural views all the way."

"Okay, I get the drift, but I still don't understand the attraction of a pokey little village with a handful of shops."

"I've always fancied life in a small, picturesque village. Probably read too many English classics in my youth."

In answer to his questions about the people in the village, she found herself talking about Emma and what a kind little soul she was.

"I'd like to meet her."

"Unfortunately, she's in New Zealand right now."

He looked closely at her. "What's wrong? You looked worried just then."

Glad of an opportunity to voice her concerns, she said, "I don't know. Something's just not right."

"*What's* not right?"

"Well, she's painfully shy and totally under the thumb of her husband. Now she's suddenly joined a photography group and taken a trip with them on her own. Her husband came home without her."

"Nothing wrong with that. Maybe she's always wanted to be a photographer. Shy people like to hide behind cameras."

"My neighbor tells me Emma never does anything without her husband. I have a hard time believing she could change so much in the space of a few weeks."

"Maybe it's the New Zealand air."

When she didn't laugh, he said, "If you're really worried, why don't you call her husband and find out?"

She bit her lip. "I guess I could." It wasn't until she voiced her thoughts that she'd recognized how much it was bothering her. Over the weeks, Emma's invitations when Adrian was away became less important for the dinner than her genuine concern. Her sympathy and understanding when Nicole was aggravated with her job, or worn out from travel, made Nicole subconsciously look forward to their evenings together. Now the thought that something might have happened to defenseless Emma kept her awake at nights.

However, she could tell by the look on Jerry's face that he was merely indulging her. "I know, I'm overreacting. Worrying about nothing."

With a quirky smile and twinkling eyes, he said, "Well, I was tempted to say you're acting like a mother hen and should probably just adopt a puppy with big brown eyes to worry about. However," he added quickly before she could speak, "due to the proximity of a tall, vertical cliff conveniently near, I decided to hold my peace. I've a feeling you'd shove me over."

"How right you are!" She laughed. "Whenever I think about it logically, I agree with you. But that uneasy gut feeling keeps creeping back. Something's wrong."

He leaned forward, looking into her eyes. She shifted uneasily. "Talk to her husband. He'll set your mind at rest."

"You're right. I'm probably being stupid. I'll give Adrian a call when I get home." And as she got to her feet and put on her jacket indicating the long lunch break was over, she added, "I think it was that private eye course; I see a villain behind every bush these days."

He stopped in the middle of picking up his jacket. "What private eye course?"

"I went to one in Seattle. Hah! I even have a private investigator's license." She saw no point in mentioning it was only valid in the States.

He roared with laughter. "You've got to be kidding."

"No. I'll show it to you sometime."

"Uh oh – are you inviting me up to see your etchings?"

"Stop kidding yourself."

The return hike took longer. The sun warm on their backs, their stomachs still full, their pace slowed until by mutual agreement they went over to the cliff's edge and sat with their legs dangling watching the yachts off-shore for a while. Arriving at the parking lot at five o'clock, Nicole said, "There's an express to London in about thirty minutes. Want to catch it or do you want a cup of tea first?"

"Let's go for it. I'll get tea on the train"

When Nicole drove up to her garage, she saw Iris working in the garden. She parked and went over to the fence. "Hi, Iris. How are you?"

"Good thanks. Have a good hike?"

"Yes, great, lovely weather. Heard from Emma yet?"

"No, not a peep."

"Don't you think it's strange she hasn't called or sent a post-card? She seems like a postcard sending person."

"You're right, she does usually. Bombards me with them. I'm glad she isn't, means she must be having fun."

"But it's been weeks. I'm worried. What if something has happened to her."

"For goodness sakes there's nothing to worry about. Adrian says she's having a ball. I think he's miffed she's having a good time without him."

Unconvinced, she persisted, "I don't know. Can I have Adrian's number? I'll call and see if he's had any word."

Iris straightened up, displaying mud encrusted knees. "Better than that, are you free for dinner tonight?"

Puzzled, she answered, "Yes."

"Okay, then seven o'clock. I'll invite Adrian too. He can tell you all about it. I think you're worrying about nothing."

CHAPTER 15

Nicole sat with Adrian, Martin and Iris nibbling pate with French bread and smoked salmon wrapped around a soft cream cheese. The table set with a bowl of fresh spring flowers in the center, a cheerful check table cloth and blue and brown stoneware plates felt as welcoming as the food. She noted with some surprise that even the floor was temporarily devoid of dog hair.

Adrian regaled them with stories from his trip to the States, and when Iris went to the kitchen to bring in a rack of lamb, he asked Nicole where she was from. After raving about the delights of New Zealand, he asked about her job. He leaned forward, listening intently and barraging her with questions. She told him she had been recruited from New Zealand by an English company and soon had them all laughing about the perils of consulting.

As Iris served a trifle, fruity, creamy and delicious with just the right amount of too much sherry, Nicole asked "How is Emma doing Adrian?"

"Having a great time."

"When's she coming home?"

"Damned if I know. She finished her photography trip and now she's decided to become a writer."

"What!" Iris and Martin chorused.

Adrian grinned broadly. "Yes, after they finished the photography boondoggle, the group decided to put a book together. They want it to be a travelog and photo journal."

Puzzled, Nicole asked, "Is Emma a writer?"

"Emma a writer!" Adrian guffawed.

Martin and Iris both laughed. Feeling confused, she asked, "Well, if she isn't, why is she staying to write the book?"

"According to Emma, all the other members of the group have full-time jobs. She's the only housewife. So she ended up volunteering to do it.'

Iris, wiping tears of laughter from her eyes said, "Oh, dear, I just had this wonderful vision of Emma as a best-selling romance writer running around in sunglasses beating off the paparazzi."

"You never know," Martin added. "She may surprise us all yet."

Adrian, frowning, said, "She's taking a one-week writing course in Auckland before she starts."

"You mean she thinks she'll be able to knock out a book in a couple of weeks after that?" Martin asked.

"That's the plan. She says she just has to gather all the info from her New Zealand friends then come back home and finish it."

Nicole helped Iris take the dishes to the kitchen, and made coffee while Iris loaded the dishwasher. Iris, adroitly pushing away a spaniel that was trying to get his tongue on the dirty dishes said, "Don't forget to ask Adrian where he stayed, and the hotel Emma is in. I'll give her a call tomorrow."

Jolted, she realized she was so charmed by Adrian, she'd totally forgotten her earlier misgivings. She carried the coffee through to the dining room and as they sipped, Martin, reminded by a none too subtle nudge from Iris, leaped to his feet and asked, "Who's for a B & B?"

Nicole declined on the grounds of an early start in the morning, and as the other three sampled their drink, asked Adrian, "Where did you stay when you were in New Zealand? You were in Northland weren't you?"

"Yes, not too far from that little place where you can have a fish and chip lunch on the jetty."

"Mangonui!"

"That's it. We sat down. Started off with a crayfish salad." Turning to Martin, he added, "Salt water crayfish are the size of lobsters and just as delicious. Then ate fish and chips out of fake newspaper with our fingers. All washed down with a good bottle of chardonnay."

"I'm glad you didn't miss that. Where did you stay?"

"Damned if I can ever remember the name. It was a Maori one. Think it began with a K or something like that." He turned to Martin. "You'd love that place. They let you pick out your fish, and then cook it while you eat your salad or whatever. Fish is straight out of the ocean; the fishing boats come right into the same harbor."

Why do I keep thinking he's being evasive? He certainly remembers a lot of details about everything except where they stayed.

CHAPTER 16

"Hi Nicki, want to come to an antiques show next Sunday?" Jerry's call surprised her. He normally waited two or more weeks before suggesting another outing.

"Not much. Had a friend who wanted to furnish her house with Victoriana. Spent too many hours trailing through shops packed with furniture smelling of must and dust. Gave me the creeps."

"Oh!" His deflated voice picked up as he added, "But I'm talking about the Art & Antiques Fair at Grosvenor House. Strictly up market – have to have a ticket. Won't be dusty. And the only smell will be of money – the rich and famous fly in from all over."

"In that case, it sounds fun. I've never been to Grosvenor House." She paused. "Wait a minute though. How did you snag a ticket to mingle with the mighty?"

"Ahah, my dear! You are privileged to know a man of influence." He waited a dramatic moment before adding, "Actually, there was a special offer in the Sunday Telegraph."

"What time?"

"I'll meet you at Waterloo at 10:30 a.m."

Ringing off, she made a mental note to get a manicure and hairdo next Saturday and then rummaged through her wardrobe for a suitable outfit.

◄►

Swept along by the hurrying passengers, Nicole stepped from the train into the melee of Waterloo. Jerry stood waiting at the barrier. Dressed in a custom tailored suit, he looked as if he had just stepped off the pages of the Tatler. The tailor had taken full advantage of his broad, square shoulders and slim frame. But he looked as comfortable in high fashion as he did in his usual sweat-shirt and jeans. As he caught sight of her, his eyes flickered over her, widened and a slight smile curled the corners of his mouth, but as she came up to him he simply crooked his arm, gave a slight bow and said, "Madam."

She sedately placed her arm through his, feeling the firm mus-cles beneath the soft wool. "Sir."

Arm-in- arm they wove their way across the concourse packed with passengers hurrying to their platforms. Past the smell of hot bread at a food counter, the tempting display of best sellers in W.H.Smith's window, and out through the arched exit to the taxi rank.

During the ten-minute wait on the diesel smelling forecourt, buses and taxis disgorged passengers in holiday garb dragging large suitcases or hefting bulging backpacks. Others, casually dressed, seemed to be off to the country or seaside.

"Where to, guv?" the cabbie asked as they clambered in.

"Grosvenor House."

The taxi accelerated out of the forecourt and they sat hanging on to the straps as he wove his way through the crowded streets. Past Buckingham Palace gardens, the Wellington monument and on to Park Lane, where it flew alongside Hyde Park to Grosvenor House. While Jerry paid the driver, a top-hatted, liveried door-man helped Nicole out of the taxi with a gloved hand.

Heads high, they sailed through the lobby to the entrance of the Great Room; a banqueting room capable of seating two thou-sand guests. For the Art & Antiques show – a show that had run each June for seventy five years – it had been converted to a series of rooms. Each room a stage set showing off vendors' wares. Jerry showed his tickets at the entrance and they followed the well-heeled viewers into the show.

For a moment they stood, savoring the scene, listening to the muted buzz of conversation, and wondering where to start. Picking a vendor at random, they wandered through the rooms. Previous experience of antiques' stores left Nicole cold. Overcrowded and musty they bore no relation to these rooms of gleaming furniture. Nary a scent of dust, but the rich smell of lemon wax polish mingled with the delightful aroma of expensive perfume.

As they moved through the rooms with their magnificently laid out displays, they felt as if they were in an enormous, elegant mansion. Engrossed in the furniture and taken by a splendid oak chair, Nicole took a peek at the price tag "£100,000". She moved on quickly. Jerry, who had disappeared, was found busy haggling with a vendor over two magnificent life-size bronze hounds. She loved them. However, commonsense prevailed, and she whispered in his ear, "If you buy them, you are going to have to buy a country estate to go with them." Ruefully, with a last pat on one of the dog's heads, he followed her to the next room.

After a couple of hours, they began to wilt. Jerry leaned over, "How about we find something to drink?"

An inviting champagne bar lay in their path, the shelves behind the bar displaying a bewildering array of different vineyards and vintages. The bar stools adorned with long-legged Sloane rangers and their elegantly tailored escorts.

"Since my intentions are not nefarious, we shall go in pursuit of tea. Were you to ply me with champagne my resolve might weaken." He steered her past the bar toward the exit.

With a faint feeling of regret, immediately stifled, Nicole followed. They slipped into a tearoom and sat nibbling tiny sandwiches and drinking tea from bone china cups as their feet recovered.

"Let's take a walk across London. I love the side streets – particularly all those blue plaques on walls. I swear everybody famous has lived in London over the past couple of centuries." He glanced under the table at her feet. "Perhaps not, you're wearing fancy shoes."

"They just look fancy. I learned early in my career to wear comfortable shoes. In foreign cities people invariably want to show you some sights on their way to dinner. After scaling a park hillside in Austria wearing spiky high heels one time to admire a view, I learned the error of my ways." She swung round in her chair, crossed her legs and wiggled a foot. "Behold Swiss footwear at its finest. Elegance and practicality combined. These soft-leather shoes can walk across London and back."

They spent an enjoyable few hours walking and window shopping. At a charming old pub they found on a corner, they sat outside with a soft drink and people-watched. Fortnum & Masons was too much for Nicole to resist, so they went in and browsed the food hall delighting in the magnificent displays of food and the seductive smell of exotic meats, cheeses and pastries. Salivating at the French pastries and savory venison pies, Jerry said, "Let's buy some goodies and take them back to my place. You can admire my great new decorations while I make coffee. Then we'll get you to Waterloo for a 5:30 p.m. train."

While Jerry went to the kitchen to make coffee, Nicole wandered around the living room admiring his two new paintings, and selection of books. As she perused the bookshelves she saw a large silver-framed collage of photos set squarely in the middle of the shelf. She decided it would look better off to one side, and in moving it, took a moment to look at the pictures. The first was of a stunning woman in a bikini. The skimpy bikini showed off a perfect figure, long elegant legs, and a cascade of shining red-gold hair. Other photos showed her laughing up at Jerry on the ski slopes, dressed in a long gown beside Jerry in a tux and standing in front of a huge Christmas tree. Nicole noted with an unworthy feeling of satisfaction that the later photos showed a fuller face and figure.

Jerry came in with a tray laden with coffee pot, cups, cream jug and a plate of goodies from Fortnum & Mason. She waved to the framed photos, "Is this Madison? Wow! No wonder you don't want to lose her."

His face lit up. "You're right. She's gorgeous isn't she?"

He busied himself pouring coffee and bringing in plates and napkins while she tried to decide what to eat first. After she'd made her selection and settled back on the sofa with a cup of coffee, he said, "Madison called yesterday."

"That's great." She knew he'd been worried about her.

"Yes, it was a surprise. It's been a while. Anyway, it's great, she's finally figured out what she wants to do. *And* bottom line, she's coming over here at Christmas."

"Terrific. But why Christmas? Why not now?"

"This gets heavy." He stirred cream into his coffee and sat looking at it for a long moment. "She's decided she wants to come back, but she's convinced that when she's with me she must be her own person."

"Uhh?"

"With the aid of a counselor," - he gave an involuntary shudder - "she decided that she had been so busy running around after me while I was flat out building my company, that she had no time for herself." He paused a moment and then added wryly, "Although she did manage to fit in regular visits to the spa followed by lunch with her friends."

"Okay," Nicole said dubiously.

He continued with a rush. "Even after I slackened off, she still felt she had to look after me to the point where she lost all sense of who she was." He looked up quickly, studied his cup and continued, "She's decided she must have a career of her own and she's training to be an interior designer."

"That's going to take until Christmas? Why doesn't she come over and take a course in London?"

Now he looked embarrassed and took a long drink of coffee, smothering his face behind the cup. "She's sure if she comes back to me before she qualifies, she'll slip back into her old habits and just run around after me. Apparently, I dominate her."

"Whew!" Not quite sure what to say, Nicole laughed it off. "Since you are such a dominant type, I'd better drink my coffee quick and be on my way before you turn me into a scullery maid."

Visibly relieved, he grinned and looked at his watch. "Actually, you're right. You do need to be on your way. I'll call a taxi or you'll miss your train."

As the taxi hurtled toward the station, snaking its way through traffic snarls, Nicole caught sight of Martin handing a very elegant woman into a large Mercedes. She glimpsed just a flash of dark blue silk, tan sports jacket and brown slacks before she was jostled into the corner of the back seat as the taxi shot down a side street.

"Hey, I know you must be a Le Mans driver, but could you just slow down a bit."

"You want to catch your train don't you love?"

"Preferably in one piece."

"Okay, we're through the worst of it now, we can take it easy."

She relaxed and sat back. Decided it couldn't have been Martin. She knew he was in Dorset. Iris had said she was looking forward to the party they were going to on Saturday night.

CHAPTER 17

Three weeks later, Nicole sat at Iris's kitchen table luxuriating in the aroma of fresh baked pastry and coffee. The apple turnover crumbled as she bit into it and oozed tangy apples and Devon cream. "Mmmm, you've surpassed yourself."

Steadfastly ignoring the imploring eyes of the overweight pug that sat on her foot - presumably to anchor her to the spot - she added, "How on earth does Martin stay slim married to a fabulous cook like you?"

Iris, her face flushed from the oven, said, "He works out at the gym about four times a week."

As Iris put a tray of scones to cool, Nicole told her about the antiques show. Iris showed scant interest, and instead raved for a solid twenty minutes about visiting Crufts Dog Show two years before. A tired old border collie at her feet yawned.

Agreeing with the collie's opinion, Nicole looked desperately for a change of subject. Spotting an elegant silver gray outfit hanging on the back of the laundry door, she gushed, "That's nice. Going somewhere special?"

"I'm off to the symphony tonight. I tell you, dinner at a swish hotel and the symphony."

"Great. What are you celebrating?"

"Oh, nothing. Martin just feels he's been neglecting me lately. We'd arranged to go out to dinner last Sunday with friends and he had to cancel at the last minute."

"That's too bad." Nicole took another bite of turnover and broke off a tidbit for the pug.

"Not really. Mitzi had an operation on her paw on Saturday and I wanted to be home with her." Mitzi was an incredibly ugly bulldog.

A flash back of the Martin lookalike with that elegant woman crossed her mind but she decided not to mention it. If it was Martin, the woman could have been his latest divorcee client. But why on a Sunday?

"Any news of Emma?"

"No. Still not a sausage."

"That's weird. I'll give Adrian a call. See if he's heard from her. He'll be at home won't he?"

"No. Didn't I tell you? He's in New York again – seems to have a lot of business there these days. No need to worry about Emma, Adrian says she's taking a writing course in Auckland this week. Too busy to call him often. He sounded quite miffed." She gave a snort of laughter. "Serves him right. About time she started enjoying herself instead of running around after him." She gulped down the last of her coffee, brushed pastry crumbs from her blouse - the crumbs immediately attacked by the pug - and stood up. "I need to get moving. Have to clear up the kitchen, feed the pooches and spruce myself up before Martin comes home."

The following Sunday, Jerry bounded off the train in Poole, a deerstalker hat flapping around his ears and a woolen Sherlock Holmes' cape streaming behind him.

"Don't you know Hallowe'en's in October?" Nicole said through her laughter.

Unperturbed, he rummaged around in the cloak's cavernous pockets and produced an oversized magnifying glass. "Madam, it is time to stop fretting about your long-lost friend and start looking for her."

He took off the hat, stuck it on her surprised head and gave a short, courtly bow. "Watson at your service ma'am."

"You're nuts."

He looked at her with serious eyes. "Every time we meet, you talk about Emma." He fidgeted with the lapels of his coat. "Damn it Nicki – I find *I'm* worrying about her now."

Uncomfortable under the amused glances of people on the platform, she urged, "Come on. Let's go to the car and shed our fancy dress."

Once in the Renault, she added, "You're right. I've always believed worrying is futile. If you're worried, do something about it and if there's nothing you can do, forget it."

"That's my girl. This is your opportunity to put all those skills you learned in that private eye course to good use."

"It's a bit difficult when she's on the other side of the world."

"No, it's not. Let's have a quick hike around the heath and then go back to your house and get to work. We can make a few phone calls to New Zealand, see if we can track her down."

A few hours later they sat in Nicole's kitchen enjoying a cup of tea.

"Okay, super sleuth, where do we start?"

"Let me see," she pondered, pinching the bridge of her nose between thumb and forefinger. "The instructor told us 'the first thing to do when seeking a missing person, is to list all the things you know about them, because somewhere in their background lurks a clue to their whereabouts.'"

"Right." Jerry pulled his laptop out of its bag. "Dictate a way. You knew her."

"She likes cooking and gardening. Grew up in Bath and went to a fancy girls' boarding school somewhere near there. Got her degree in London – that's where she met Adrian – worked for a publisher for about a year, then married him."

"That's a bit stark. Do you know any of her friends?"

"I met a few of them at a tea party she had, but never since. She hasn't talked about anyone else."

"She must have friends somewhere and what about her family?"

Nicole shook her head in dismay. "It's ridiculous. I just don't even know where her family live, or whether she's got any other friends. She never talked about them. She was painfully shy when I first met her, and then when I got her to open up, all she ever talked about was Adrian and how marvelous he was. And all the places they had visited together."

"Didn't she have any interests outside the home?"

"No. She just ran around after Adrian. His annual sojourn in Bermuda meant her life was disjointed and pretty busy anyway. I gather he's a demanding sort who needs lots of backup."

"Really?"

"He was always writing articles and giving talks, and I believe Emma is a pretty good editor. Although I never heard him say so."

He put down his pen. "Somehow I don't think we're going to get very far digging into her background. Fact is, she's right out of her home environment. Why don't you give Missing Persons in New Zealand a call and put them on the job?"

"That's part of the police I think."

"You think? What sort of a Kiwi are you?"

"To tell the truth, I never knew anyone who went missing so I haven't a clue how it works."

"Let Watson go to work." He clicked away industriously. "Okay, here we go. You're right, the police handle it. The Salvation Army too, but let's try the police first. Hmmm." He sat reading for a few moments. "Eight thousand people reported missing each year. Fifty percent found within forty eight hours – seems a lot of folks just go back home. Then a full 95% within 14 days."

"Okay – now tell me what they need to start a search."

"This is encouraging. If you fear for their safety, you can report right away. You don't have to wait."

"Interesting. But let's concentrate on Emma – she's been missing a long time."

"They need all sorts of info like where she was last seen, what her full name is, photo, what your relationship with her is, her credit card details."

"Somehow I don't think we've got a very convincing case if her husband isn't worried." Nicole got up and poured more tea into their cups. "Think about it. They'll ask all the standard questions – for which we have few answers – then they'll ask why we're worried. We say we fear foul play and they'll ask what evidence we have." She gave an exasperated sigh.

Jerry grinned. "They would have a point. What is the evidence, and if Adrian isn't bothered, why are we?"

Her mouth set in a grim line. "I think it's downright suspicious. No one just disappears off the face of the earth. Certainly not a sweet little soul like Emma. She would be sending postcards. Iris says she normally gets at least a dozen from her on every trip."

Jerry's grin grew wider. "So you think Adrian has a dark secret and has buried Emma somewhere deep in the bush? Has it ever occurred to you that you read too many mystery novels?"

"You're probably right, but every time I try to rationalize it, it doesn't work. Something isn't right. It's totally out of character for Emma. And when I had dinner with Adrian, his reactions were off. If his wife hasn't come home, why is he taking it so calmly? With his overbearing personality, why would he accept her absence so meekly? He just keeps shooting off to New York, and according to Iris, seems very happy. Why? My gut says something's awry."

"Hah! The famous woman's intuition."

"No, bimbo, it's more like when you have to deal with difficult people all the time - and let's face it, the software industry has them in spades: introverts by the bushel, oversensitive ones and super egos - you get a feel for how people react in different situations. And Adrian is the classic big ego, but he isn't worried the little woman is making a fool of him by not coming home."

"Okay, Dr. Freud, so what's next?"

"Let's think about this. There has to be something we can do to trace her." She stared into the cup of tea for inspiration. "I know. Adrian said she took a writing class in Auckland. They should have an address and phone number for her. I'll look up writing classes and you can do the phoning. Ninety percent of them are run by women and you can charm them to death – see where that gets us."

It didn't get them far. Emma had not enrolled in an Auckland class, but a helpful woman there gave Jerry a list of regional chapters of the Writers Association. After six phone calls they looked at each other in disgust. "Now what? It's hopeless." Nicole picked up their cups and put them in the dishwasher with an unnecessary clatter.

"No, it's not. Judy – the last fair damsel I talked to – said there are a bunch of small writing groups in the regions but we'd need to go to the local areas and ask around."

"Great!" She tried unsuccessfully to keep the sarcasm out of her voice.

"The answer's clear. Hop on a plane and hunt her down. You know the territory and face-to-face people are going to give you answers. You have that effect on them. That poor cop won't know what hit him. He'll probably tell you the trouble he's having with his son too!"

Stunned, Nicole looked at him for a long moment. A trip home. A bubble of excitement welled up inside her. A walk on the beach. A swim in a warm ocean. Fishing. Sailing. Just as quickly the bubble was replaced by a lump of lead. Jay wouldn't be there.

Looking faintly puzzled, Jerry stood up. "Let's have another cup of tea and think about this a bit." He filled the kettle and flipped the switch, took a fresh couple of mugs out of the kitchen cabinet, rinsed out the teapot and came back to the table. "You do have enough vacation don't you? I bet you haven't had a long one in ages."

"I took that trip to Seattle."

"Yes, but you're a workaholic. I bet you've got weeks stacked up. You're due six weeks a year, and my bet is you didn't take any of them last year."

Nicole sighed. Was she that transparent? "Yes, I have the time and things are fairly quiet at work at the moment, but I don't know, I don't have too many friends there now. I'm not sure I want to go running around on a wild goose chase."

"Ho! So now you don't care about Emma. Okay, let's shelve the project. Adrian's probably right she's just enjoying life."

"Dammit. You know I'm worried. I just don't want to take the trip."

"Look, it doesn't have to take long. We can just zip down, find Emma and be back in no time."

"*We!*"

"Yes. I'm coming too. Sherlock has to have Watson along. I'll even carry the magnifying glass and rent a bloodhound when we get there."

"Rent a bloodhound?"

"That damn little country seems to have everything else. I'm sure they'll have a Rent-a-Bloodhound at the airport."

In spite of the leaden lump, she found herself laughing. Maybe she could do it. If she just concentrated on Emma, perhaps the demons would stay at bay. "Okay, I'll go, but I don't need you along."

"Yes, you do. I'll be invaluable as your gofer. Anyway, I've always wanted to take a trip to New Zealand and it would be great to have a native guide." As she started to protest, he added, "I think it'll only take a couple of days to run her down, then I'll leave you to it."

He went over and poured some boiling water in the teapot, tipped it out, put in the teabags and filled the pot. Returning to the table, he leaned back in his chair balancing on the back two legs and said, " I like the idea of staying at one of those fancy fishing lodges where they spoil you to death and have guides that take you out and put you right on the fish. I figured trout fishing first, then a bit of the deep sea stuff. Catch myself a marlin."

She took a deep breath and exhaled slowly. "Okay, you're on. I'll see how the workload looks on Monday and then book some flights."

Excited at the prospect of seeing her dad again, she called on Monday evening. His answering service told her to leave a message. She tried again the next day; still no response. Exasperated and anxious to let him know she was coming, she called one of his Auckland friends. "Sorry, luv, he's sailing round the islands with his mates. Should be in Fiji about now. He's not expected back for another three weeks."

Her shoulders sagged, but she took a deep breath, swallowed the threatening tears, and chatted for a while with his Auckland friend. The Kiwi voice made her homesick. She found herself looking forward to the trip.

CHAPTER 18

Warm moist air, rich with the delicate scent of Jacaranda, caressed her face. Why on earth had she stayed away from New Zealand for so long? Before the black cloud of memory had time to ruin the moment, Jerry bounded out of the motel office with a pile of brochures in his hands.

Nicole looked at the jumbled papers. "Ye gods, I've got a tourist on my hands!"

"No, me darlin', I've got a map so we can find our way around Auckland – you haven't been back for years so you'll have forgotten where everything is. Brochures too, so I see all the attractions. I'm going to have a ball after we've found Emma."

"Whew! Are you done? I thought lunch sounded like a good idea."

"No, work first. Police station's not far. We can walk from here. We'll go talk to their missing persons guy. Get him to work. *Then* lunch, and a cold beer. It's hot."

With long, steepled fingers under his chin, the policeman listened, his eyes not wavering from Nicole's face. When she finished expounding her reasons for the need to find Emma, he sat back. They waited.

"So to summarize, you want me to help you trace this woman. Someone who is not a relative, just a friend, and one you know very little about." As she leaned forward ready to interrupt, he continued, speaking rapidly. "It's obvious that you are very concerned, and it's good to have a friend that cares about her this much. However, hasn't it occurred to you, that maybe she doesn't want to go home to her husband? He sounds the overbearing type. Perhaps she decided it was a good time to do a runner."

Jerry, who had sat quietly listening to Nicole's impassioned arguments and watching the policeman with amused eyes, grinned broadly. She shot a murderous look in his direction, and said, "I know, but it's just so out of character for her. There's not a strong-willed bone in her body." She tried to suppress her growing irritation. "I think it's downright suspicious. I need to find her, then I'll believe you."

"Ah well, if you don't believe the magic of Godzone captured her – think you must have been living in England too long – maybe her husband told her to stay for a while. Is he playing outside the family circle, back home?"

"I've no idea. He travels on business so often, no one would ever know."

"Look Mrs. Jensen, I appreciate your concern, but I don't think there's any reason to list her as a missing person."

As Nicole rose slightly in her seat, ready to explode, Jerry intervened, his voice quiet, conciliatory. "I know this sounds like a flimsy case from where you are sitting, and I'm sure you are overloaded with work as it is, but couldn't you just give us some help so that we can get started. We'll go and look for her, and apologize if we've wasted your time."

The policeman looked at Nicole, long experience telling him there was no way she was going to leave before he agreed to help. She'd already been harassing him for over half an hour in this room, and had made several lengthy calls from the U.K. He looked at his watch. "I'll make a few phone calls. Why don't you go get yourselves some lunch and come back and see me in a couple of hours."

As they left the building, Jerry laughed. "That poor guy. I made a mental note never to bother arguing with you when you're intent on achieving something. You sure there isn't a bulldog somewhere back in your ancestry?"

She took a deep breath of salty air. "Between us we did get him to take some action though." She laughed. "I do tend to get a wee bit carried away I must admit." She skipped down the steps. "Come on. Let's go eat."

They walked down to the Viaduct Basin and settled down outside a restaurant with a great view of the yachts. People sauntered by, paused to read menus, and kept an eye on children who ran perilously near the edge of the wharf. Nicole and Jerry ordered Steinlager shandies.

"Hey, these shandies taste good. I thought the combination of lemonade and lager sounded gross."

"Oh ye, of little faith! When are you going to bow to my superior knowledge?" Nicole was saved from Jerry's retort by the arrival of the waitress.

After she had finished reciting the specials and departed with their orders, Jerry watched her shapely rear end disappear from view before turning to Nicole. "Heck, I thought I understood the language, but it took me a while to work out that frish was fresh. I thought for a minute she was offering me fish tomato soup!"

The meal was delicious and the service excellent. As Jerry paid the bill and added a large tip, Nicole intervened. "No tipping in this fair land."

"You're kidding?"

"No, it's true. Makes life a lot simpler. Think about it. Tipping implies that you are superior to the waitress."

"Wow! I'm beginning to like it here. Lead on, trusty guide, and show me the sights. Sandy, in the motel, told me the maritime museum is on the quay. Can't be far. We still have an hour before we can go back and beat up on that poor policeman again."

"You're right, it's just over there." She pointed toward the harbor mouth. They walked along the quay, the sun warm on their backs, a light breeze keeping the temperature perfect and creating a medley of jingling yacht riggings.

As they approached the museum, she attempted a light tone to mask her impatience. "This has to be a fast tour – I want to get back to talk to our buddy at the police station."

She gave an impatient glance at her watch, but it was too soon to return and there was nothing they could do until they had checked with the police. Maybe he could come up with something. If not, what then? Seeing Jerry's avid interest, it struck her that Emma would have been a tourist too. She would have hit some of the sights. Or rather, she would have looked at the sights Adrian wanted to see. One of the guides, ticket sellers or coffee shop waiters might remember seeing her. A slim chance, but with precious few clues to follow anything would help.

She grabbed Jerry's elbow and whisked him through the exhibits inside the museum. They were arranged as a progression through the maritime history of the country including the voyages of the settlers. Jerry was fascinated by the waka, a long canoe with outriggers propelled by oars and a small sail, used by the Polynesians.

As she dragged him away, he turned to her with a puzzled expression. "If this thing is called a waka – what's the haka?"

Laughing she said, "That's a Maori chant the All Blacks – New Zealand's rugby team – do before games."

"What?"

"It goes like this." She bent her knees, crossed her arms across her chest and chanted:

Ka mate Ka mate

Ka ora Ka ora

Tenei Te Tangata Puhuruhuru

As she chanted, she slapped her knees and pulled a face at him.

Some amused German tourists stopped to watch. Before she got half way through, Jerry grabbed her hand and pulled her up. "Okay, already, I get the picture."

"Yah, come on, you've missed the best bit where I leap in the air with my arms wide and stick my tongue out."

"Thank god for that. Your going native was a bit more than I bargained for."

"Come on then. Let's hustle through to the immigrant ship."

On the way, she fished out her photo of Emma and showed it to a guide. He shook his head. "No, sorry, but try the souvenir shop before you leave the museum. She's sure to have gone there." Thanking him, she followed Jerry to the ship.

The guide at the entrance shook his head when Nicole showed him Emma's photo, "Sorry, don't remember her." Then turning to include Jerry, he said "The ship's a replica of one of the sailing vessels used in the 19th and early 20th century to bring European settlers – a preponderance of English and Dutch – on the long, slow voyage from England. Go take a look. I'll be glad to answer any questions."

As Nicole and Jerry boarded it, the timbers creaked, the light grew dim and the decks began to rock beneath their feet. "Jeez, this thing is floating!" Jerry exclaimed.

"That's why the museum's on the waterfront."

As they drew back a curtain and looked at the huge bunk, Jerry said, "This cabin is pretty darn luxurious. I've been on cruise ships with less room."

"But this would have been for a family of seven or more. They had big families in those days, and the mother might well have had another one right here in the middle of them all."

Jerry looked startled. "There's a lot to be said for a 747!"

They moved on and stood outside on a balcony overlooking the outdoor exhibits tied up beside the museum. "How about we take a tour around the harbor on that old scow?"

"No, it will take too long. However," she pointed to a dinky tug boat, "we could take a trip on that one. It only takes about twenty minutes." The boat was small and round with just enough room for the captain, a boiler and stoker, and about four passengers.

"I doubt there's room for my knees on it, but let's go, looks like fun."

Although they were the only passengers, the captain welcomed them aboard and prepared to cast off. The stoker scowled in their direction and threw a shovelful of coal in the boiler.

Nicole pulled out Emma's photo. "Did this woman come on a trip with you? She's a friend of mine from England."

The captain looked, "No. Don't remember her. You, Bruce?" The stoker leaned over to look and shook his head. Nicole pocketed the photo and sat back to enjoy the ride.

With a toot on the horn, they were off and chugged around the harbor getting wet when a bow wave from a ferry hit the tiny craft. Damp and laughing, they clambered back on to the dock and checked the souvenir shop. Nobody remembered seeing Emma. With spirits dampened to match their clothes, they headed for the police station.

Within a few minutes, they were greeted by the same policeman. "Did you have a good lunch?"

They answered and Jerry told him about their short visit to the museum.

"Good, glad you enjoyed it. I made a few calls."

Nicole held her breath.

The policeman continued, "I talked to her husband, nice bloke. He was surprised you're here, but he said he isn't worried."

Nicole started, "But . . ."

He cut her off. "I'm not worried either. She's still using her credit card. He says she's not spending much so she must be staying with friends, but he doesn't know where she is. The credit card has been used in several different locations. Sounds like she's moving around."

Still not convinced, Nicole said, "But why do you believe him about the credit card?"

He looked volumes, but answered quietly, "I made a call to the bank. She's been using it alright."

Nicole persisted quietly through pursed lips, "He's working a scam somehow. I'm sure something's wrong."

After a quick glance in her direction, Jerry intervened. "Could you give us one of the locations on the credit card to get us started?"

"No, sorry, that's confidential, but if I were you I'd head north. Didn't you say her husband talked about being up there?" He turned to Jerry, his stern face relaxing. "Great fishing in the north and a couple of dynamite golf courses."

Nicole had a hard time accepting the dead end and muttered under her breath. The policeman stood up and came over to her. He said quietly, his sympathetic eyes focused on her face, "I think you need to find her to make you feel better. " He paused a long moment and then added, "I know how hard it is to lose a friend, and how difficult it must be for you to come back home." *Dammit, he'd been checking up on her. He knew all about Jay's accident. As the searing misery of Jay's death swept over her, she realized this trip had been a huge mistake. She'd kidded herself it would be okay after all this time. People would have forgotten. And the first damn person she talks to reminds her of him.*

The policemen continued, his voice soft. "You'll feel happier after you've found her and had a good laugh about it." He handed her a piece of paper. "This is the name of the senior sergeant up in Mangonui. You mentioned her husband talked about that area. He'll give you a hand. Good luck."

Eyes clouded by tears, she stumbled toward the door. Gritted her teeth, straightened her shoulders and by the time she reached the street, had the tears stifled.

Jerry, puzzled by what had been said, but sensitive enough not to ask for an explanation, took her arm reassuringly. "Let's go get the car and head north. We'll find her in no time."

CHAPTER 19

After leaving the police station, they walked towards their car without exchanging a word. "Let's sit and have a cup of coffee," Jerry suggested quietly. "We can figure out what we're going to do when we get to the north." He steered her in the direction of a coffee shop. Cool air, coffee and a babble of voices greeted them in the crowded restaurant. Jerry surveyed the scene. "Let's try outside, it'll be quieter."

Outside, a scattering of shoppers tucked into pastries and a lone business-type hunched over his laptop. Jerry led her over to a corner, well away from the other customers. "You get settled, and I'll get the coffees."

The few moments alone helped, and after a cup of coffee Nicole began to feel better. Taking a deep breath, she forced herself to concentrate on the problem of locating Emma. "Let's start by advertising in the Herald. I'll write a small ad telling Emma I'm here and would like to talk to her. My cell can be the contact point." She clicked her tongue as she drafted it on a napkin. "Maybe, just maybe, she'll look at the ads while she eats breakfast. I do. The agony column and the small ads are more fun than the news."

His eyebrows went up. "Somehow I never visualized you reading advice columns."

"You don't know what you're missing. Agony aunts come up with some of the most hysterically ridiculous solutions you have ever heard. However, time is a-wasting." She slid the napkin across to him. "We need to get things rolling before we leave. Emailing an ad to The New Zealand Herald will do it."

He fished in his bag for his laptop and got started. "Just one off, or a few days?"

"Let's try it for a week. Then we'll put one in the Northern Advocate once we get up north. She's less likely to look at the local paper but you never know."

She tapped her fingers impatiently on the table as he typed, but as she started to tell him about another idea, he interrupted. "Let's just finish our coffee and hit the road. We can make plans as we drive." He stopped. "How long does it take to get to that place?"

"'Bout four hours. Motorway peters out after a while, then it's two-way roads all the way. Lovely scenic drive, but a lot slower."

He took a last sip of coffee, packed away his laptop and followed her out of the café. "Guess we'll have to start at that place you mentioned. You said Adrian raved about some place with a great fish and chip shop on the wharf. What are you going to do when you get there?" His grin was sudden. "That is, while I eat fish and chips . . ."

"Yes, that's our best bet. We've nothing else to go on. We'll talk to the local cop, then the postie."

"The postie?"

"The mail man. They know where everyone lives and most of their business. They're all gossips."

"Great. Let's go."

As Nicole slipped into the driver's seat, she asked, "Did you do any driving in England?"

"No. Don't need a car in central London. Walked to work and took the bus or train everywhere else. Think a car would be more of a hassle than an asset. I'll rent one if I need to drive some place."

"Okay, then take a seat and enjoy the scenery. I'll drive until you get the hang of being on the left hand side of the road."

But after she fastened her seat belt, moved the seat forward and adjusted the mirrors, she couldn't press the starter. Her hands shook. She closed her eyes tight for a moment, opened them and with gritted teeth and white knuckles grasped the wheel. Beads of perspiration coated her upper lip and dampened her armpits. She took two deep breaths to steady her nerves. *Why, oh, why, did I come back?* The memory, suppressed for so long swept over her.

Jay wheeled his bicycle out of the drive, mounted and turned to wave, a big morning grin on his face. Brakes squealed, the sickening crunch as the car's fender hit the bicycle and Jay – Jay – went hurtling into the air, falling like a rag doll into the path of the truck. The truck driver screeched to a halt, flung himself out of the cab – burly, clean jeans, bright red shirt, ashen-faced – ran to Jay. "Call an ambulance, call an ambulance." And as she stood rooted to the spot in horror, he yelled at her, furious, "NOW!"

She fumbled for her phone. A tall man in a business suit leapt out of his car waving a cell phone. "I called 111."

She ran back to Jay. Knelt beside his limp body as the truck driver tried CPR. The clang of the ambulance, the frenetic pace of the response team, the long minutes in the waiting room, the carefully arranged face of the doctor as he came out to tell her. Something in her died too.

Jerry looked startled as the color drained from her face. He tapped her gently on the arm. "Let me drive. You're tired."

She closed her eyes to hold back the tears as a wave of sheer misery swept over. Horribly aware of Jerry sitting beside her, she sat back in the seat, exhaled slowly, loosened her grip on the wheel and said in a shaky voice, "No, I'm fine. Just a jet lag moment. Once we're on our way with the window open, it'll be okay."

He turned toward her, edging closer, his arm sliding along the back of the seat behind her. She pushed against the door protecting the space between them. Finally, she hit the starter and biting her bottom lip, concentrated on the traffic.

Arms rigid on the steering wheel, stiff back, eyes glued to the road, she maneuvered through the city traffic. Once on the open road, her shoulders came down a fraction. She felt Jerry's eyes on her, but knowing they would be full of concern, kept her head averted. Finally, he started asking questions about places they passed. Her body slowly relaxed. It was going to be okay.

After about two hours, Jerry pointed to a billboard advertising a tearoom at the top of a long winding hill. "Let's have a coffee break. Looks as if there'll be a good view from the top. Then I'll drive – think I've got the hang of this wrong side of the road stuff."

Glad of a break, she drove into the parking lot, turned off the engine and rolled her shoulders to get rid of the tension. "Let's sit outside." She pointed to a deck jutting out from the elevated shop. "You can enjoy the view while I slurp tea. Good strong, stand-your-spoon-up-in-it Kiwi tea."

Beneath the deck, a rolling sheep-dotted pasture provided a verdant foreground for the breathtaking view of a dramatic coastline: a headland stretching out into the sea like a sleeping dragon and off-shore islands seemingly floating on a glassy ocean. The smell of new mown grass from the tearoom's garden and salt air mingled with the appetizing aroma of Jerry's meat pie. She grinned across at Jerry as she spread a thick layer of jam and cream on her scone.

Arriving too late to catch the postie or bother the cop, they found a beachfront motel, went to their rooms to change and took a run along the beach reveling in the fresh salt air. The shallow blue water with gentle surges of incoming tide lapped the shore, and a fringe of dark green pohutakwa trees hung out over the sand providing welcome shade for a few sand-encrusted families.

Hot and sticky after their run, they walked up the beach to their towels which lay on the soft dry sand above the waterline.

Nicole shed running shoes, shorts and shirt, until she was down to her swim suit. She turned to ask Jerry if he was ready and saw him staring at her. "What's the matter?"

Confused, he looked away. "Nothing. Just daydreaming."

Puzzled by his unconvincing explanation, she let it pass. "Okay, then hurry up. That water looks great."

He stripped down to his swimsuit and they splashed out through the shallows, dove in and swam the length of the beach. Nicole loved the silky feel of salt water on her hot skin. Refreshed after the swim, they plodded up the beach to the motel, took showers and went out to dinner. Feeling relaxed and sleepy after dessert and coffee, she tried to suppress a yawn. Jerry gave an answering wide one. "I'm whacked, Sherlock. Let's head home and sleep. We can start our sleuthing in the morning."

The next day, they started early in an attempt to catch the postie before he began his round. He listened to Jerry's description, looked at Emma's photo, took off his hat and scratched his iron gray hair. "Dunno, she looks a bit like a checker at Pak'nSave in Kaitaia, but no, sorry, mate, can't help. Go and ask Jenny behind the counter, she's worked here for ages."

The post office sat at the back of a small grocery store stocked with every conceivable need. Dairy goods, greengrocery, bread, cakes, wines and beer. Freezers brimming with ice, icecream, frozen meats and fish bait. Newspapers, magazines, cigarettes and candy mixed companionably on the shelves. The bare wooden floors felt gritty from sand tracked in by children's flip flops.

Jerry gave Jenny his most winning smile. "Can you by any chance help? We're looking for this lady. The postie didn't know her." He slid Emma's photo across the counter. "She's about 5'1", brown hair."

"Course he doesn't." She sniffed in disgust. "Didn't he tell you he's the sub. Only started yesterday. Jim, our regular postie's taken off to Oz to visit his daughter. She lives in Perth so he'll be away for about four weeks."

A deflated, "Oh!"

She gave him an encouraging smile. "I did see her a few times. Couldn't help but notice the first time. She came to the counter with half a dozen postcards and asked how much the stamps were. Very shy, could hardly hear what she said, but she seemed pleased with the cards. Just as she's digging in her purse for some money, her husband –– or I assume he was –came over and picked them up. 'You don't need those.' I was gobsmacked. They were on sale – hardly a major purchase. She looked crushed but didn't say anything. Then he puts his arm around her and says, 'Let's surprise them this year. We'll take a whole bunch of photos instead and give them a real presentation when we get home.' She went all pink and beamed at him. I'd have clobbered him. Think he must have read my mind so he turns a beaming smile in my direction, then goes and buys some magazines and cokes instead."

Jerry looked equally surprised. "What a control freak."

"I saw her a few times after that. Sweet little thing but painfully shy. I haven't seen her for months though."

"Do you have any idea where she lived?" Nicole intervened. "We're friends of hers. I'm working in England. Didn't expect to be coming on vacation so soon, so I want to find her, give her a surprise."

"Neat. She was living out at Kingfish Bay. Go down there and ask around, someone may know where she is. Try the camp shop."

They headed back south on the main road, then turned down the road to the bay. A winding country road passed hills dotted with sheep and flat ranchland where magnificent Santa Gertrudi bulls pulled at the grass, black flanks glistening in the sunlight.

Finally, they wound down a long hill lined with tree ferns, tea tree and graceful fronds of toi toi waving in the light breeze. Once down on the bay, Nicole parked on the sea front. A mile-long semi circle of golden sand with a massive bush-covered bluff at one end spread out before them. Long lazy swells rolled in to the beach, and a large island stood some three miles out to sea providing shelter from the open Pacific Ocean.

"How come that bluff over there is so pristine. Looks like a wonderful spot for a house."

"You Philistine, that's national forest. Can't be touched."

"Let's climb up there. We'd get a terrific view."

"Maybe later." She was beginning to feel as if she was dealing with an impatient child. "Right now I am off to the shop to see if they know Emma."

Outside a small campground, a weatherworn sign tipped drunkenly to one side and announced – Kingfish Camp, Dairy, Bait, Icecreams. A few late campers had pitched tents and parked RVs but not a soul stirred. Even the children's swings hung forlorn and neglected. As they pushed open the door of a two-storied building, a bell rang and a sleepy-eyed man came through from a back room. After greeting them, he waited patiently as they looked around the shop. The shelves were packed tightly with anything a camper might need – tinned and packaged food, T-shirts, beach shoes, fishing rods and tackle, first aid items, shampoo, candy, cigarettes, magazines and books. A large freezer hummed in a corner, the list of contents helpfully listed on the lid.

Nicole picked up a bottle of water and a paperback. Jerry a coke and a bag of potato chips. The man behind the counter rang up their purchases. "Welcome to the bay. You staying down here? Need any milk or bread. Got plenty out back."

"No, we're just visiting." Jerry said. "I like your shop. You seem to have packed an awful lot of useful items in a small space."

"Folks drive up from Auckland with sacks of groceries, but they've always forgotten something. They hate to waste good fishing time driving to the supermarket."

Nicole slid Emma's photo across the counter and asked the man, who introduced himself as Murray, if he had seen her. "Yes, she came in quite a few times. Quiet! Could hardly get a word out of her. Her husband though, Adrian, he liked to talk. Full of good stories. Spent a lot of time talking to customers. One pretty young Maori girl took a real shine to him. Looked really down in the mouth when he left."

Nicole felt a bubble of excitement rising. "Were they here long?"

"Oh yes, for weeks. Used to have people up to their house for parties. They rented that big one that's tucked back there in the bush. Lucky for the owners, that little woman didn't talk much but she certainly did a great job on the garden."

"Do you know where they went when they left?"

"They went back home to England." He looked puzzled. "How come you know her? You're a Kiwi." He turned to Jerry. "You're American, aren't you?"

"We're both working in England and Emma's a friend. Adrian came back but she didn't. We're on vacation and wanted to find her and give her a surprise."

He ran his hand through his short, curly hair. "She didn't go back to England?"

"No, and no one's heard from her. Do you think Adrian and Emma changed their plans?"

"They had a farewell party the night before they left. Great fun. Then they left very early next morning. Ryan came down fishing at 5 am. Passed them on the road."

"They both left?"

"Well, he saw their car. She's so tiny I could never tell whether she was in the car when she passed me, unless she was driving, in which case it gave you a bit of a turn seeing this car coming along with no driver." He chuckled at his own wit.

So they left together. Curious. "Did she make friends with anyone?"

"No, too shy. Although come to think of it, Ben – he lives down on the seafront – he had quite a chat with her. I remember I was surprised, he's a miserable old sod. So give him a try. Fifth house on the left."

They thanked him, dropped off their purchases in the car and went in search of Ben. He lived in a white wooden house with colorful flowerbeds surrounding a shorn lawn, and an uninterrupted view of the ocean. Well into his eighties, clad in a long-sleeved shirt and a big floppy brimmed hat, he was working on a flower bed. They introduced themselves and told him they were looking for Emma. He got creakily to his feet, brushing sandy dirt from his knees and invited them in for a glass of lemonade. "Too hot to talk out here. Make yourselves at home while I wash up." He led the way into a comfortable, colorful room. "Norma?" he yelled. "Come on down, we've got guests."

Norma, a slim, energetic, white-haired woman with a darkly tanned face, ran down the stairs and greeted them. "I'll just get you a drink. Want a coffee, or lemonade?"

They both opted for lemonade and she appeared two minutes later with a tall glass jug, chinkling with ice and four glasses. As she poured, they looked around the room – a comfortable chintz-covered sofa and two wicker chairs – the walls pristine white to highlight the photos lining the walls; sensationally beautiful photos of cliffs, flowers, birds, driftwood.

Nicole took a sip of lemonade. "Delicious. Real lemons!"

"The tree's just behind the kitchen. Didn't have to go too far to pick them. Want some? I've got more than I know what to do with."

"Thanks, but we're only here a short while and we're in a motel." She got up and walked over to take a look at a photo of an oyster catcher at dawn on the shoreline, the sun glistening on the wet sand. "This is fantastic. Who's the photographer?"

"Here he comes, right on cue." Ben came into the room, helped himself to a glass of lemonade and sat down.

"Are all these yours?" Nicole asked indicating the framed photos that lined the wall.

"Yes, but they're nothing to skite about. I've a long way to go yet." He leaned back in his chair and turned to Jerry. "You wanted to ask me something about Emma."

Jerry pulled Emma's photo out of his pocket and showed it to Ben. "That's her all right. So what do you want?" His tone had an edge.

Nicole worried that he would clam up, said, "We're friends of Emma and we haven't heard from her in a long time. Since we're on an unexpected vacation we wanted to give her a surprise."

"Occur to you, she doesn't want to see you?"

"Could be, but I'm worried. No one has heard from her. Her husband came back to England without her, and I don't know, it just doesn't seem like something Emma would do. I want to be sure she's okay. Her husband doesn't seem bothered."

"She didn't come home?" His lined brow furrowed. "Norma went to her farewell party. They were off the next morning."

"She didn't turn up in England and her husband said she'd decided to stay, but Murray at the dairy said there wasn't a peep out of her about staying, the night before she left."

He ran a finger around his glass, leaving a thin trail in the frost, studied it for a while and said, "That *is* odd. Sweet little thing, really interested in photography. Hope she's okay."

"That's why we're trying to find her. Make sure she's alright."

" 'Fraid I can't help."

Norma leaned forward in her chair. "Didn't you put her in touch with that photography group on Ninety Mile Beach? You thought they might help her get started."

He looked at her with surprise, smiled, and said, "You're right. Why don't you go look up Mike Francis. He'll probably be able to help."

Jerry asked gently, "You got a phone number for him?"

"No way. He doesn't know beans about photography. He's a right bore."

Norma suppressed a laugh. "Hang on. I'll look in the phone book." She took down a slim book with a yellow cover. "No, he's not listed. Just go to Awanui and start asking around. Someone in the post office will know where he is, or for sure they will in the pub."

Walking back to their car, Nicole realized they hadn't talked to the police yet, so they stopped in Mangonui and walked up to an attractive white wooden house overlooking the harbor that served as the police station and residence for the Senior Sergeant's family. His wife answered their knock. "Hello, come in. What can I do for you? He's out on a call right now. It'll be a while." When they hesitated, she continued, "Shall I call him? Is it urgent? I can get someone from Kaitaia to come out right away."

"No, thank you, we just wanted to chat with him to see if he could help us find a friend we're worried about." Nicole fished in her bag and pulled out Emma's photo. "Don't suppose you know anything about her?" She added hopefully.

The slight, dark-haired woman peered over the top of her glasses. "No, sorry. Don't know her. Can I get you a cuppa while you wait?"

Itching for action, Nicole said, "No, thank you, we'll be on our way. We'll drop in on our way back. We're off to Awanui right now."

CHAPTER 20

A co-operative woman in the Awanui post office told them that Ben, the photographer, lived about half way along Ninety Mile Beach. "Trim looking white house with a metal roof. A real oldie, just in behind the dunes. Flag pole out front."

"Grief," Jerry said as they left. "Do we have to walk forty five miles to see him?"

Nicole laughed. "No, in the first place it isn't ninety miles, only fifty five. Way back, the missionaries' calculations were a bit off."

"Whew! That's a relief."

"And anyway, we can drive along the beach."

"You're kidding."

"No, it's a public highway. Quite legit. Even the tour buses do it. You just have to make sure the tide isn't coming in. You need a four-wheel-drive too."

"Lucky you rented one. How did you know we'd be coming here?"

"I didn't, but since Adrian talked about them renting a house in the boonies, I thought we might need one."

Down at the waterline, where the firm wet sand glistened in the sunlight, they jumped out of the car and stood admiring the wide, wide sweep of sand that stretched as far as the eye could see. The massive surf crashed on the beach, a dull roar in their ears. Seagulls wheeled and cried overhead while industrious oyster-catchers, shoulders hunched, pecked within inches of the foaming tendrils of spent waves. The wind whipped Nicole's hair into her eyes and the air, freshly laundered by the ocean, cooled her hot cheeks.

Jerry watched fascinated, as three little girls planted their feet in the wet sand at the edge of the waves and wiggled their bodies in unison. One squealed. They all rushed to the spot, dug with their bare hands, and pulled out small shellfish which they tossed in a red bucket.

"What are they getting?"

"Tua tua - small shellfish, good to eat in chowders, dipped in hot sauce, or they make great bait."

He laughed. "Handy to have around."

"Hop in, time's a-wasting." Closely followed by Jerry, she jumped in, slammed the door, buckled her seat belt, and they set off, tires hissing on the wet sand.

Off-shore a limitless Tasman disappeared over the horizon to collect more perfect, impossibly long waves that rose in the shallows, curled, toppled and broke on the beach; their spent energy sliding gently on the sand. Beyond the dry mounds of sand at the top of the beach, the evergreen Aupori Forest stretched into the distance.

A land sailer hurtled by, people walked their dogs, and isolated pockets of fishermen surf cast waist-deep in water. Other fishermen sat on low canvas chairs, rod stuck in the sand beside them, tackle box, thermos and a boxed lunch at the ready. Nicole smiled as she inhaled salt, seaweed and fish. After driving for twenty minutes, they pulled up beside a fisherman. Jerry jumped out of the car and asked him how he was doing. He showed them some sizeable snapper, and after Jerry had plied him with a dozen questions about bait and tides, Nicole asked if he knew where Ben lived.

"Yes, couple more miles, keep your eye open for a white house with a flag pole out front. Weird character. Welsh. He flies the Welsh flag at half mast whenever they lose to the All Blacks - which is always. Last time Wales won was back in 1953. The Welsh are still singing about it!"

A few minutes later, they walked up Ben's flagstone pathway and knocked on the door. Silence. They looked at each other. Jerry shrugged and turned ready to leave. Finally, the door opened and Ben emerged, blinking in the strong sunlight. He squinted at them. "Hello. What can I do for you? Come inside. I just came out of the dark room and can't see a thing in this sun."

Nicole explained why they were there. "Yes, she came. Funny little soul, seemed scared to death of me but dead keen on photography. I don't have a group anymore, but there's a bunch meets in Kaitaia once a month. I gave her their number." He chuckled. "She scuttled off – I don't know whether she was going to call them or was just glad to get away from me."

Nicole looked around the cramped, dimly lit bachelor quarters that smelled of dust and chemicals. Incredible Emma had come to this isolated house in the first place. The man went over to a bureau laden with a tripod, books and a wobbly stack of photos. He rummaged through a drawer. "Ah, here it is. Give Phyllis a call, she'll be able to help you." He gestured to a wall-mounted phone.

Jerry continued to chat to the man about photography while Nicole called.

The voice on the other end of the phone was buoyant, full of life. "Oh yes, Emma. We all know Em. Came to South Island with us. We had a blast hiking and getting some great shots of Alpine flowers. Marvelous that time of year." Nicole's eyebrows went up, *Emma*?

"Do you know where she is now? I want to catch up with her."

"She was off back to England last I heard. We had such fabulous shots of South Island we decided to put a book together. Reckoned it needed some explanations – sort of a travelog. No one had time to write it though." She stopped and Nicole could almost see her smiling to herself. "What a sweetie Emma is. She offered to do it. Once she'd said it, she looked terrified. But took a deep breath, gathered all our notes and promised to put a book together. Said she could polish it off in England just as easily as here …. What? You say she hasn't gone back? That's rum." A long silence ensued.

Nicole prodded gently. "Do you think maybe she stopped to do some more research before she left?"

"Hardly, but wait a tick, she was really nervous about writing. Said she needed to learn some more. Somehow didn't think a bachelors in English would be enough."

"You think maybe she went to a writers' workshop or something. Are there any held locally?"

"Haven't the foggiest. See if you can catch up with Susie; she used to belong to a writers' group, she might know. I'll just get her number." A few minutes of rustling at the other end of the phone and she said, "Hang on. Just give me your number and I'll call her then call you back."

After a five minute wait, she called. "No luck. She's not answering. Probably out in the garden and hasn't got her phone with her. Typical." She paused and Nicole expected her to say goodbye. Instead she continued, "Look you're very close to where she lives. Drive round and catch her in the garden. Once she's done there, she'll be in the house and will squirrel herself away for three hours. Won't answer the phone."

Puzzled Nicole asked, "Why not?"

"She'll be writing. Deadly serious about it. Says she has to have three clear hours every day and if she answers the phone, she never gets back to her writing. Daft if you ask me. So, go catch her, she'll be in the garden for an hour or so yet. If you don't catch her, it'll be forever before she gets back to you. Say hello to Emma when you find her and tell her to hurry up with that book. Oops! Nearly forgot to give you directions." She rattled off an address and how to get there. Nicole wrote it down on the back of a crumpled receipt.

She thanked Phyllis and said goodbye to Ben, who looked keen to get back to the darkroom. On the way to the car, she explained to Jerry they'd have to drive to the end of the beach and loop back to find Susie's house. Jerry stopped in his tracks. "Don't you think this is getting a bit ridiculous? We're yo-yo-ing around. I think we're on a wild goose chase."

"No, we're getting somewhere. We know Emma took a trip to South Island – which is pretty darn amazing – and then they planned to go back to England. Had a farewell party the night before. So what the heck happened after the party?"

"The guy in the beach shop said someone saw them both driving away from the bay in the early morning."

Nicole's skepticism spilled over. "Maybe she wasn't in the car. Bruce said she was so small the driver couldn't see her."

"Jeez, what are you saying? He buried her in the bush before he left? As I just said, we're on a wild goose chase. It's a waste of time."

Irritated, Nicole's response was sharp. "No, it's not. So far we've followed her trail. I'm not giving up until I've talked to Susie and the police up here." She set off for the car, saying over her shoulder, "You don't have to come along. I'll drive you to the Whangaroa Fishing Club. They'll set you up with a skipper, boat and accommodation. Go have a thrill catching kingie's."

Jerry's long stride caught up with her. "Hell no." Nicole suppressed a surprised sigh of relief. "If you think you can find out what happened, I'm not giving up on the hunt. I'm enjoying watching this great logical mind of yours figure out all the clues. Can't wait to see if you can catch him!"

"Can't say you're coming up with too many ideas."

"Not my job. I'm the Watson observer and chronicler." His grin was broad, eyes twinkling. He put a loose arm round her shoulder and gave it a light squeeze. "You don't get rid of me that easily."

Glad to have his company, she didn't flinch under his touch. "Okay, then let's go. I'll drive to the end of the beach, and take the highway back."

They bowled along scattering flocks of terns and sending them wheeling gracefully into the air. As they bumped their way off the beach up the Te Paki stream, Jerry exclaimed, "Wow! I feel like I'm in the Sahara – look at the size of those dunes!"

Feeling slightly guilty about telling him to take off, she realized letting him play for half an hour wouldn't do any harm. It might also help dispel her nasty sense of foreboding. What had happened between the party and Adrian's flight back to England?

"We've got a bit of time before we have to be at Susie's. Want to go surfing on them?"

Jerry looked at three youngsters hurtling down the side of a dune, two on their rear ends hanging on to the board for dear life, the other arms wide, knees bent, blond hair streaming out behind him, sped down the slope like an Alpine skier. "Yes ma'am. Looks like fun."

They rented a couple of boards and slogged their way to the top of the dune, the soft sand sinking beneath their feet. At the top, Nicole looked down and took a deep nervous breath; it looked way higher than it did from the bottom. A slight, blonde woman sat on her board trying to pluck up the courage to get started. Jerry pushed his board at maximum speed, jumped on and sat hanging on to the sides as he flew down the slope, going airborne whenever he hit a bump. As the board accelerated on the last steep incline he tipped over ending up in a tangle of limbs, flat on his face.

Nicole, having done it once before, and witnessed a similar performance from Jay, pushed off gingerly. The board accelerated to an exhilarating speed and she whizzed down laughing at the thrill. At the bottom, she laughed even harder when she saw Jerry's sand-covered face. She stood up, brushed off her shorts and went over to give him a hand. He shook himself like a retriever, scattering sand in all directions, and started laughing too. "And to think I used to be a surfer."

With the beach a couple of miles behind them, Nicole pulled over and looked at her scribbled directions. "Okay, look for Carpenter Road. Should be coming up on the right any minute now."

They arrived at Susie's house ten minutes later, a sparkling white wooden house with wide verandahs shaded by curved green iron overhangs supported by patterned white columns. Long and wide, seated on the top of a hill, with a sweeping drive and gardens blazing with color the house was an impressive sight.

They found Susie at the back of the house carrying a tray of plants to a newly turned flower bed. The smell of freshly turned earth mingled pleasantly with the aroma of lavender from a large bush besieged by bees. Dressed in shorts, dirt smeared pale blue shirt, sandals and a floppy brimmed hat, she stood clutching the tray of plants as Nicole explained their mission.

Susie plonked the tray unceremoniously on the ground, abandoned her trowel and rake, and ushered them towards the house. "Yes, I talked to Emma. Come on in. I'll make us a cuppa." She stretched her back. "I could use a break."

Urging them to make themselves at home, she tossed her hat on a chair, releasing a mop of light brown curls, and disappeared in the general direction of the kitchen. When she emerged a few minutes later with a tray laden with tea and scones, she had washed her face and hands and dragged a wet comb through her hair. The combing had done little to restrain the buoyant curls.

Nicole bit into a light, crumbly scone that brought back memories of her mother's kitchen. "These are great. Wish I could make them this light."

Jerry, not to be outdone, a smudge of butter dribbling down his chin, added, "Amen to that." After a few more cook-gratifying bites, he said, "This is a great old house. Have you lived in it long?"

"No. We bought it last year. They've been tearing down some of these old beauties in Auckland to make way for blocks of apartments. Outrageous." Her rapid fire speech hard to follow. "We saw one was for sale. Bought it and had it moved out here. Great location."

"What an awesome idea putting it on a hill. How the heck do they move a house this size?"

"No problem. Just pick it up, load it on a truck and bring it to your site. Mark you they had to move it overnight before the traffic started. Can't have these old monsters holding up the commute."

She laughed, gestured to the teapot, and when they declined, poured herself a second cup of tea. "Anyhow, you were asking about Emma. Why are you looking for her? I gather she's a friend and you're on vacation. But why is it so important?" A keen look at Jerry. "You after her while her husband's in England?"

As Jerry choked on his tea, Nicole intervened. "We're just worried about her. Did she ask you about writing courses? I wondered if maybe you ran one."

"Course not. No time for that. Want to write, not talk about it." This in staccato bursts. "Anyway, told her we're all romance writers. Not much use to her. She wants to do a book about photography." As Nicole started to speak, another burst. "Told her about a man in South Island, Glen Gerrard. Book doctor. Non fiction. Wife a romance writer. Met him at the Auckland Writers' Conference. He's writing a book on Hillary. Can't imagine the world needs another one. Difficult to know what they want. Except steamy romances – they always sell." This accompanied by a wolfish grin.

Nicole laughed. "Really! "

"Yep. Seventy percent of the market. Sure fire winners. Wouldn't waste my time on anything else."

Jerry's grin widened. "Personal experience?"

"Don't get any ideas. My husband's an ex All Black."

Having seen the size of the rugby players down under, Jerry responded with a deferential, "No, ma'am. Just kidding."

With an exasperated glance in Jerry's direction, Nicole interjected. "Do you have a phone number for that writer? Think he might be helping her?"

"Number's in my study. Probably is."

Nicole followed her. The writer's haven was spacious, light and airy. A purpose built desk and work table in some attractive glowing wood filled the back wall and wrapped around one side.

A filing cabinet of the same wood was within easy reach of the desk. A multi cubby-holed piece of furniture above it contained every type of office aid imaginable – stapler, paper clips, post it notes. A wide window above the desk showed a blaze of bushes in the foreground and a green sheep-dotted hill in the distance. The smell of new-turned earth, grass and hydrangeas wafting through the window mingled pleasantly with the smell of furniture polish, paper and books.

On the other side of the room, shelves of books in untidy rows – reference books, dictionaries, thesaurus, word finder, novels. And an impressive row of colorful titles by Rosie McCready. As Susie rummaged in her desk drawer for the writer's number, Nicole picked up one of Rosie McCready's books. A more than well-endowed brunette sat astride a magnificent white stallion. Susie turned, caught sight of the book and laughed. "Do you like it?"

"I've never read her. Is she good?" Nicole indicated the long row. "You must think so!"

"Of course. I think she's fabulous. She's me."

"But why McCready? Was that your maiden name?"

"No. I didn't think Susie Cook had the right ring to it for a romance writer. Sounds too much like a nice little homebody. My maiden name was Brown so that wasn't much better. Thought Rosie McCready had a nice sexy ring to it."

"You're right. I'll enjoy reading it." Nicole ran her hand along the row of Rosie McCready books. "You must be doing very well."

"Not bad. As they say if you want to make money writing, write checks. However, with ebooks we romance writers are expecting a bonanza."

"Why? Ebooks are way cheaper than hard copies aren't they?"

"Yes, but it's the number you sell that counts. With ebooks, all those little old ladies that were embarrassed to be seen on the plane or in waiting rooms reading steamy romance novels can read one anywhere on their Kindles or Ipads."

Susie handed Nicole a filing card with a name and number. "Here's the number you need. Give him a call. Come on, let's go gather up the boyfriend and you can be on your way." She stopped and looked hard at Nicole. "You're really worried aren't you? Emma's just a friend isn't she? You can't be going to all this trouble just to pop in and say hello before you take off for England."

"Yes I am. It's really peculiar. Emma usually sends oodles of postcards and phones her friend frequently. Nobody has heard from her. Her husband came home without her. Everyone in Kingfish Bay said Adrian and Emma had a farewell party and were planning to fly back to England the next day. Adrian came back. But no Emma."

"That sounds weird."

"I know. Something's happened to her, I'm sure. But the police think I'm nuts. Apparently she's still using her credit card."

"Oh well then." Susie shrugged and smiled. "She must be okay."

"I don't know. It's just not like Emma. Seems fishy to me. What the heck could have happened to her between the time everyone left the party that night and the flight home?"

"They probably had an argument. It happens after parties."

"Come on now. You met Emma. Did she look like the sort of person who would stand up to her husband?"

"No. She nearly ran away when I opened the door. Saw the house. Saw me, and panicked. Don't think I look that scary. I had to grab her and pull her in for a cup of tea. She calmed down after a bit. After slopping half the tea in her saucer."

"You see what I mean."

"Aha, now. But she's the sort who suddenly has had enough. Grinds up some glass and pops it in the husband's mashed potatoes. Now if Adrian had gone missing, *I'd* have been suspicious."

As Nicole laughed, Susie said, "Okay time to pick up the boyfriend and be on your way."

"He's not my boyfriend, just a good friend."

Susie, suddenly serious, looked her in the eye. "Make sure you keep it that way."

Nicole bit her tongue to hold back a caustic retort. *Stupid woman. Just because Jerry's always flirting with women doesn't mean a thing, he's still very much married.* Since pointing out that he was married would probably make it worse, she decided to hold her peace.

With a polite smile, she walked through to the living room. "Come on, Jerry, time we were on our way. Susie needs to start churning out another romance."

He grinned when he saw the book in her hand. "One of Susie's? Great, can I read it after you?" He got up and moved toward the door. "You can't start writing yet, Susie. What about those poor plants out there?"

Susie stood up and stacked the cups on a tray. "Enough of the garden. I'll bung the plants out of the sun, damp them down, and plant them tomorrow." She took a quick glance at her watch. "Time I started writing, or Graham will be home crashing around and asking what's for dinner." She put down the tray. Gave them a quick hug – she felt soft, cuddly and smelled of scones - with an extra squeeze for Nicole. "Good luck. Hope you find her soon." Then as they made for the door. "If you find out she's turned into a femme fatale and lured that poor bloke in South Island away from his wife, give me a call. Make a dynamite plot."

CHAPTER 21

A few minutes after they left Susie's house, Nicole pulled over and called the number in South Island. An automated message told her Glen Gerrard was on vacation, but to leave a message and he would get back to her on his return next month. "Damn."

Jerry looked across at her. "Another dead end."

"Yep, he's on vacation. Will get back to me next month."

"We'll have left before then. Ah well, let's go see the cop. Maybe he'll know something."

With a growing sense of frustration, Nicole shrugged her shoulders and set out for Mangonui. Frustration changed to amusement when they finally caught up with the senior constable in the harbor. In paint-speckled T- shirt and shorts, skin bronzed and hair bleached by the sun, he was lying on his back painting the underside of a boat. Not exactly what she expected after the serious-minded policeman in Auckland.

The boat, a fourteen-foot runabout, was propped up by two chisel-scarred benches, and sat on a flat, parched grass area just above the tide line of a small bay. Well off shore, a few power boats and a twelve-foot sailing dinghy, tied to colorful buoys, bobbed in the wash of small trawler that had just pulled out from the nearby quay. Behind the trawler, seagulls wheeled and quarreled.

A rack at the far end of the bay housed a collection of overturned dinghies and kayaks. Some colorful and new, others thick with dust. The smell of paint mingled with salt air brought back warming memories of sun-washed hours beside her dad painting the family boat.

She squatted down beside the policeman's boat. "Sorry to bother you, but your wife said we'd find you here."

The policemen shot her a friendly grin, carefully balanced his brush on a can of paint and rolled out from under the boat. Springing nimbly to his feet he pulled himself up straight. At over six feet, with shoulders like a line backer and powerful legs, he towered over Nicole. He ruffled his hair with an enormous hand to get rid of the sand. "What can I do for you?"

Before she could respond, Jerry asked, "Is this your boat?"

"No, just giving old Alfie a hand. His arthritis is playing up and he can't do it himself anymore. Makes him madder than a hatter." He gave a self-depreciating grin. "I just do it to keep the peace between him and his missus."

"I was hoping you might be able to give us some information on this woman." Nicole hauled out the photo of Emma that was starting to look a trifle weatherworn. "She's a friend of mine and I'm worried about her."

"Why are you worried?"

Nicole explained the reasons for her concern.

"Ah, yes. Bill gave me a call about that. She's still using her credit card so she must be okay. Obviously enjoyed herself and decided to stay over. It happens."

Before Nicole got beyond "But . . ." Jerry interrupted. "Did you meet them?"

"Yes, bumped into them in town several times. Seemed a happy couple. She was beaming and he was always holding her hand. One time Fred let his ridgeback out of his truck and she nearly jumped out of her skin. Her husband immediately put his arm round her and moved her away from the dog. Protective sort by the look of him. Rodney the ridgeback looked offended."

"Don't you think it was bit strange – her not turning up in England?" Jerry persisted.

The policeman's grin was wide. "No. Why wouldn't she decide to stay a bit longer? She didn't have to go back to work."

Then noticing their questioning looks. "Okay, it's a small place. Everyone knew all about their lives before they left."

Nicole, dispirited by yet another dead end, smiled weakly. "Well, thanks for your help."

On the way back to the car, Jerry said, "I'm sorry to sound like a broken record, but there's nothing more we can do. Why don't you just accept it? Emma must be okay if she's still using her credit card." He put his arm loosely round her shoulders and gave a light squeeze. "Look, forget it, she's a grown woman and I'm sure she's okay. You've done everything you can. Just relax and enjoy the rest of your vacation. It's beautiful up here. Enjoy the sunshine, go fishing. Forget Adrian."

Nicole's shoulders stiffened under his touch. "Okay, I'll try." She had to get away. Spend some time on her own and think.

A few minutes later, she added, "Do you mind if I take off for a while? I'll give you a ride back to the motel before I go."

"No. That's fine. I'm going to go to the pub and have a beer, then walk back to the motel. I'll give you a call at dinnertime."

With no idea what to do next, but determined not to give up, Nicole seethed with frustration. She decided to take a walk along the long stretch of sand in Kingfish Bay. Maybe returning to the area where Emma had stayed would give her some fresh insight. She knew Jerry was talking commonsense, but the thought of going back to England and seeing Adrian's smug face tied her stomach in knots.

She parked beside the beach in Kingfish Bay and set out at a fast pace for the far end. The taste of salt on her lips and the warm air fanning her face soothed her. The sea always did it. She knew the scientists said it was the ions coming off the ocean, but she believed it was the restlessness of the sea. If you looked at it long enough when you were stressed, the sea's constant motion meant you could relax – the sea had taken over. Whoever was right, it worked every time for her. She knew if she stayed here long enough, she'd be ready to face Jerry and even Adrian.

It was an exceptionally low tide and when she reached the rocks beneath the headland at the end of the beach, she was able to walk out past rocks normally immersed in water. Clusters of green lip mussels clung to the sides of the rocks. In the pools of water left by the outgoing tide, tiny crabs scrambled to bury themselves in the sand.

She walked out to the waterline, clambered up on a large rock and sat, oblivious to the world around her, as she tried to wrestle with the problem of Emma. Her mind went round and round in circles but although her gut still told her something was wrong, she could think of nothing else to do to find out what had happened.

Deep in thought, she lost all sense of time and was startled by the sound of splashing. As a man waded out towards her, she looked around and saw the tide had turned and was moving up the beach.

"Hi, I'm Pete. You're going to get awful wet if you stay there much longer. It's an exceptional tide, must be an equinox or something, and it comes much farther up the beach than usual. You'll have to swim for it pretty soon."

"Hello. Thanks for the warning, I was daydreaming and didn't notice the tide had turned. Dumb."

"Don't thank me. It's my wife, Zoe. She's been outside on the deck all afternoon trying to paint the ocean. She's a pretty good artist, but the sea defeats her. Anyway, she said she's been watching you and the tide and got worried. She's probably just ticked off because she can't capture the scene, so she decided to worry about you instead. I was commissioned to leap on my white charger and rescue you!"

"Thanks again. I'll get back to the beach now." She jumped down off the rock and the water, coming up above her waist surprised her.

Together, they waded back to shore. He looked at her dripping shorts and the bottom of her wet blouse. Laughing, he said, "Come on up to the house. I'll give you a towel to dry off."

"No, I'll be okay, they'll dry on the way back down the beach."

"But it'll be awfully uncomfortable with those flapping around your legs. Come on up to the house and dry off then we can have a glass of wine. I was looking for an excuse to open a bottle."

Nicole grinned. "Okay, thanks. That would be nice."

She followed him up the beach and was soon wrapped in a towel while her shorts and blouse rolled around in the dryer. Jerry told her to take a seat on the deck and poured three glasses of wine. Zoe appeared a few moments later with a dish of olives and a large platter containing a huge wedge of cheese and crackers spread with paté.

Nicole sat back enjoying the wine and the comfortable feel of the voluminous towel. After a while, she caught sight of the submerged rocks and laughed. "Great that you came to my rescue. I would have got awfully wet." She sank back in the deckchair. "Mmmm, this is the life. Have you lived here long? This is a fabulous spot."

"Don't I wish. Unfortunately, we've just rented it for a couple of weeks." Zoe looked rueful. "I could do with another four."

Pete snorted with laughter. "Imagine four more weeks without capturing the scene. You'd have been a basket case."

"Nah, with this air, I shall be so relaxed, I shan't care. Probably paint a masterpiece when I return home."

"Fat chance of that. It's back to the treadmill. You slog at figures all day and then you teach art classes in the evening. " He put his hand up to his face and tried to look serious. "Mark you, you do have plenty of time on the weekend while I'm playing golf."

Nicole interrupted. "Where is home by the way?"

"We live in Hamilton; I have a car dealership and Zoe's an accountant. So life is pretty busy. It's good to come up here where there's nothing to do except swim and play golf. I enjoy the breeze off the ocean too. Makes a pleasant change from sweltering inland."

"More paté?" Zoe picked up the plate and offered it to Nicole. "Where are you from?"

"I'm living in a lovely little country village in England at the moment. Just came back for a vacation."

"On vacation!" Zoe looked stunned. "Why on earth were you sitting there so deep in thought all afternoon?"

Maybe it was the effects of the second glass of wine, but Nicole suddenly found herself telling them about Emma and her misgivings. "The reason I'm so frustrated is that nobody believes me. The police just look at me and tell me over and over, she's still using her credit card so she must be okay. I still think something's wrong."

Pete sat back in the deep deckchair, contemplated his glass of wine, and then said, "Okay, let's suppose your theory's right and something has happened to Emma."

Zoe broke in. "Come on, Pete, get real. The woman's still spending money, she must be okay. He can't have done anything to her."

"Yes, but let's look at the credit card. If he is guilty, it's the perfect alibi. The police buy it. You buy it. What if it is just an alibi?"

Nicole's spirits lifted. He had a point. "How could someone – on the other side of the world – continue to spend money here? I know he could order stuff from stores but the police would have easily found that out."

"You can always get someone to buy a debit card. If they didn't have an account with a bank already, they'd just have to go in and set one up. You could give them some cash to do it. After that you just transfer money to them on a regular basis." Zoe interjected.

"You're right." Nicole's mind began to work. "Parents give kids debit cards when they go away to uni and set it up so that they can only take so much money per month."

"That wouldn't work. The police would see a record of the transaction on his bank statement," Pete said. He looked at the almost empty bottle for inspiration. "Hang on a minute. I know.

He could just set up a separate account under a business name. I'm sure he's got a friend or two that would be happy to let him use their address as a business office."

Zoe's voice was excited. "That would work. Brilliant. But who on earth could he trust enough to accept a debit card without telling anyone about it? I could see one of his long time friends in England letting him use their address, but here he'd no one he could trust to use the card and keep quiet."

"I wonder if he made friends with anyone. You said they stayed her for a few weeks, didn't you?" Pete turned to Nicole.

"Yes, it was long enough. There are a lot of men here who think he's great."

He polished off his glass of wine. "You need to go back to the shop and ask them who Adrian's friends were. That couple know absolutely everything that goes on in the bay."

Zoe got to her feet. "Your shorts will be dry by now. Come on through and get changed. I'll walk back to the shop with you. We can do some undercover work." She looked apologetically at Pete and said defensively "I need some cream for this recipe I want to try. It will make a perfect excuse for going in there. Then Nicole can come back and have dinner with us. I know you're dying to do some more of this Inspector Morse stuff." She turned to Nicole. "You risk life and limb eating my cooking but we'd love to have you."

"Thanks." Nicole shot a glance at her watch. "It's time I was getting back. I'm having dinner with a friend. You've been great. Wine and another approach to the crime. What more could a woman want?"

"It's fun playing detective. We're always watching mysteries on the telly. I'll just shoot into the shop, wander around a bit looking for some other bits and pieces to give you a chance to start a conversation. You can stand around near the counter waiting for me and they're bound to start chatting. They love a good old gossip."

They walked back along the beach to the shop. With the tide high they were forced to walk on the deep, dry sand. Nicole's legs began to ache, but Zoe seemed oblivious to the effort and kept up a constant stream of chatter about life in Hamilton.

Just before they went into the shop, she said, "I'll give you plenty of time to get the conversation going, then I'll pay for my cream and take off." She dug in her pocket and came up with a pen and wrote her phone number on a scrap of paper. "Let us know how you get on." She bustled into the shop and wandered around the shelves.

As Nicole loitered close to the counter waiting for Zoe to pick up her purchases, the woman behind the counter asked, "You here on holiday?" She appeared to be about the same age as the owner so presumably was his wife. She looked a lot livelier than her husband.

"Yes, but I'm not staying on the bay. Just came down to see if I could get some more information about the couple who stayed here a couple of months ago. Emma and Adrian."

"Why do you need it?"

Nicole explained that Adrian had returned, but not Emma, and she was worried about her. Wanted to find her. The woman looked sympathetic. "Does sound odd that she didn't turn up. I can see why you'd worry. Have you talked to the police?"

"Yes, but they say she's still using her credit card so she must be okay."

At this point, Zoe came up to the counter and as the woman rang up her purchases, she asked, "You are coming back to dinner aren't you?"

Feeling as if she was in a second rate movie with an inferior script, Nicole answered, "No, thanks all the same, but I'm having dinner with a friend in Mangonui."

"That's too bad. Maybe some other time. If you're going to the hotel, don't forget to order the crayfish. It's great."

Nicole said goodbye and with a large wink Zoe left.

She looked around to make sure the shop was empty. "I've got my doubts about the credit card. Maybe someone else is using it. Did he make any close friends while he was here?"

The woman's eyes lit up. She could see a good dramatic story coming up. Life wasn't too exciting at this time of year. "Let's see now. He was always having a good old gossip with Bill and his mates, and I know he played golf with Ken a lot. Can't see any of them being daft enough to do it for him."

"Wasn't there anyone else?"

"Not really. He always chatted to everyone but didn't spend much time with anyone other than those I told you about." She patted her untidy mouse-brown hair. The door bell chimed and a young Maori boy came in asking for an ice cream. She served him then watched him leave. "Hang on a minute. There was someone else. He was cagey about it, but Betty up on the hill, she cottoned on to it. Jennifer, Maori girl. Pretty as a picture and not too swift. She was besotted with him."

"Does she live on the bay?"

"Yes, right down on the waterfront. She really moped around after they left. Daft thing."

"Can you tell me where? I'll go and have a chat with her."

"She's away for the weekend. Gone down to Auckland. Think she must have a new boyfriend now. She's certainly perked up and bought herself some nice looking clothes. Was in here a couple of days ago buying twenty ciggies and a box of chocolates. Think the new boyfriend must have a few bob."

Nicole, picked up a magazine, thanked the woman and left. On the drive back to the motel, she wound down the windows of the car, letting the salt air rush through her hair, and sang along with the radio. Jennifer was spending money. She must have the debit card. Adrian's alibi could be broken.

CHAPTER 22

Freshly showered and in pale linen pants and a light green blouse, Nicole walked briskly across to the motel office where Jerry was waiting. "You're looking a damn sight chirpier than you did earlier in the day." He looked closely at her. "What have you been up to?"

Nicole tossed her head and answered nonchalantly. "Nothing much. Just think I can break Adrian's alibi."

Jerry, beginning to walk up the road, stopped in his tracks. "*His alibi!* What are you talking about?"

"It suddenly struck me - well, to be quite honest it struck Pete first – that the credit card is the perfect alibi."

Jerry's brow clouded. "Who's Pete?"

"Just a bloke I met over at the beach. We had a couple of glasses of wine together."

"Clearly." His voice dripped disapproval.

"Don't be stupid. His wife was there too. She put my clothes in the dryer."

"Spare me the details. Just tell me what on earth you are talking about. Adrian has an alibi? No one's accused him of anything."

"I know. That's the point. The police should, but until I find out how he did it, they won't."

"Did *what* for gods' sakes?"

"Knocked off Emma."

"Two glasses of wine and you've gone from vague suspicions to concocting a whole murder plot. I'm going to feed you orange juice at dinner tonight or you'll accuse me of being his accomplice next."

"Come on now. Be reasonable. From the time of their last night party, no one has seen Emma. She's disappeared. You think someone swallowed her? Everyone is convinced she went back to England. In England, they think she's here. Where? We've found no trace of her."

"Whew!" Jerry shook his head. "You're being ridiculous. Take out your phone and give Iris a call. bet she's sitting having a cup of tea with Emma right now."

Nicole felt stricken. "Whoa! Hadn't thought of that. You're right, I could end up with egg all over my face. I'll give her a call." She looked at her watch. "Darn, can't do it now. She's always helping at the pound this time of day. It's still morning there. I'll give her a call tomorrow." Sadness swept over her. In spite of her earlier feeling of triumph when Pete came up with the alibi theory, she hoped desperately she was wrong.

Nicole heard the phone ringing and could almost see Iris dodging dogs on her way to pick it up. "Hello."

"Hello, Iris, it's Nicki. Just called to see how you are doing."

"I'm fine but poor Mitzi has been throwing up all morning. Think she must have eaten something outside – probably the ginger tom from next door!"

Nicole chuckled, she knew Mitzi, the bulldog, was famous for defending her territory against cats. Foxes, hedgehogs, and other dogs were just fine with Mitzi but cats were definitely off-limits. "Sorry to hear that. Leave her outside and she'll find a nice stalk of grass to cure her. Has Emma turned up yet?" She held her breath.

"No. Still not a peep from her. Adrian's started to worry about it. He didn't say so outright, but I think he's going to hop on a plane and go looking for her. He was quite upset when the New

Zealand police called him. Said the whole thing was ridiculous."
She paused. "By the way, he was really ticked off about you being
down there trying to find her."

An icy shiver went down Nicole's spine. She said goodbye to
Iris and put down the phone with a shaking hand.

The debit card was a perfect alibi. No one, none of Adrian's
friends and certainly not the police, suspected foul play. She was
a lone voice crying "Wolf". He had a picture perfect plan. It had
only one flaw – her.

Now Adrian was furious and on his way to New Zealand. No
doubt to engineer another suitable accident. She tried to convince
herself she was overreacting. It didn't work.

That night she tossed and turned for hours. He might turn up
at any time.

CHAPTER 23

Jerry plowed into the pile of scrambled eggs and bacon Nicole had whipped up on the motel stove. Swallowing a large gulp of orange juice, he asked, "Have you called Iris yet?"

"Yes. No sign of Emma." She sighed and pushed her piece of toast to one side. It had suddenly lost its appeal. "However, Iris thinks Adrian is coming here to fetch her. I gather he's a bit miffed with me."

He crunched on a piece of toast. "Can't say I blame him. Anyway, that means you can relax. Let her husband find her. It's his job after all."

"Okay." She drank the last of her fruit juice. "I think I'll just pop down to Kingfish Bay again this morning. I'd like to tie up a loose end before I give up."

He swallowed the last of the eggs and started smothering his toast with honey. "Need company?"

"No. I'm going to talk to a young Maori girl and I think it will go a lot easier without you. Women tend to open up more when a man isn't around." She leaned back in her chair. "With you leering at her, she'll be twittering all over the place and I won't get a word in edgewise."

A deprecating eyebrow went up. "Can I help it if I have that effect on women?" He sat looking smug for a few minutes. "Good. That means I can go fishing. Bob at the pub said he was going out after kowhai this morning and invited me along."

"Aren't you supposed to get up at dawn and catch the first tide?"

"No. He maintains the kowhai run all day when they're around. You just need to know the right spots to fish."

"Good. While you're out there, don't forget to mark an X on your map so you can sneak back to the same spot another day."

"Don't try to make fun of an expert. I'll be hauling in fish right, left and center."

As soon as he had finished eating, Nicole picked up the plates and stacked them in the dishwasher. "Okay, off you go. I'm going to hop in the car and head for Kingfish Bay."

"I'll catch up with Bob before he takes off." Jerry jumped to his feet and set off up the road.

Nicole watched him disappear round the corner with a furrowed brow. She felt disappointed. He hadn't been a bit excited about her alibi theory. She thought it was pretty darn clever, but he wasn't at all impressed. It wasn't as if he ever came up with any helpful suggestions. He just seemed to enjoy seeing how she worked. She gave a mental shrug, and decided he was fun to have along anyway so what did it matter.

Twenty minutes later, she knocked on the door of an attractive beachfront house. Its rather sandy looking front garden had a perfect view of the beach, ocean and an off-shore island. The sea was calm but a long lazy swell rose up just off-shore, curled as it approached the beach and toppled sending tendrils of foam up the sand. The only people on the deserted beach were a couple launching their boat.

The man sat on a rust-encrusted tractor, behind him he trailed a sleek white boat equipped with a cuddy cabin and two outboards. The woman stood in the boat watching him closely as he swung the tractor around and backed it into the water. She then climbed nimbly out of the boat, exposing bare suntanned legs and feet. Her red, skimpy shorts were topped by a loose linen shirt and a faded blue baseball cap. As her husband hit a lever and the boat, still chained to the trailer, slipped slowly into the water, she sloshed around to the bow. Once it hit the water, the man jumped off the tractor and the woman grabbed the bow just as he unhooked the boat. Leaping back to his seat on the tractor, he hit a lever and the loose chain rolled back into place. Meanwhile, his wife had pushed the boat out until it was well afloat, then swung it bow-out to face the swell. She appeared totally oblivious to her saturated shorts

The man drove the tractor up to the soft sand at the top of the beach, then ran, full tilt, down into the water to join his wife who was hanging on to the boat as it bobbed up and down in the spent waves. He clambered aboard and readied the engine. She waded out pushing the boat until it was well afloat and she had water up to her breast. As the engine roared into life, he turned and yelled something swallowed by the sound of the engine and she climbed up the ladder and fell into the stern of the boat. He gunned the engine just as a wave rose in front of them and they powered out through the following swells. A few seconds later and they would have been swamped by a breaking wave.

Fascinated by the spectacle, Nicole turned reluctantly to the front door. As she lifted her hand to knock, it opened and a beautiful young woman with long dark hair and deep brown eyes, said, "Hello, I saw you watching Teena and Dick. They're quite the team aren't they?"

"Incredible. Is it always that difficult to launch off this beach?"

"Generally. Launching off a flat sandy beach is never a breeze," the young woman answered complacently. "We do get a few days when there's no swell at all, but it can get quite hairy out there. They've timed it right. That's an outgoing tide so the swells are flat. Will be interesting when they come back-- especially if it blows up a bit."

"Do they always make it okay?"

"Oh, yes. They're a couple of hotshots, "but we do have quite a few accidents. It's a tricky coastline." She pointed toward the horizon. "One or two have gone overboard out there. Nasty business."

Her frown cleared and she looked at Nicole, her dark, lustrous eyes bright with curiosity. "What can I do for you?"

"Sorry," Nicole said extending her hand. "I'm Nicki. Murray at the shop said you might be able to help me. You are Jennifer, aren't you?"

The smile was warm. "That's me. Can't imagine how I can help, but come on in I was just going to have a cup of coffee. Want one?"

"Sounds great." She followed Jennifer into a spacious living room furnished with deep comfortable looking off-white upholstered chairs. In the corner of the room, a piece of driftwood had been polished and inlaid with colorful stones.

Jennifer waved to one of the chairs. "Have a seat. How do you take your coffee?"

"Black no sugar, thanks." As Jennifer turned toward the kitchen, her very short shorts rode up over her flawless legs.

A few minutes later, she returned with two large blue mugs of coffee and a plate of muffins. "No thanks, just had breakfast. Coffee smells great though." Nicole took a small sip of the scalding brew, then swept her arm around the room. "What an attractive house. Have you had it long?"

"Heavens, no. I couldn't afford this place. I just pay a nominal rent. The owners live in Auckland and need someone to keep an eye on the house when they're not using it. They only come up for the Christmas holidays and I go to the rellies for those, so it works out great."

"Sounds like a heck of a deal." She sank back in the comfortable chair and looked appreciatively around the room. *I could get used to somewhere like this in a hurry.* Then suddenly remembering why she was there, she asked, "Did you know Emma and Adrian that rented the house on the hill?"

"Yes. They were a lot of fun."

"I'm over on vacation from England and Emma's a friend of mine. I'd like to look her up. Do you have any idea where she is?"

"She went back to England. Didn't she tell you?" Her eyebrows went up. Even they were perfect.

"No. She isn't back yet. I got a bit worried about her and since I was coming on holiday anyway, I decided to see what she's up to. Emma said she was in Kingfish Bay." Nicole mentally crossed her fingers as she lied. "Thought she'd still be here, but they told me at the shop she left quite a while ago."

"Adrian said they were going back. I didn't know she'd stayed." She looked taken aback.

"Would you have any idea where she is?"

"I haven't a clue."

"Did she ever talk about things she'd like to do here?"

"I really didn't know her that well. And she never seemed to say anything. Adrian was the fun one." Her eyes sparkled. "He used to make me laugh all the time. He said he wished Emma had a sense of humor like mine."

"Did you see much of him?"

"Oh yes." Her face was guileless. "We went to the pub quite a bit and to a few of the cafes that serve wine. He'd sit around and talk for hours. Even took me to the movies in Kerikeri. Said Emma didn't like going out. I felt quite sorry for him."

Nicole bit back a caustic comment, and forced a smile. "He does sound fun. You must have missed him when he left."

Jennifer looked wistful. "Yes, I did. But he'd even thought of that. He told me I'd made him so happy, he wanted me to continue having a good time." Her look was smug. "Gave me some money so I could go out and buy myself a few nice clothes."

"Wow, he's generous! Did he go with you when you bought them?"

She looked shocked. "No. You don't understand." She leaned forward to make her point. "He loved me. He wanted to make me happy even when he was gone. He left the money and told me not to touch it until after he had left." She topped up Nicole's cup and filled her own. "He's going to come back. I think, and please don't breathe a word of this, he planned to take Emma back to England and divorce her so that he could come back here and marry me." She looked dreamily out of the window. "We could live in one of those fancy new apartments on the Auckland waterfront. We could go out clubbing every night. Even go to the theater." She sighed. "But he's been gone a long time."

"It hasn't been long, Jennifer." Without a trace of artifice, she tried another question. "Did you buy some nice clothes?"

"Yes. He told me to go down to Auckland and go to Smith & Caughey's. No expense spared. Even gave me enough for the bus fare and an overnight at a motel." She jumped to her feet. "Would you like to see them?"

Finding it hard to believe the woman could be so naïve, Nicole struggled to keep a straight face. "Yes, I'd love to."

Beaming, Jennifer disappeared in the direction of the bedroom. After about ten minutes, she reappeared in a striking red dress that emphasized her dark hair. Teetering on perilously high heeled shoes she twirled and struck a pose. "What do you think?"

"You look gorgeous."

"Hang on a minute." She reappeared a few moments later in a silver gray pantsuit and another pair of spiky heels. This time, she had added earrings sparkling with some unidentifiable stone. In this outfit, she looked almost sophisticated, apart from the sparkling eyes and delighted smile.

"You're a regular knockout. You must have all the men after you in these outfits."

Jennifer blushed. "Er, yes. I finally caught the eye of Jason. He's a real hunk. We have fun together."

"Did you buy all these clothes at the same time?"

"No. I bought the first outfit in Auckland and the second one in Hamilton."

"Hamilton! Why on earth would you go that far to buy clothes? They have some nice shops in Kerikeri just down the road."

"Adrian wanted me to see a bit of the country. So he gave me enough money to take the bus down and stay there overnight."

"The bus?"

"Actually, don't tell him but I didn't do that. Jason gave me a ride in his car as long as I paid for the gas, so it worked out just the same as the bus fare."

"Heavens! Did he leave you all that cash before he left?"

"Of course not." She looked at Nicole as if she had just stepped off the Ark. "I have a debit card."

"He paid it into your bank for you?"

"I didn't have a bank account. Don't make enough money to save any, so he gave me thirty dollars and told me to go in and open one." She walked over to the bureau and pulled out her wallet. "Look. A Bank of New Zealand one."

"Wasn't he afraid you would blow it all on one big spree with the rellies?"

Jennifer let out a delighted peel of laughter. "He even thought of that. He knew if the rellies found out about my windfall they'd all be over helping me spend it. He's very clever you know."

"So what did he do?" Nicole tried hard to look mystified.

"He set it up so that I could only take out so much each month. And he made a real game of it to make it more fun for me. He sends a sealed envelope every few weeks telling me where I should go and spend it. He really wants me to move around and see more of the country. Help decide where we're going to live."

"What fun for you." *You poor naïve little creature.*

"Yes, Jason and I are having a great time driving around seeing places. We quite often stay with his friends. That means we can spend the motel money on drinks." *Maybe you aren't so naïve after all.* She grinned at the thought of Adrian imagining this sweet little thing still pining for him.

"Good for you, enjoying life." She got to her feet. "Thanks for the coffee. That just hit the spot. Must be on my way now."

Jennifer stood up and gave her a hug. "Glad you stopped by. If you see Adrian when you get back to England, tell him I miss him."

Grinning to herself, Nicole drove back toward the motel but as she drove, the good mood evaporated. If Adrian had murdered Emma – and between the beautiful young Jennifer and the debit card alibi – it looked increasingly as if he did, it would be easy arrange an "accident" in the boat.

Jennifer pointed out launching boats could be hairy and several people had gone overboard. All the locals recognized the hazards of boating. If he found a nice convenient spot to toss Emma overboard, and came up with some story about her falling off the boat, people would believe him. Of course, he'd need to take Emma out somewhere other than Kingfish Bay because everyone had seen her the night before they left. But it wouldn't be difficult to take sweet little submissive Emma boating in Auckland, and no one would ever know.

She began to feel sick.

CHAPTER 24

Nicole woke with a start. Eyes wide, nerves on end, not moving a muscle, she listened. Nothing. She moved her head cautiously. Sunshine streamed in around the blinds. Still not a sound. She slipped out of bed and padded barefoot to the door. Scarcely breathing, she moved soundlessly. Still locked. Nothing moved behind it. No telltale breath. She crept along the wall to the bathroom. Listened. Nothing. She pressed the door open inch by inch. The shower empty and the washbasin untouched. With a quick intake of breath, she looked behind the door. All clear. She breathed out.

Back in the living area, she moved stealthily to the window, lifted the blind half an inch and peeked out. A car started up and pulled away. She slapped her forehead. *You idiot! It was a car door slamming that woke you. Just a bunch of early-bird tourists.*

After a long exasperated breath, she wandered over to the kitchen and filled the water jug. She took a quick shower followed by a comb flick through her wet hair then made tea and contemplated the day ahead. The tea did little to clear her tired brain.

She needed to think, and think fast. Adrian was coming after her. No point in hoping he couldn't engineer some plausible accident. Emma's disappearance looked too authentic.

She decided to go to the police and tell them about the debit card scam. But remembering the I've–seen- everything eyes of the Auckland policeman, she doubted the police would be convinced it meant foul play. The jaded man could probably shrug it off saying there's nothing wrong with someone setting up a mistress. Morally wrong yes, but nothing illegal.

She racked her brain but couldn't think of anything else to do. Jerry might be able to help, but as she stopped and thought about it, she doubted it. Even he'd decided she was being ridiculous. So no point in waiting for him to wake up. She drained her second cup of tea and made for the door. She'd drive up to the Pa. Sitting up there watching the sun paint the scenery might help. She drove along the road for about a mile, turned off on a little gravel road and made her way up through the trees to the Pa. Or, as the sign told her Rangikapiti Pa Historic Reserve. On the crest of the hill, she parked her car and ran up the wooden steps to the top. The view took her breath away.

The Maoris fortified village commanded a view of all points of the compass. No one could approach by land or sea without being spotted. The village was long gone, but a monument marked the spot and offered an unbeatable view.

She felt sure the slight chill in the early morning air, the panorama of sea, town and sweeping bays spread below would bring inspiration. Pivoting slowly, she absorbed the sparkling ocean, tranquil harbor water and the toy town windows glinting in the sun. How could it fail? It did.

She took a deep breath of the salt laden air and sank down on the cold stone step of the monument to think.

Could she really be sure of what Adrian had done? Or was she just imagining the whole thing? But if so, why hadn't Emma contacted anyone? Where was she? Why was young Jennifer being told to run around the countryside spending money? She had a hard time believing that naïve little soul's conviction that Adrian planned to come back and marry her.

It was pointless going to the police with her debit card story. They would take one look at Jennifer and be convinced Adrian was keeping her on a string. Maybe not to marry her, but what red-blooded man would turn down a beautiful young thing like that flinging herself at him?

She looked inland toward the sweeping green vista dotted with trees and houses. Cars pulled out of driveways. Time to move. She had to continue her search. Unless she eliminated all possibilities of Emma staying in the country and playing possum somewhere, no one would believe her.

She must stay ahead of Adrian. But where should she go? The only lead left was the man in South Island. She had his name and phone number but who knows how long he would be away? She got to her feet and walked down the grassy slope on the far side of the monument. As the grass tickled her bare legs, inspiration struck. She took a quick look at her watch. Too early yet. She'd call the Auckland Writers Association. They would know who he was, where he lived and whether he would be likely to help Emma. Maybe they'd know someone else Emma might have contacted. When she'd talked to them initially, all she had asked was whether Emma had been to a writing class.

By the time she got back to the motel, had some breakfast and packed her bag, it would be time to call. Then she could head down to Auckland.

Poking her head in the refrigerator to get out milk and orange juice, she saw she still had several eggs and some bacon left. Her stomach rejected the idea. Pity, she'd have to toss the eggs and bacon or leave them in the refrigerator for the cleaner. Maybe Jerry would like some. She needed to talk to him before she took off anyway. She was sure he'd lost interest in the hunt and was keen to go fishing and golfing with his new found friends. Not that he had been enthusiastic about finding solutions. His only interest had been in seeing how she did it. She shrugged and accepted that he just wanted a vacation in New Zealand.

"Like some eggs and bacon? I'm cooking." It was a while before Jerry picked up the phone.

"Sounds good. I was in the shower – just got back from a run. I'm wrapped in a towel right now but could be over in about ten minutes."

While she waited for him to turn up, she called the Writers Association. Predictably, no one answered, but she left a message. Hopefully, they would call her as soon as they opened up the office or finished giving their family breakfast.

Jerry came in looking bright-eyed and bushy-tailed. "Wow, that smells good!"

He walked over to the refrigerator and helped himself to an orange juice. Nicole poured two cups of coffee and as soon as he sat down, placed three fried eggs – proud of herself for not breaking the yolks – and several slices of bacon in front of him.

"Thanks." He reached for a slice of toast and spread butter on it. "The butter's great here. Tastes real. Good thing I'm not staying long or I'd have to pay extra baggage for myself on the flight back."

As she spread butter and Manuka honey on her toast, he asked, "What's that honey made from?"

"Manuka trees, more commonly known as tea trees. It's those white blossoms on the low trees in the bush. The bees love them. Supposed to be very good for you. Cures everything."

"To heck with cures. It tastes good." Eyeing the honey, he attacked his eggs and bacon with relish.

When he had finished, he reached for his coffee cup. "How did your trip to Kingfish Bay go? Did you get anywhere?"

Nicole told him about her visit to the ravishing young Jennifer and the clever debit card scam.

"That's not a scam. If she's as good looking as you say, he's just keeping her on a string."

She shook her head in disgust. He'd reacted in exactly the way she anticipated.

At that moment the phone rang. "Excuse me. I need to take this. It'll be the Writers Association." She got up from the table and moved over by the window.

"Good morning. I wonder if you could help me. I've been trying to contact Glen Gerrard in Nelson but he's away on vacation. I have a friend who was looking for someone to help her write a nonfiction book."

"What's the subject? Birds? Memoir?"

"No. One about photography. Do you know anyone else she might have contacted?"

"No, no one in Auckland. Glen's the best there is in that field."

Nicole let out an exasperated breath. "I have to go back to England in about a week and I really need to contact him. Would there be anyone else down there who works with Glen?"

A long silence ensued. Nicole tapped her fingers impatiently on the window sill.

"I just looked up some meeting notes and it says Janice – who lives in Nelson – does editing for him from time to time."

"That's great. Do you have a phone number? No – oh."

She listened again as the woman began making helpful suggestions. "Okay, that sounds the way to go. I'll get a flight down tonight. Thanks for your help. I really appreciate it."

She turned, beaming, from the phone. "What a sweetie that woman was. Had a name but no phone number for her. So, instead, she gave me the number for a friend of Janice's who would probably know where she is."

Ignoring Jerry's dumbfounded expression, Nicole dialed the number in South Island, and was delighted when a woman answered. "I was wondering if you could help me. I want to get in touch with Janice. Kelly at the Writers Association thought Janice'd be able to help me. Problem is she is away on vacation. Kelly thought maybe you'd know where she is."

"Janice. 'Course I know where she is. Why do you need to know by the way?"

Nicole gave her standard explanation about wanting to surprise her friend who she knew would be delighted to see her.

"Okay, sounds neat. Janice isn't too far from here. She's got a little beach house up on Marlborough Sound. No landline and cells don't work worth a damn. Always goes up there. Likes to get away from it all. Lazy creature. Just lies around on the beach all day. Wish I was with her!"

"Can you give me directions?"

"Bit difficult to find. Where are you now?"

"Northland. But I can fly down."

"You'd better come to my house. I'm right in town. You can stay over and then I'll drive you there in the morning. You'll be lost for days on your own."

"Thanks, that's brilliant. I'll give you a call when I know how soon I can get there." Grinning broadly, she put down the phone.

Jerry pushed back from the table. "What on earth are you up to?"

"I'm going down to South Island to see a woman who may be helping Emma."

"Maybe? Do you know for sure that she is?"

"No, that's why I'm going."

He looked incredulous. "You're going to travel seven hundred miles on the off-chance."

"How do you know it's seven hundred miles?"

"I've studied my Lonely Planet guide by the hour. I'm a walking encyclopedia of mostly useless New Zealand information." His brow clouded. "Don't change the subject. Why are you going all that way?"

"I broke Adrian's alibi, but I can't go back to the police unless I've exhausted all hope of finding her. Once I have, maybe then they'll believe me."

"You're liable to get locked up somewhere. You do realize you're being completely irrational. He doesn't *need* an alibi. He hasn't *done* anything. When will you see sense?"

She could feel her temper rising and forced her words out through tight lips. "Why would he have Jennifer running around the countryside spending money, if he wasn't using the debit card to create the illusion Emma is still around?"

Jerry got to his feet, came over and stood in front of her. "When are you going to get real? According to the guy in the shop she's 'a pretty young thing'. Even you conceded she's beautiful. Adrian's just keeping her on a string. Dollars to doughnuts he'll be setting up a lecture tour in Auckland and Sydney pretty soon. And guess who'll be keeping him company?" Jerry's voice had a hint of admiration.

"*You* may be convinced. *I'm* not. I'm going to find her or go back to the police."

"Nicki." His voice was soft and conciliatory. "I know it was rough losing your husband the way you did." And as she glared at him, he added "Yes, after the episode at the police station I looked up some old newspapers. It had the whole thing laid out."

"I don't want you prying into my life and I don't need your false sympathy. Back off. Leave me alone. I'm going to find Emma come what may."

"Okay, so you lost your husband and now you've lost a good friend. Has it occurred to you Emma is so vulnerable it's brought out your suppressed maternal instincts. Occur to you, maybe all these years of avoiding men has left you a wee bit frustrated?"

Nicole's temper reached breaking point. "Get out. Go fishing. I don't need you around trying to psych me out."

At this, he stepped forward grabbed her roughly by the shoulders and pulled her to him. Reeling with shock, she had no time to react before he kissed her, very hard, forcing her head back. She felt his hard body against her, and feelings suppressed for years, came surging back. She put her arms around him. At that, he slackened his hold, kissed her again. Gently this time.

As she relaxed in his hold, welcoming the gentle touch, an icy finger of cold crept into her consciousness. No, not this again. Raw feelings exposed. The blinding pain and sheer misery of Jay's loss came back to haunt her. No way, was she going through that again.

With shaking hands, emotions tumbling, she pushed him away with all the force she could muster. "Keep away from me. I don't want this."

He moved to take her in his arms again. His voice hoarse, barely more than a whisper, he said, "But you know you do. Stop fighting it . . ."

Trying to block out his words, she yelled with unnecessary force, "YOU'RE MARRIED. YOU HAVE A WIFE." Then through gritted teeth. "Now for the last time. Get out of here. I don't want to see you again."

He reeled back as if she had slapped him. Without another word, he turned on his heel, stomped toward the door and went out, crashing the door behind him.

CHAPTER 25

" **N**icki's in New Zealand looking for Emma! That's ridiculous. You must be mistaken Iris." Adrian shook his head in disgust. *That woman is as nutty as a fruit cake.*

"No, Adrian, I am *not* mistaken." Iris's voice rose in indignation. "She just called and wanted to know if I had heard from Emma. She's worried about her."

"Why on earth should she be worried about Emma? I told you she had stayed behind to write that silly book of hers."

"I was surprised too. But I thought you'd like to know."

"Thank you, but I've never heard such nonsense. Emma is there trying to get that book done so that she can come home. The last thing she needs is that darned interfering woman going to see her. Why doesn't Nicki mind her own damn business?" Unable to control his anger any longer, he said goodbye through clenched teeth and switched off the phone with unnecessary force.

What was she doing? Why was she so concerned? She was the last person he expected to be a friend of Emma's. A software type, and damned intelligent too as he recalled. All Emma's other friends were homebodies who liked to quilt and crochet – none of them the sharpest tool in the box. Then, of course, there was Iris. Completely potty about dogs, always made him suspect she was one sandwich short of a picnic. No wonder Martin spent so much time up in London with his rich divorcee.

He closed his eyes and pressed on them with thumb and forefinger to fend off an impending headache. He had to stop Nicole looking for Emma. Just when he'd finally worked out what he really wanted in life, along comes a busybody. He racked his brain trying to work out where Emma met Nicole. It had to have been at Iris's house. Emma probably went over with some plants, or something, and Nicole was having coffee with Iris. Iris loved to keep tabs on her neighbors.

He sat for a long time trying to work out what to do, and decided on the straightforward approach. He'd call Nicole and tell her Emma was just fine and didn't want to be disturbed while she was researching her book. Then he realized he didn't have the wretched woman's phone number.

"Hi, Iris, do you know Nicki's phone number. I'll give her a call."

"That's a good idea Adrian. But I'm afraid I don't have her number. She told me she'd picked up a new phone over there. She said it's always cheaper to go with a local phone, if you use your US one it's horribly expensive." She chuckled. "Oops! Forgot to ask her for the number."

Damn silly woman. "Do you know where she is staying? I can get the number for her hotel."

"Sorry, she didn't say. Didn't think to ask."

"Ah, well Iris, never mind. Talk to you later.

He spent long, frustrating hours trying to track Nicole down. Calls to Auckland hotels and motels were unsuccessful. The one useful piece of information Iris had volunteered was that Nicole's boyfriend was with her. On the assumption Nicole would show him the sights, Adrian checked a few of the major tourist spots. Still no luck. Frustrated, and determined to stop her from ruining his plans, he decided to jump on a plane.

On the flight to New Zealand, he tried to work out ways of finding Nicole. She'd probably start in Auckland, but phone calls to hotels and motels there had drawn a blank. It was while the stewardess was serving his dinner that it struck him. When he was eating dinner with Iris, Martin and Nicole, he'd started telling Martin about the great fish and chip shop in Mangonui. He hadn't mentioned the name of the town, but since Nicole had lived in Auckland, ten to one she had spent vacations at one of those gorgeous beaches near Mangonui.

◇

As Adrian came out of customs and through the exit at Auckland International Airport he paid scant attention to the people who sat watching a large screen that displayed a picture of people approaching the exit after clearing customs. He knew they were waiting to catch a glimpse of friends or family. All of them, poised ready to leap to their feet the minute the person reached the exit. A big improvement on the scrum at most international airports where you have to push through crowds and stand for ages waiting for someone to arrive. He hurried on, intent on reaching the Information Desk before the tourists found it.

"Welcome to New Zealand. What can I do for you?" A suntanned young woman with dark hair and a beaming smile greeted him at the desk.

In an exaggerated English accent, he asked, "I wonder if you can help me. I need a list of motels in the Mangonui area."

The young woman behind the desk flipped open a folder and handed him a list. "What type of accommodation are you looking for?" She indicated several names. "These motels are all close to Mangonui and there are also B & Bs and house rentals listed. You might consider some of those, they can be nice."

"To tell you the truth," he gave her his most engaging smile, "I'm looking for a couple of friends. A man and woman traveling together. She's about this tall," he indicated a spot on his shoulder, "dark curly hair, attractive. Don't know what he looks like, but he's an American. She's a Kiwi. Don't suppose they happened to talk to you, did they?"

She looked puzzled, but smile firmly in place, asked, "When was she here?"

"Very recently." He leaned on the counter, looked her in the eyes, and said, "You see they're a very nice couple. I had some problems at work and was really strung out, and you know they just jumped in and helped me. Sorted out a really sticky problem I had with a client and even did my garden for me. I'd have been sunk without them and wanted to do something to thank them." He smoothed his hand over his forehead and hair. "Wouldn't accept anything."

"That's nice." She smiled encouragingly.

"I had to come down here on business anyway so thought I'd charter a fancy boat with a fishing guide. Take them out for a fishing trip and have it catered so we could have an exotic meal out there with a drop of bubbly. I'll just tell them I was chartering the boat for myself anyway. They know I do that from time to time." He smiled ruefully. "Seemed like a good plan until I realized I don't exactly know where they are!"

She laughed with him. "See what you mean!"

"I thought Mangonui was the most logical place for them to go. But . . ." he looked very dubious, "I could be wrong." The engaging smile again. "Do you happen to remember them coming by and asking for motel recommendations?"

"No, sorry. Hang on a minute though. I'll give Jordan a call. He's been on for the last couple of days. He might remember them." She picked up a phone and explained the situation to Jordan. "Too bad. 'Fraid he doesn't remember them either. I think your best bet will be to drive up – assuming you've got time – and ask locally. Someone may know."

"Thanks. That's kind of you. I'll make a few calls. See if any of the motels you gave me can help."

He found a quiet corner in the coffee shop and started dialing, ticking off each motel and hotel. With reluctant pen and deep sigh, he ticked off the last item on the list. Another dead end.

Turning his attention back to his lukewarm coffee, he sipped and pondered the problem. If she isn't staying anywhere there, maybe she's not as smart as I thought. Or maybe – he tapped his fingers on the tabletop – she's been to Mangonui, asked around, and those nosey parkers had told her Emma had been staying in Kingfish Bay. No, she couldn't have got there that fast. A small smile crept across his face. I know, I'll just head straight for Kingfish Bay and beat her to it. I can tell the folks at the shop I'm picking up Emma, so they can tell Nicole, if she turns up, not to bother looking.

He gulped down the last of the tepid coffee and headed for the car rental desk.

Adrian settled himself in the seat of his rental car, adjusted the leg room and rear view mirror, and did a quick check of the control panel. All set and ready to go. He stopped in the act of fastening his seat belt. Where to? Kingfish Bay for sure, but he had a sneaking suspicion that last motel manager in the north he'd questioned had been lying. He was just too quick in saying Nicole wasn't there. All the other motel managers had consulted their registers before answering. He was ninety percent certain if Nicole had headed for Mangonui, someone there would have told her Emma had been staying in Kingfish Bay. So first stop, Kingfish Bay Dairy.

CHAPTER 26

Nicole slammed the breakfast dishes in the dishwasher and hit the start button. She strode to the bedroom, threw the last bits and pieces in her travel bag, did a quick check of closets and drawers, picked up purse, bag and motel key and headed for the office.

The man behind the desk, short, mildly overweight, brown hair, newly pressed crisp blue shirt, looked up and tried to suppress his surprise. She made a valiant attempt to readjust her scowling face as she slapped the key on the counter. He pushed his glasses up his nose. "All set to go then?"

"Yes, time to be on my way."

He clicked away at his computer, and while he waited for her receipt to print out, he asked, "Where are you headed today?"

"Auckland." Some inner voice of caution urged her not to give away too much information.

"Off back to work then?"

" 'Fraid so."

He handed her the receipt. "That's always tough. Hope you enjoyed the stay. Take care. Bye." Then as she turned to go, he added, "Wait a tick. I nearly forgot. Someone called very late last night. Wanted to know if you were staying here. Said he was a looking for a friend who was here on holiday." He took off his glasses and massaged the bridge of his nose with a pudgy thumb and forefinger. "I didn't like the sound of him. I thought maybe he was a drunk or something. So I told him to call again this morning. I wasn't sure if you'd want to see him." He hesitated, bit his lip. "Thought I'd ask you first."

"Thanks, that was good of you." As Nicole saw his look of relief, she asked, "What was it that bothered you? Did he slur his words or something?"

"No, no. Nothing like that." He frowned. "He didn't sound quite right. I think it was his accent. I got the impression he was trying to fake a Scottish accent, but every once in a while he sounded as if he came from the south of England."

"Wow! Can you pick where people come from? I still can't recognize all the regional accents in England and I've been over there a few years now. There's oodles of them."

Laughter lines crinkled around his eyes. He leaned on the counter, his smile wide. "Nothin' to it, luv. I'm from good old Pompey – well, Portsmouth to you Kiwis – and that's pretty well as south as it gets."

"You fooled me."

"Been here more years than you've had Sunday dinners."

It was her turn to smile at the exaggeration. "Doubt it! Anyway, thanks for screening the call. I know who you're talking about and you're right on – he's from Dorset. He's a regular pest. Can't stand the man, and he's always trying to get me to go out with him. If he calls again, don't tell him I was here. I'm off today, so hopefully he won't be able to follow me and I can enjoy my last couple of days in New Zealand."

He winked at her. "Can't blame a man for chasing a good looking chick like you." He touched the side of his nose with his index finger. "But, Bob's your uncle, I won't tell him you were here. I enjoy a bit of cloak and dagger."

Still smiling, she headed for the car, only to stop in her tracks when she saw Jerry standing beside it, his travel bag slung over his shoulder."What do you think you're doing? "She walked to the driver's door. "I thought I made it crystal clear. I'm leaving without you." Then as she felt a fit of remorse. "Get your friend from the pub to give you a lift to Kerikeri. It's only twenty minutes from here. You can hire a car there. Or like I told you before, just get a ride over to Whangaroa Harbor. The fishing club there will set you up with a skipper and accommodation. Anyway," suddenly annoyed again, "you've got your damn phone. You don't need my help."

He stood hands wide, his face contrite. "Nicki, I'm sorry about what I said. I was totally out of line. I've no right to tell you how to live your life. God knows, I've messed my own up enough." His hands dropped to his side, his shoulders drooped. "I'm ashamed. Truth is, I was the one who was frustrated. I like you. It's great having you as a friend and it worked like a charm in England. But here, in this climate, with you in a swimsuit and then just across the courtyard every night. Dammit, woman, you're disgustingly attractive." A small smile crept across his face. "Even more so when you're being totally ridiculous."

"I was not being ridiculous," she started hotly, but then stopped and laughed. "Well, maybe just a bit. I do tend to get carried away." She stuck out her hand. "Okay, apology accepted. Can't say I was totally blameless. Let's just shake on it and I'll be on my way."

He ignored her hand. "No, you don't understand. I *like* you. I want to come along. It occurred to me this morning, you could be in danger. If that theory of yours is right – and you've a lot of evidence to show that it is – Adrian may come after you. Take me along to ride shotgun. I promise not to make another pass at you. Let's go back to being friends. I was having fun."

He looked at his feet, wriggled his shoulders. When he raised his head, his eyes were earnest. "You're right, I've got a wife who'll be with me by Christmas. I should not have acted the way I did. "

"That was quite a speech." She paused. Having him along would save her from getting the jitters about Adrian. Deep down she knew she would miss his company too, so ignoring the niggling thought that she was becoming far too involved, she said,

"Okay, you're on. Hop in. But first swear scout's honor you're going to behave."

His grin was wide. "Okay, I promise not to molest you again. But damned if I'm going to be a Boy Scout. I intend to leer at all the other women. Window shopping doesn't count."

CHAPTER 27

Adrian caught sight of the lopsided sign for the Kingfish Bay Camp and swung hard right to cross the bumpy little bridge that separated the camp from the road. He drove into the parking lot and walked round the corner to the shop door.

A stretch of grass and trees offered camp sites only a few steps from the long, sandy beach. As he opened the door, an automatic doorbell announced his arrival, and produced a delighted, "Adrian! What are you doing here?" from Murray, the shopkeeper, who was stacking cans of meat on a shelf. Adrian returned the beaming smile. "Good to see you too." He rolled his tired shoulders. "Got a cup of coffee for a weary traveler?"

As Murray moved over to the coffee pot, Adrian looked around and felt the tension melt away. The gritty feel of sand on the floor, the sound of the waves outside, and the appetizing smell of coffee and pies competing with a faint odor of fish. It all brought back memories of a great vacation. The shelves were not as tightly packed as they had been during the peak holiday season, but still contained just about everything a camper would need.

Murray gestured with the pot toward a pile of brand new T-shirts that sat on top of the freezer. "Those just came in. Doris came up with the idea of selling Kingfish Bay T-shirts. Daft. But in the season, they'll buy anything." He grinned. "If they don't, I'll dock her pay."

"What's that you're saying?" His wife came through from the back of the shop and gave him a friendly poke with her elbow.

"Nothing, darling, I was just going to give you a shout to come and say hello to Adrian."

She echoed her husband's welcoming beam. "Great that you could get over here again so quickly." She looked out of the window, and then at the door. "Where's Emma?"

He picked up the cup of coffee Murray had set on the counter and took a sip. Hot, rich and fresh. He looked puzzled. "She's here already isn't she?" He knew they handled house rentals for absentee owners. "I just popped in to ask which house she's in."

"What are you talking about? She went back to England with you." Doris stopped, looked dubious. "Didn't she?"

Adrian hung his head. "No, she didn't after all."

"But you left together," Murray interjected.

Adrian gave an audible sigh. "I know. We drove down to Auckland. Left early because she wanted to go and talk to someone in the city before we caught our flight. It was about this book she's writing for the photo club." He took another sip of coffee. "The man she wanted to see wasn't there and was going to be out of town for a while." He sipped some more, thinking fast.

"So why didn't she get on the plane with you?" Doris was starting to scowl.

Adrian shook his head in wonder. "She was in a right tizz about it. Thought she'd never be able to write the book without some more information. Got herself in such a state, she started crying."

"Poor little love. She would too. She was really nervous about that book."

"Yes," Murray added heavily. "But I still don't see what that had to do with your flight home."

"Well," Adrian's words came out reluctantly. "I tried to console her. Told her we could call or email from home, but she was adamant. Said she must have some more information before she left or she'd never be able to do it." He leaned on the counter so that he was eyeball to eyeball with Murray. "Would you believe she wanted us to stay over for another week?"

Doris's tone had an edge. "So why didn't you?"

He turned toward her, his face softening. "I wanted to. Anything to stop her being so upset. But I had to get back to work. I had a week of appointments scheduled – had been putting them off because we were having such a good time here – but I couldn't stay any longer."

"That's tough." Murray was all sympathy.

"Long story short. I ended up agreeing to let her stay for another week or two to get her act together while I flew home and went back to business."

"Good on you." Doris now looked equally sympathetic. "Why don't you come through to our living room. You must be tired after your drive. I'll make you a fresh pot of coffee and I've a pie just out of the oven to perk you up."

"Thanks, that sounds great. The thought of your pie makes my mouth water, but I really just came in to find out where Emma is. You do handle all the rentals for the bay, don't you?"

"Of course. Not too full this time of year. But she isn't here. Did you expect her to be?"

"Yes, I felt sure she'd come back to the bay once she had the info from Auckland. The photo club is here."

"Sorry."

A camper, dressed in shorts and heavy wool shirt, came in and bought a packet of cookies and some potato chips. Adrian watched him leave, then asked Doris, "Do you have any idea where she would have gone?"

"No idea." She paused, looked blankly across at the pile of T-shirts. "Tell you what though, when that woman came looking for Emma I sent her to see old Ben. He's big on photography. Thought he might be able to help."

Adrian's stomach clenched. "What woman?"

"Kiwi. Friend of Emma's from England. She's over on vacation and wants to surprise Emma."

"Nicki?"

"Yes. That's her name."

"Damn woman. She's going to spoil everything."

"Why? What's the harm in her popping in to see Emma?"

"She's going to ruin everything. All my planning. Hell's teeth," he blurted out, "why does she have to interfere?"

"What planning?" she persisted. "You mean picking up the phone and booking a flight?" This laden with sarcasm.

"I came over to bring her back home. To tell you the truth, it's lonely without her." He gave Doris a bashful smile destined to melt any woman's heart. "I know she hates flying, so I've come to keep her company. She'd be terrified on her own making the flight transfer in Los Angeles. That airport's a zoo. I plan to give her a few days of luxury at Huka Lodge. Then we can go home together."

"Neat – she'll love that."

"Huka Lodge?" Murray exclaimed. "Phew! You're pushing the boat out."

Adrian gave a slight shrug. "You know me – nothing's too good for Emma."

"You'd better get a move on then."

"Problem is, I don't know how to find her. Where was that Nicki woman going?"

Doris leaned over the counter. "To see old Ben. Perhaps he knew."

"Who's Ben?"

"The old guy who lives on the beach. Just to the left of the slipway. Always has a beautiful garden."

"Oh yes, I remember. I'll go have a chat with him. Thanks for your help." Adrian made for the door.

"Good luck. Say hello to Emma from us."

As Adrian opened the door, the sound of the sea increased to a low-pitched roar. *Incoming tide* he thought. He drained his coffee cup, the warm liquid and caffeine easing the ache in his shoulders. He decided to leave his car and walk the short distance to Ben's house. It felt good, his legs welcoming the stretch after hours on a plane and the fast three and a half hour drive from the airport. As he rounded the corner to the beachfront, the breeze coming off the ocean ruffled his hair and blew away some of the cobwebs in his brain.

However, when he reached Ben's house, he received scant encouragement. Ben was working in the garden and when Adrian explained the situation and asked for help, Ben muttered darkly, "People should leave the poor little lassie alone."

His wife, overhearing him, smiled apologetically at Adrian and told him to come inside. Once there, she looked in her bureau and produced the telephone number of the photographer on Ninety Mile Beach. "I gave this to Nicki when she was here, so hopefully it will be a help." She looked at his crumpled shirt and tired eyes. "Can I get you some tea? Why don't you sit down for a while. You look as if you've been traveling a long way." She gestured to one of the comfortable chairs in the living room. "I can make you a sandwich too, if you'd care for one."

The offer was tempting, but he knew he had to move quickly if he was to catch up with Nicole. "Thanks, you're very kind, but I really must be going. I just can't wait to see my wife and find out how much she has written."

She looked inordinately delighted by his words. "Good on yer! She's going to be glad to see you." She followed him to the door and waved when he looked back as he reached the corner.

Once in his car, he tried calling the number. No reply. Just an answer machine. He decided to head out of the bay, and try again before he reached the main highway.

On the third try, he managed to contact the photographer on Ninety Mile Beach. But a long and frustrating conversation only resulted in another phone number. He rubbed his hand across his forehead and sighed. With scant hope of success, he called a romance writer called Susie. He was surprised when she told him Nicole and Jerry had come to see her.

"Can you give me some help? I'm trying to locate my wife. We were over here on vacation and I had to go back to work. Emma wanted to stay and talk to a writer to see if she could get some help with this book she's writing. It's her first attempt at producing a book so she's pretty nervous about it. In fact, she was in such a state and so adamant that she must get some help before she left that we agreed she would stay an extra couple of weeks." He paused for breath.

"So what's the problem?" Susie asked.

"She's been running around chasing information for quite a while. Then almost two weeks ago, she called and said she had been advised to stay some place without a phone and just write non-stop. Some dimwit told her that was the only way to get a book done."

"They were smarter than you know." Susie stated dryly.

"But that leaves me with a problem. She hasn't called and I'm a bit worried. So I came over to see how she's getting on, and offer to travel home with her. She's very nervous about flying at the best of times. I don't know how she'll do on her own."

"Don't worry about her. Sounds as if she's found a group of writers somewhere who are looking out for her. And anyway, friends of hers from England came to see me. Nicki, and um, Jerry, were the couple. They were looking for her too." She gave a mirthless laugh. "Popular lady, your wife. Anyway," she added, her voice dismissive, "they're going to see her. So she'll be fine."

Adrian gave a rueful laugh. "I know about her friend looking for her. That's part of the problem. I want to surprise Emma and whisk her off for a weekend at Huka Lodge. If Nicki finds her first, I'll be a bit of an anti-climax." He paused, letting the silence hang for a full minute. Getting no response from Susie, he continued, "I miss Emma. I want her to come home. I don't mind how long she spends writing. I just want to be near her." He hesitated again. "Silly after all these years I know."

"How long did you say it has been since Emma contacted you?"

"Two weeks now."

"Occur to you, maybe she doesn't want to see you."

"No," he said in an aggrieved voice.

"Didn't she say where she was?"

"No, not exactly. I know she's in South Island but I'm not sure who she's visiting. Last I heard, she was looking for a non fiction writing coach or something equally harebrained."

Susie's voice dripped with disgust. "Nothing harebrained about that. The only one I know is Glen Gerrard."

Bingo! He slapped his hand on the dashboard. Then, voice once more worried and sincere, he thanked her and ended the call.

Stood to reason, Nicole would fly to South Island. All he had to do was find out where this Glen Gerrard lived and then he'd know where Nicole was heading. When he phoned the airport, he discovered a plane would be leaving in thirty minutes. Unfortunately, that didn't give him enough time to get back to the motel and get his things. He decided to go to the airport anyway. There, he would be able to find out when Nicole left. After that he'd be hot on her trail.

CHAPTER 28

As Nicole drove out of the motel and headed north, Jerry looked puzzled. "Where are we going? You have to go south to Auckland, don't you? Or am I completely turned around?"

"I'm heading to the airport. It's just 15 minutes away. A flight leaves in half an hour."

"You can't go by air, that's crazy."

She slowed to let some pedestrians cross the road, then put her foot down. "I want to get there before Adrian. He's probably on his way here by now. Driving will take hours. We can be in South Island in two hours if we fly."

"I thought you were worried about Adrian catching up with you? You seemed pretty edgy about it earlier."

An irritated, "Yes. That's why we're flying."

"Perfect." Jerry's voice dripped sarcasm. "You'll leave a trail a mile wide. All he has to do is check at the airport."

Surprised, she glanced across at him and grinned. "Smart thinking. You been on the run before?"

She passed a car meandering its way to town, and continued, "It's a long haul by road. About four hours to Auckland, then say another seven or eight to Wellington. Three hours on the ferry between North and South Island. One and a half hours or so from the ferry to where that woman lives."

"Hey! I've driven across the States. That doesn't sound too tough. After all, we can just keep switching drivers and bowling along."

"Yes, but there's still that long ferry ride," Nicole persisted.

"According to my handy dandy guidebook, that's supposed to be one of the most beautiful routes in the world."

"Sure. But Cook Strait can get awfully rough sometimes."

"Isn't this a maritime nation? What a chicken you are. No wonder they deported you to England."

"Okay, smart Alec, you're right. The rough bit – and that's only if it blows up – isn't that far, and then we're cruising down the Marlborough Sound. Even I couldn't manage to get seasick there."

He looked behind them. "Okay, so turn around and let's start beetling down to Auckland instead of yakking." Then as an afterthought. "You didn't buy a ticket for the plane did you?"

"No, I was going to do that at the airport."

She drove along the road, but seeing no place where she could turn, yelled, "Hang on tight!" Swung the car across the path of an oncoming car, and gunned the car into a driveway on the opposite side of the road. Fortunately the house had a circular drive, so with a sedate wave of apology to the surprised woman who stood in the garden, trowel in hand, she drove around and they were on their way to Auckland.

After a couple of hours, Jerry tapped her on the shoulder. "Okay, hotshot, pull over when we get to that park." He pointed ahead to a city park. "Don't want you harassing any more poor people en route. I'll take over. We'll keep up a faster pace if we switch before you're tired."

She was glad to relinquish the wheel, and as he pulled away from the park, she took out her phone. "I'll give Iris a call, and see if Emma has turned up."

Nicole could hear the usual yelps of protest from the spoilt pug as a flurried Iris answered the phone. "Hi, Iris, that dog giving you trouble again?"

"She's always trouble, this one – unless I feed her non-stop. But she gives me a good laugh every day so she's worth her overweight self in gold."

"Don't suppose you've heard from Emma yet, have you?"

"No, dear. Adrian's on his way, so I'm sure he'll find her and bring her back. I hope it's soon. I miss her."

She rubbed her arms against the sudden chill. Adrian would be here soon. He must be coming to make sure she didn't find out what had happened to Emma. She swallowed, and tried to sound casual. "You mean he's left already?"

"Oh, yes, dear, he left a couple of days ago."

She looked nervously over her shoulder. Searching for a quick change of subject, she asked, "What are you up to these days?"

Iris sounded buoyant. "Would you believe we are off to the Outer Isles of Scotland? Martin's between cases and thinks we should get away. He's spent so much time on that wretched divorce case up in London, I've hardly seen him. A rest will do him good." Nicole's mind flashed back to the day in London when she saw Martin with another woman. *Martin's conscience must be getting to him.* Iris babbled on. "We're going sailing. Martin says there are some fantastic winds off the islands, it should be really exciting."

Knowing that Iris was notoriously inept in a boat, Nicole cautioned, "Be sure to wear your life jacket. It's one thing to fall overboard in Poole Harbor where the water's warm and there are plenty of boats around. If you go overboard up in the isles, you'll be in Scandinavia or the Arctic before you know it. My geography's not good enough to know where those currents go, but wherever you are up there is going to be darn chilly. In fact, hypothermia will probably get you before you wash up anywhere."

Iris roared with laughter. "Don't be silly. Martin is an excellent sailor. I'm safe as houses with him. Marvelous surprise having him take me along on this trip. I can't wait." Nicole heard a bell in the background. "Oops! Must go, someone's at the door. Lovely hearing from you. Take care."

"Bye, Iris. Have a good time in Scotland."

After she put her phone away, she sat silent for a long time. She remembered seeing Martin with that filthy rich woman in

London. Before that, over coffee at Iris's house, he'd told her how the rich women he represented in divorce cases ended up with a pile of money. Now, with a rich woman on a string, he's taking Iris on a very risky trip. She shook her head. This is ridiculous. It must be worrying so much about Emma that has me suspecting every man of skullduggery. She decided to say nothing to Jerry or he would go ballistic. Worse than that, she would lose all her credibility if he knew she believed Iris was in danger too. She leaned back against the seat and closed her eyes.

CHAPTER 29

A s a crocodile of toddlers crossed the road, Adrian tapped his fingers impatiently on the steering wheel. Once clear, he sped along a straight stretch of road bordered by flat pastures where self-satisfied cattle cropped lush grass. Turning off at the narrow airport access road, he checked his watch. Still ten minutes until the Auckland plane departed. He slowed down. A Camry came screaming up behind him and honked impatiently. Adrian pulled over and waved him past, then sat consulting the map to let three other cars by.

A few minutes later, engines roared and a small plane took off. Grinning, he put down his foot, sped along the road, pulled into the open air parking lot, jumped out of the car and ran full tilt toward the terminal. He wove his way through passengers heading for their cars narrowly missing a young couple hand-in-hand, a middle-aged woman in a pathetic shift and a woman hauling two unwilling tow-haired boys.

He ran to the departure gate and arrived red-faced and breathless. Fumes from the flight hung in the clear air. The airport official clad in light blue shirt and navy pants, was busy fastening the departure gate. The official raised bushy eyebrows that spread like an overgrown hedge across his narrow face, as Adrian gave a heartfelt "Damn."

"What's up mate?"

"Just missed it. Wanted to catch my girlfriend before she took off."

"Too bad. Give her a call when she gets to Auckland."

Adrian hung his head and let out a pathetic sigh. "I really needed to see her. We had a pretty bad argument the other day. You know, one of those where you've had a jug or two, and you're not too careful what you say."

The other man laughed, his eyebrows keeping time. "Been there. Done that." He straightened up and started toward the departure lounge.

"Excuse me, but did you see her? Tallish, dark curly hair, great figure." Then another sigh. "Probably with a tall streak, an American bloke."

The man stopped. "Like that is it?"

"Yes, she's got this old boyfriend over visiting. That's really what started the argument. Says he's just a friend. Huh!"

"See what you mean."

"So I must catch up with her. Don't want her off having a fling with that joker and getting ideas." After a suitably dramatic pause, he asked, "Was she on the flight?"

"No." He gave a quiet grin. His eyebrows twitched in unison. "If she's the knockout you say she is, I'd have noticed her for sure."

Adrian managed to look even more dejected. "Don't suppose she was on last night's flight, was she?"

"No. I was on all day yesterday. Didn't see her then." He fidgeted, anxious to get back to work. "Hop on down to Kerikeri. Maybe she flew out of there." Then, as he began to walk away, he shouted over his shoulder. "There's a flight to Auckland from there in about an hour."

"Good idea. Thanks, you're a star." Adrian, knowing it was only half an hour down the road, sauntered across to his car and took a leisurely drive to the airport. He intended to repeat the same stunt and arrive just after takeoff.

The Kerikeri airport had a narrow access road, an air stocking, a smallish control tower and a diminutive booking office. He wouldn't have been surprised to see sheep grazing in the surrounding fields. But the greenery encircling the efficient air-strip was freshly cut and the personnel all business.

He tried the same approach he had used at the last airport, but this time the man securing the gate was skeptical. "Girlfriend, huh? That's a new one." He locked the gate and leaned on it to make sure the airstrip approach was secure. "Can't help you I'm afraid. Not supposed to disclose information about passengers. I'm after a transfer to Auckland International, so I have to obey all the rules." He drew himself up to his full 5'4", and a small grin spread across his face. "Of course, if there'd been someone that good looking, I'm sure I'd have noticed."

With a mouthed, but not articulated, "thank you", Adrian took his leave. He slumped in his car seat feeling totally defeated. If Nicole had gone by road, he had no hope of catching her. They may even have left the previous afternoon.

With an extreme effort, he pulled himself upright and wiped his hot face with a crisp white handkerchief. Crying over spilled milk wouldn't get him anywhere. He needed to think. He closed his eyes, pressed thumb and forefinger on the lids. He didn't have a clue where Nicole was going, so how on earth could he catch up with her? Think, Adrian, think. His stomach growled, reminding him he hadn't eaten all day. The last food he'd had was dinner on the plane the night before. He'd skipped breakfast, much preferring to get over the landing rigmarole and sit down later in a hotel and have a good solid breakfast. Unfortunately, he'd been in such a hurry to catch up with Nicole he'd driven straight to Kingfish Bay. So, step one, food. Maybe a few calories would fuel his imagination.

He decided to head for a small café he'd visited on vacation with Emma. He swung the car around and headed for Kerikeri. As he drove past the citrus orchards, where the dark green foliage glistened in the sunlight, he passed fruit stands brimming with large bags of oranges and piled high with kiwi fruit. Stalls crammed with bags of onions, potatoes, nuts, dried fruit and flowers abounded. The colorful scene and moist warm air began to work their magic. His shoulders relaxed. His worries started to melt away.

Past the stalls, he admired the trim freshly painted houses fronted by shaved lawns, colorful bushes and flower beds. Occasional signs advertised tucked away riverside motels. Finally, he reached the small town and parking in an open lot he sauntered along the main street enjoying the small shops: arts and crafts, fishing tackle, men's clothing, jewelers, photographers and cafes.

When he reached his favorite tearoom, the delicious scent of pies and coffee gave him an idea. Quite busy, but not enough. He hastened past and spent some time admiring paintings in a small gallery, then tried on a snappy wide-brimmed hat in a clothes store; great for the sun, but not too useful in the English winter. He returned to the tearooms, and looking through the large window pane saw most tables were full and a short line had formed at the counter. Perfect.

He took his place in line behind a woman, who in the past had eaten well and often, and saw her select a large glistening pastry from the display case. A quick glance around the tables revealed exactly what he needed. Picking up a roll filled with ham, cheese, and an ample supply of green and red vegetation, he added a sausage roll, ordered tea and made his purchase. As the cheery motherly type behind the counter gave him his receipt, she said, "We'll bring your tea over in a couple of ticks."

He wound his way through the tables to one at the back of the restaurant where two smartly dressed elderly ladies were enjoying coffee, pastries, and a good gossip. Looking around for a place to sit, he made a pretence of seeing them for the first time and asked, "Would you mind very much if I joined you? It's awfully crowded." He indicated the holiday-makers in shorts and flip flops tucking enthusiastically into salads, and steaming bowls of soup with scrunchy looking bread rolls.

"Of course," they chorused and moved their cups and pastries closer to the edge of the table to give him ample room.

"Thank you so much, I've been running around all day so sitting down is going to feel great." He placed his food on the table and then turning to the lady on his right he extended his hand. "Hello, I'm Adrian." He held her hand a few seconds longer than necessary. She smelled of Chanel No. 5.

"Pleased to meet you. I'm Jessie," and indicating her friend she said, "that's Rachel."

As Rachel extended her hand he noticed a beautiful bracelet of woven gold and silver. "What a lovely bracelet. My wife would love that." Important to assure them he was a respectable married man.

She put her arm on the table to let him see the bracelet. "It is lovely, isn't it? My daughter bought it for my birthday. Actually it was made right here in Kerikeri. You should check the jewelers. They're on the other side of the road, not too far from here. They have some nice pieces. This was made specially for me."

"I'll take a look after lunch. I'd like to buy her something special." He reflected ruefully it was just the sort of thing Cindy wore – but then her husband probably had things custom made at Tiffany's.

"Are you on holiday here?" Jessie asked.

The waitress set a pot of tea, jug of milk, cup and saucer beside him, and he busied himself pouring a cup of tea. "No. Wish I was, I had a lovely time here in February. Spent it on Kingfish Bay – delightful spot."

"That is a lovely beach. We always go there to welcome in the New Year. It's fun having a bonfire on the beach and counting down the last seconds of the year with all the other holiday makers." Jessie's cheeks dimpled.

"So you're on business," Rachel prompted.

"No, believe it or not I'm looking for my wife." They both looked puzzled. He gave a reassuring smile. "She isn't lost. She's off some place writing a book, and wherever she is they told her the only way to get it done was to go to a writer's retreat and ignore all phone calls."

"How long has it been since you heard from her?"

"Over two weeks." He gave a bashful smile. "I know it's silly, but I miss her. So I just jumped on a plane to find her, take her to Huka Lodge for the weekend and then fly home with her. She's very nervous about flying so I thought we could travel back together."

"That's really nice," Rachel said, "she's a lucky woman."

He looked at her gratefully and gave a shy smile.

"So why are you looking for her? Don't you know where she is?" Jessie asked.

"No, part of this 'writer's retreat' thing is that you have to be cut off from all your friends so they can't come barging in and interrupt the great Kiwi novel or whatever you're doing. She's writing a nonfiction book, by the way, about a group of photographers who spent the summer in the Southern Alps." He took a sip of tea. Hot and strong. His stomach gurgled its appreciation. "So problem is, I caught a plane on an impulse. Now here I am, and I haven't a clue how to find her."

Jessie laughed. "Now that wasn't too smart."

"Charming though." Rachel, a lovely fair-skinned woman who must have been beautiful in her day, looked wistful as if she remembered the days when someone would have done the same for her.

"So call the Writers Association in Auckland. They'll be able to help you, I'm sure."

"Better than that," Jessie intervened, "go talk to Andrea. She lives about ten minutes from here. She's been writing for donkey's years. She'll know who's who and where."

"Good thinking, Jess. Now eat up your lunch young man. You've got work to do."

CHAPTER 30

Adrian was mystified by the sturdy chain-link fence surrounding Andrea's charming little house. The necessity for the fence came bounding toward him the minute he let himself in through the latched gate. A huge black Newfoundland skidded to a stop, licked his hand with a massive tongue, then tail wagging furiously bounded up to the front door. With a joyous bark, he turned around, raced back to Adrian and stood on his hind legs, front paws on Adrian's shoulders. Luckily, In spite of his bulk, the dog exerted no pressure.

"Alexander, down." A gray-haired lady commanded as she opened the door. She smiled an apology in Adrian's direction. "Sorry about him. He loves company." The dog obeyed instantly and sat down in the middle of the path. "The fence is to save the world from him. He went missing a few months back and finally turned up in the back of a VW. Some couple had seen him in the middle of the highway chomping on a possum. They decided he was a driving hazard and coaxed him in to their car. He was only too happy to accept a ride. They drove all around the neighborhood trying to find the owner. Heaven knows how they managed to cram him in to the back of one those little cars."

Adrian stepped off the path and walked around the genial dog. "He's no problem. I've a friend with a houseful of psychotic dogs." He put out his hand. "I'm Adrian. Jessie said she would give you a call to say I was coming."

"Ah! So you're the young man who bewitched Jessie. She's been twittering over men since she was in grade school. Old enough to know better by now I would have thought." She shook his hand with a remarkably firm grip. "I'm Andrea. Come on in and tell me what I can do for you."

Adrian followed her through the door, the dog hard on his heels. "Thank you." Noting the open newspaper and glasses on a table beside a comfortable looking leather chair, he added, "Sorry to disturb you, but Rachel and Jessie assured me you are the local literary expert."

"Hardly," she grinned, looking ten years younger, "but I have had a few books published. Now what do you need to know?"

"As Rachel probably explained, I'm trying to find my wife. She's writing a book – well not exactly – she's agreed to do a write up on a series of photos for the photographic club at Kingfish Bay. She went on a hike with them in the Southern Alps earlier this summer." He hesitated a moment, before adding, "It's her first try at writing and she's very nervous about it."

"That's understandable." Andrea settled herself in her chair. "Sounds like a nice project. But why don't you know where she is?"

"We had a long holiday in Kingfish Bay. Delightful spot. However, when we drove to Auckland for our return flight, she was so worried about the project, we decided she would stay here for a couple more weeks and get some help, then follow me home."

Andrea frowned and tapped a long skinny finger on the arm of the chair. "To cut a long story short," Adrian continued, "she met some writer who gave her help in getting started, then suggested Emma go on a writer's retreat to get it finished quickly. Of course, that means she hasn't been taking any phone calls or contacting me."

"Of course not. That's the whole point. You need complete quiet and sometimes that's the only way to do it. I have grandsons galloping in and out and the phone ringing its head off. Can't get a damn thing done." She gave him a long look. "Jessie said your wife hadn't told you where she was and you want to surprise her."

"That's right. All I know is that she was looking for someone who could help her with her project. Would you have any idea who that could be? She did mention South Island."

"Humph, there are quite a few folk around, but there aren't many places that provide writing courses, *and* offer a writer's retreat. Your wife must be pretty good." She scratched the top of her head with her glasses. "I'll give Debs a call; she edits non fiction, maybe she can help."

Adrian looked around the small comfortable room with its sheepskin rugs and a bookcase crammed with books in all shapes and sizes. Andrea picked up her phone. "Are you there Debs? How's it going, got that 500-pager off your plate yet?" She laughed. "I'll tell him that next time I see him. Okay, now to business. I've got a young man here who's trying to find his wife. She's at a writer's retreat – nonfiction, photography. Any clues?"

She listened attentively and with phone balanced between head and shoulder made a few notes. "Thanks, that's great. Come on over for a cup of tea sometime." With a few more pleasantries the conversation ended.

Adrian brightened up. "So you found out where she might be?"

"I'm not that smart. But I do have a number of leads. May take a while. Why don't you make yourself at home, while I make some calls."

"Thanks." Adrian settled down on a wonderfully squishy sofa. Alexander immediately followed and put a massive head on his lap. He smelled of doggy shampoo.

"Alexander, go to your bed!"

"He's okay," Adrian said, scratching the dog behind the ears.

"Alexander you're off the hook this time, but don't think you can do it to all my visitors. Dumb dog thinks he's a spaniel." Her amused and affectionate tone caused Alexander to thump his tail.

Andrea moved over to her desk and started making calls. On the third try, she said, "I think I know where she'll be. There's a place at Lake Taupo. Unfortunately, no one's there at the moment, and we need to make sure before you go beetling off. Let's have a cup of tea while we wait."

She bustled off to the kitchen. Adrian decided to look around, and the minute he moved Alexander obliging removed his head and looked hopefully toward the door. "No, I'm not going for a walk, just stretching my legs. I've done too much sitting down in the last two days." *Grief, I'm getting as batty as Iris talking to a dog.*

He wandered around looking at photos of Andrea with a tall, lean man, arm draped around her shoulders, and then others of three strapping boys their eyes full of mischief. On her bookshelf, casually mixed in amongst best sellers, classics and romance novels were three books by Andrea Black. He felt sure that was the Andrea who right now was making him a cup of tea. Riffling through the first one, he was impressed. He read the dust jacket. It looked good. Book in hand he poked his head round the kitchen door. "You have had three published. That's terrific. *The Ones Left Behind* looks fascinating."

Andrea poured boiling water into the teapot to warm it, then added three spoonfuls of tea. Pouring the kettle until she was satisfied the teapot was full, she put the lid on the teapot, firmly encased it in a cozy, and set it on the tray. Adrian tucked the book under his arm and hastened over to pick up the tray and carry it through to the living room.

Once settled with teacup in hand, he nodded toward the book which he had placed on the coffee table. "It's WWII isn't it? The women?"

"Yes, all the war books are about brave men and the battles they fought. If women get a mention, they were nurses on the front line, WRNS, WAACs, or WAAFs. No one has paid any attention to the women who were left behind. *They* were the heroes. All on their own having to bring up the kids, look after the garden and the house, work double time on the farm, or some other enterprise, keeping their husband's businesses going."

"Wow! That's interesting."

"And the loneliness. Think about it. Years of maybe nothing but the house and the kids. Young women. No wonder a bunch of them went off the rails when the Americans moved in to protect us while all our forces were off saving Europe and the mid-East." She shook her head.

"Yes, but . . ." At that moment the phone rang. Saved by the bell. Adrian had a feeling Andrea was about to jump on a soapbox.

"Hello, Marcie, thanks for getting back to me. Do you have a woman, Emma, scribbling away in your cottage?"

She listened for a while, thanked the woman and put down her phone. Adrian moved to the edge of his chair. "What did she say? Is Emma there?"

"Marcie is on her way back from some conference in Sydney so doesn't know. She said her husband called and told her he'd let some pommie woman have the cottage. Apparently, a friend convinced him he should. However, he's way back in the bush somewhere trout fishing. She can't raise him on the phone. Probably in a dead phone zone – or more likely, he's just switched it off so it doesn't disturb the fish!" Her laugh was a short bark.

"But isn't the cottage close enough that a friend could just go across and ask if she's Emma?"

Andrea gave him an exasperated look. "She's in a retreat. The whole point is not to disturb her."

"But come on, I'm her husband for goodness sakes."

"If she wanted to talk to you, she would have called. Leave her alone, let her do her thing."

Trying to curb his impatience, he asked, "How long before I can call?"

"Really don't know. Maybe a couple of days."

"Since the woman in the cottage is English, sounds like it must be Emma. I think I'll just go now. I'll be there by tonight or early tomorrow. Another friend of hers from England is heading that way. I don't want her to get there first and ruin my surprise."

He'd go straight there and be waiting when Nicole arrived. Grinning to himself, he got to his feet. "Thanks so much." He suppressed his feeling of triumph and managed to look bashful. "You'll excuse me if I rush off, I'm really anxious to see my wife." He stood hesitant for a moment and then said, "It's been a pleasure to meet you. As soon as I've found my wife, I'll be sure to buy your book. I know she'll enjoy it too." He walked over, kissed her lightly on the cheek and enjoyed the comforting smell of lavender soap.

The dog fell in step behind as he headed for the door. Andrea got to her feet. "I'll see you out and make sure Alexander doesn't jump on to your back seat. He'd love to take a trip to Lake Taupo and splosh around scaring all the trout."

Adrian said goodbye and set off making sure to latch the gate carefully behind him. As he waved goodbye and gave a farewell toot on his horn, he grinned from ear to ear. Nicole was in for a big surprise.

CHAPTER 31

Nicole sat back and relaxed. Still two hours to Auckland, and then the next leg of the long haul to South Island.

Jerry drove fast, and the scenery slipped by in a blur of green fields and fern clad slopes. Nicole tuned the radio to a classic station and as the strains of a Tchaikovsky symphony swept over her, she put her head back and let her mind drift aimlessly. The beautiful landscape and the blue sky scattered with fluffy white clouds, made her realize how much she missed New Zealand and its laid back charm. *Why don't I move back and buy a neat little place on the beach? It would be easy to work from home.* Then as she began to daydream, the nightmare reason for her departure to England came back to haunt her. Shying away from the thoughts of Jay's accident, she tried to remember the good times, but they eluded her. Seeking diversion, she flipped channels to a news station. 'The All Blacks will be playing the Springboks in Cape Town. University fees are rising. The Chinese want exclusive rights to New Zealand oil. A massive search for Judd Jason is under way.'

"Who's Jud Jason?" Jerry asked.

"He's a pop singer – idol of every teenager on the planet." Frowning, she added, "Remember I told you before his plane crashed in Oregon."

Jerry grunted a disinterested "Oh."

Nicole shook her head in disgust, and found a talk show. She listened with half an ear to a discussion on roses, but a fascinating interview with an author made her suddenly sit bolt upright in her seat. "Ye gods, I'd forgotten all about that nice woman in South Island. I need to give her a call."

Jerry glanced across at her. "What woman in South Island?"

"The one we are on our way to see. She says she can find the writer's adviser who's helping Emma."

"Well, why doesn't she just go and look now? Save us the trip."

Nicole tried to suppress her exasperation. "Because he's away on vacation and her friend is the only one who knows how to contact him. Problem is, her friend has gone to a house on the beach and it's in a cell-free zone."

"All these people are beginning to make my head hurt. Just go ahead and call her, whoever the heck she is." He shook his head in mock despair. "I swear we've contacted three hundred people so far on this Emma quest."

"She's the one who expects me to arrive by air and stay with her. I need to call and explain that we've changed our plans and are driving down."

"Now why didn't you just say that in the first place?"

"Being a detective's assistant means you need to pay attention and remember details."

"Hey, but . . . "

"And," Nicole interrupted, "keep quiet while I make my call."

She found the number and called. "Are you there, this is Nicki. I just wanted to let you know I've decided to drive down to Nelson. So I'll be a day late."

She listened attentively, a smile creeping over her face, then fished in her purse for a pen and made a note of a number. "Thanks, that's terrific. I really appreciate your help. Come over and visit me in England sometime."

A few minutes elapsed as the woman at the other end of the line babbled on, and then Nicole said, "Thanks again. You've been great."

Jerry, glancing sideways throughout this exchange, said, "Okay, please explain what that was all about. If it means we have to go and talk to some other Susie, Ben, or Uncle Tom Cobley, I'm going to drive straight into the next wall I see."

Nicole leaned over and patted him on the knee. "Calm down. All's well. Turns out the woman I just talked to was delighted I called before I left, because her friend came home and she discovered that Glen Gerrard, the writer who we thought would lead us to Emma, is not the person we need to find." She paused, looked out of the window. "Sad really, the woman's father fell off a roof so she had to come rushing back from the beach."

"If I wasn't driving, I'd throw up my hands in despair. Why is it good our one clue has dissolved, and who on earth is the man that fell off the roof? What was he doing up there anyway? Practicing to be Santa Claus?"

"It's good, because we don't have to travel to South Island now. The person we want to see lives in Lake Taupo which is only about three hours from here."

Jerry slowed down as the traffic ahead started to thicken. "You mean *Emma* is in Lake Taupo?"

"I don't know. I was told to call someone in Lake Taupo. Apparently this woman is a non fiction writer and she has a writer's retreat on her property." She looked across at his bewildered face and suppressed a laugh. "This is the most promising clue we've found yet. The person I just talked to in Nelson thinks Emma is likely to be in Lake Taupo."

"Only three more hours in the car? Fantastic!"

"Yes!" She banged her fist on the dashboard in triumph. "We'll be able to get to the bottom of Emma's disappearance before Adrian has time to cover his tracks."

"Always assuming Emma hasn't called him in the meantime."

"Huh!" Nicole balanced her scribbled note on the dashboard and dialed the number of the person in Lake Taupo.

After about five rings, a somewhat flustered woman answered. "Sorry, couldn't find my phone. Just got back from a trip to Sydney."

"In that case, I hate to bother you, but I understand you're a writer and have a writer's retreat on your property."

"Certainly do. You a writer? Looking for somewhere?"

"No, I'm looking for a friend of mine from England. She's writing a book on photography, and someone told me she might be with you."

"Not with me. I've been in Oz for over three weeks visiting my sister." She paused and Nicole's heart began to sink. Not another dead end. "Hang on a minute, I remember now. My husband told me he'd let the cottage to a writer while I was away. It completely slipped my mind." She laughed. "I'm glad you reminded me."

"Could you ask him who it is?"

"'Fraid not at the moment. He's a trout fishing guide and he's back in the bush somewhere with a tourist who wants to catch a whopper. I tried him at the airport and a couple of times since. Unfortunately, he's in a zone where he can't receive my call." She gave an exasperated sigh. "More likely he's got his phone switched off. Hates to be disturbed. Can't blame him really. Who needs phone calls when you're fishing?"

"Do you expect him back tonight?"

"No, more likely tomorrow."

Nicole mouthed a silent damn. "Could you go over to the cottage and find out if it is my friend? Her name's Emma."

The woman's voice was patient. "I'm afraid not. The whole point of the retreat is that we guarantee not to disturb the writers. They're welcome to come over here for a meal anytime, but we've told them we'll give them total peace and quiet."

"But I've come over from England and I don't have much time left," Nicole protested. "I'd really like to see her." She suppressed the desire to scream *"Don't you realize if Adrian contacts you before I get there, you stupid woman, he will be waiting for me."* Then what? She shuddered.

However, the woman replied calmly, "Tell you what. By tomorrow, my husband will be back or maybe your friend will come over to borrow some milk or something. Why don't you wait until then? You can give me another call."

Something about the other woman's tone told Nicole she would brook no arguments, so she suppressed a sigh and forced a polite "Thanks for your help. I'll call you tomorrow."

She turned to Jerry. "We're nearly in Auckland. Let's stop there and get some lunch. We can make it to Lake Taupo easily afterwards"

"First sensible thing you've said all day."

As they drove across the harbor bridge admiring the yachts that zipped across the polished water, Nicole looked ahead to the city laid out before them. "As soon as you leave the bridge start looking for the Newmarket exit. We'll pull in there and find a restaurant."

He drove carefully over the bridge and blended in with the heavy city traffic. "This the one?" He asked as the Newmarket sign appeared.

"Yes, pull over, slow way down after you leave the ramp so I can spot a parking building. Know there's one close by. Just hope they haven't moved it while I've been gone!"

"Do I go straight?"

"Yes. It's not far."

As Jerry negotiated the traffic, Nicole said, "Okay, up on your left."

They pulled into a parking spot, locked the car, and made their way to the street. Shoppers with bags bustled by and office workers dodged around them as they sauntered along.

"This one looks good." Getting no negative response from Nicole, Jerry led the way inside and they were soon seated at a table facing the street. All conversation ceased as they studied their menus.

Finally, with lunch ordered, and a cold drink in front of them, Jerry settled back in his seat and said, "So, I gather we're headed for Lake Taupo now. We could make it tonight, see this woman and then who knows, maybe we can finally relax."

"It doesn't make any sense to go tonight," Nicole replied. "She won't let us go and check whether Emma is the writer in her cottage and her husband doesn't get back from fishing until tomorrow morning."

Jerry took a long drink of his lager. At Nicole's raised eyebrows, he said, "It's your turn to drive, and anyway, I intend to eat so much it will soak this up in no time. And I don't intend to have more than one, mother."

She laughed at the sarcasm. "I think we should push on to Lake Taupo today anyway. We'll be ready to get to that woman's place first thing in the morning."

Jerry took out his phone and started tracing their route. "Hey, we go through Rotorua. That way I can see the thermal region. Why don't we stay there tonight? We can get up early tomorrow and be in Lake Taupo in no time in the morning – it's only a half-hour drive. That'd be neat – to say nothing of the nubile Maori maidens who dance at the nightly concert."

"Jeez. For a man forsaking all women until his wife turns up, you haven't reformed much."

"Oh, come on. That's just eye candy. It doesn't count."

"Okay, you're on. It would be a shame to miss the bubbling pools."

The lunchtime business crowd had dispersed, leaving a smattering of tired shoppers to eat a late lunch, so the service was remarkably quick. Nicole laughed when Jerry's fish and chips arrived. "That piece of fish looks more like the Loch Ness Monster."

He picked up the slice of lemon and coated the fish. "I'm so hungry I could eat the plate too. Good luck with your rabbit food."

Nicole waded through a large portion of salad smothered with fresh shrimp, olives, and sliced egg. She munched a large bread roll spread liberally with butter and ended the meal with a slice of fruit cake. By the time she had finished her coffee, she felt pleasantly overfull and ready to hit the road again.

Jerry grinned at her. "I'm glad it's your turn to drive. I feel ready for an after lunch nap."

"Okay, let's get going. I'd like to clear Auckland before the commute starts."

Once back in the car, Nicole negotiated her way through the heavy local traffic. Once clear of the city center the congestion thinned and they made fast progress to the Waitakere mountains. She lowered the windows and breathed in the clean country air and the smell of fresh fruit as she slowed to look at the fruit and vegetable stalls. "How come so many?" Jerry asked.

"It used to be nothing but market gardening up here. Enterprising types cultivating the vegetables for the Auckland market."

"Right now food doesn't interest me too much. Just wake me up when we arrive." He leaned back in his seat and closed his eyes.

However, after a short time he opened his eyes and starting looking around at the rolling landscape of green. Black and white cows munched contentedly completing the picture of rural bliss. Gleaming milk trucks rolled by on their way to the butter and cheese factories in Hamilton, the center of the dairy industry.

As they approached the small country town of Cambridge, white fences enclosed pastures where snooty looking thoroughbreds tossed aristocratic manes. In adjoining paddocks, colts, manes flying, nostrils flaring, raced each other along the fence line.

Slowing down to negotiate the elegant tree-lined streets of Cambridge gave Jerry the opportunity to look around. "What is it about this place that reminds me of England?"

"Must be the narrow streets. Can't be the architecture, but I grant you the trees make it a bit like a small country town there."

The road widened as they left town and they were soon bowling along at maximum speed.

As they neared Rotorua, Jerry said, "Phew! Rotten eggs."

"Sulphur, dummy, it's a thermal region. Give it about half an hour and you won't notice it anymore. Let's find ourselves a motel as soon as we get there, freshen up and then hit the tourist spots. Don't know about you, but I am tired of sitting in a car."

"Amen, to that."

As they drove into town she said, "We'll have just enough time to gallop our way around the thermal region, then we can go to a concert this evening. Unfortunately, we don't have time for the Agradome show as well."

"What's that? A place where the sheep play basketball or something?" He chuckled at his own wit.

"I love it. Seen it several times already. It's an exhibition of shearing, and extremely funny herding. They use herding dogs with ducks on the stage. But the best bit is when the nineteen different species of ram trot out on to the stage and pose on a stepped platform like a bunch of beauty queens in a Hollywood production."

He started looking around the minute they entered the urban area. "Drive slowly and we'll pick a motel."

They soon picked out an attractive motel, its central courtyard decorated with tubbed flowers. The owner showed them a spacious, attractively furnished, double unit which boasted separate bedrooms and bathrooms and a large common living room and kitchen.

After Jerry had marveled at the well-equipped kitchen, checked the TV and his bedroom, he poked his head around the bedroom door and called, "All is well. There's a lock on the door so my virtue will stay intact."

"You really think I didn't know that already," Nicole retorted.

Nicole unpacked a few necessities from her bag, had a quick wash and changed her crumpled blouse. When she came into the living room, Jerry was already there looking refreshed and ready to go again.

At top speed they took in a large portion of the thermal region, marveling at the pools of bubbling mud and the spectacularly beautiful thermal lakes. One of the geysers obligingly blew for them and they dipped their fingers in some of the cooler pools. A Maori guide explained to them how people of the region used to use the hot pools for washing, and cleaning their clothes. And how many houses are still heated by the constant supply of hot, thermal water. After visiting one of the exhibitions they ended up spending half an hour talking to a Maori elder who was sitting on a bench, leaning on his stick, and sunning himself. He was a charming old gentleman full of stories about the old days and with very strong opinions about those lazy Maori tribes up north!

After they left him, Jerry said, "I have to take a dip in one of the warm thermal pools. He just told me they cure rheumatism and all sorts of things. I think it will get rid of some of the cricks that I have in my old bones caused by all those hours sitting in a car Emma-hunting. It'll feel great. Coming?"

Nicole remembered their argument and his remarks about her in a swimsuit. She decided a swimsuit was not a good idea. "I think I'll pass and just take a shower – freshen up that way. Need to wash my hair."

"Okay." Did she notice a tinge of regret in his voice? Unbidden, she remembered how he looked in his swim pants; long sun-tanned athletic body, muscular arms, and powerful legs. With a slight shake of her head, she decided – definitely not a good idea.

After she'd had a shower, she sat thinking about what would happen the next day. If they drew a blank at the Lake Taupo writers' retreat, it meant that Emma had undoubtedly disappeared. Even the skeptical police would have to be convinced that something fishy was going on. She stared out of the window for a while, scarcely noticing the tumble of flowers, in the planter outside as she thought it through.

She'd better do one last check with the writers' association in Auckland, make sure she hadn't missed anything. If she was going to put forward a story convincing enough to initiate an Emma-hunt, she needed to line up all her facts.

She called the Writers Association in Auckland, trying desperately to remember the name of the woman she had talked to there when they first arrived. "Sorry to bother you again. I called you when I first arrived in Auckland. I am looking for a friend from England who is writing a book somewhere. I thought she would be in Auckland but you told me no-one seemed to have met her."

"Yes, of course I remember. You said she was a beginner who needed help with a non fiction book. I've been checking with a lot of people. No joy though."

Nicole exhaled. Fabulous, the woman still knew who she was talking about. "I really appreciate your help. But I still haven't been able to find her. I've checked all over the place in Northland but she seems to have disappeared off the face of the earth."

"Surely, someone knows where she is. Couldn't anyone up there help?"

"Not so far unfortunately. However, I'm going down to talk to someone in Lake Taupo who writes non fiction books. That's my last resort. I know I've asked this before, but are you sure that Emma hasn't contacted anyone else? I'm really worried about her."

"Actually, I think you're in good shape going to Taupo. It's Carrie you need to talk to. She knows everyone and everything about non fiction writing. Has contacts all over the place. She'll put you right."

"Okay, thanks for your help." She closed her phone with a satisfying click. All bases covered.

◈

That evening they went to a Maori concert that was a delightful mix of song, dance and humor. Jerry got to see his Maori maidens a-plenty. And they laughed as they watched a little Japanese boy casting furtive glances at his parents as he desperately tried not to laugh in sheer astonishment at the Maori warriors poking out their tongues.

Tired, they returned to the motel feeling very glad they had only a half hour's drive in the morning. Nicole relaxed, happy knowing she was well ahead of Adrian.

CHAPTER 32

Adrian pulled over to the side of the country road to call the writer's retreat in Lake Taupo. What luck meeting those two, sweet, gossipy ladies in the tearoom. Without them it could have taken days to find out where Emma would go for help. He smiled at the thought of being there before Nicole.

Irritation replaced the happy thought as the phone rang, and rang, and rang. He dropped it in disgust, counted to ten, picked it up again and hit redial. As it continued its monotonous ring, he beat time on the dashboard with his fingers. "Answer the phone, you stupid woman." She didn't.

He flung the phone on the seat beside him and decided to head for Auckland. Nicole must be well on her way to South Island by now. He'd pile on a few miles, then try the woman again. Although if she was another one of those silly writers, she'd probably switched the phone off so that it didn't disturb her.

Concentrating on his driving, he soon forgot his frustration, and it was over an hour before he tried the number again. It rang interminably, infuriatingly. Swallowing his anger, he continued on his way.

The traffic thickened as he neared Auckland, and as he approached the harbor bridge that gave access to the city, it slowed to an infuriating stop-start pace. Realizing banging his hand on the wheel was not going to achieve anything, he sat back and relaxed. It needed only an occasional glance at the traffic ahead to know when he needed to move. Since it was commute hour, the barriers had been moved to accommodate workers leaving the city. There, in the multiple lanes, the traffic moved freely. However, the city bound traffic confined to few lanes, moved sluggishly.

Rolling down the window, he took a deep breath of fresh salt air and felt the breeze ruffle his hair. The blue waters of the Waitemata Harbor reflected the fading daylight, and provided a scenic contrast to the yachts tacking home or taking the long run out to sea. In the shallow water edging the harbor, wind surfers whipped to and fro in the fresh breeze, narrowly missing each other as they totally ignored the wide expanse of available water.

As the traffic crawled, Adrian's impatience mounted. The nagging suspicion that Nicole might find the woman in Lake Taupo persisted. It would be infuriating if she got there first. The more he thought about it, the more convinced he grew that Nicole was at the root of all his troubles. Single, a software hotshot, not a mite domesticated he felt sure. She'd probably been filling Emma's head with ideas about getting out and doing things. After all, the Emma he had known all these years would never have decided to take off with that group of photographers on a tour of South Island without him. She wouldn't have had the courage. Obviously, Nicole had been sowing the seeds of rebellion; telling Emma that running around after a man, keeping him happy, should not be her primary role in life.

He'd been having a great time with Emma in Kingfish Bay, when without any warning, she told him she was going to South Island with a group of photographers to take photos in the Southern Alps. Staggered, he'd asked her why she was leaving him on his own. Calm as you like, she'd told him that since he was out playing golf all the time he wouldn't miss her. Outraged, he'd asked her if she expected him to cook all his own meals. She'd even taken care of that and all his favorite dishes were in the freezer. All he had to do was warm them up in the microwave. What's more she'd arranged for the wife of one of the photography club members to come and clean for him a couple of times a week.

Nevertheless, the old Emma would never have been so sneaky. It had to be that Nicole. Never mind, she'd get her comeuppance when he caught up with her. Damn woman.

He glanced at his watch. Surely the woman in Taupo must be home by now. He tried the number again. Zilch. At that moment, the traffic began to move forward in a steady stream. As he crested the bridge, the city spread out before him with the Sky Tower poking its head defiantly above the multi-storied hotels and office blocks. Just as he cleared the bridge, his indicator flashed. Darn, he was almost out of gas. He pulled off the freeway into a service station. With another long drive ahead, he needed to take a break. He moved his car away from the pumps and took a brisk walk along the sidewalk. Although he didn't feel hungry, he bought a cup of coffee and a Kit Kat.

Back in the car, he peeled the silver wrapper from the Kit Kat and remembered how he used to relish Kit Kats as a child. Breaking off each finger to savor it slowly. Now, he crunched his way through two fingers at a time, scarcely tasting the chocolate, and gulped down the coffee.

Refreshed, he dumped cup and wrapping paper in a bin and set off again. If that wretched woman in Lake Taupo wouldn't answer her phone, he'd go anyway. Pound on her door and force her to respond. He had to find out if Nicole was heading that way. If she was, he'd be there waiting. He grinned at the thought and slipped effortlessly into the traffic.

CHAPTER 33

Jerry and Nicole checked out early intent on reaching Lake Taupo before Adrian. Knowing, with a sickening certainty Emma would not be there, Nicole wanted to be well away before he arrived.

The air felt fresh and newly laundered in the city's early morning quiet. Overhead pillow-soft clouds drifted across a blue sky. As they walked toward the car, Jerry took her wrist and held it firmly. She turned, surprised.

He looked her right in the eyes. "Today is going to be the end of the trail where Emma is concerned. You've looked under all the rocks and come to what we are being told is her logical destination. If she's not there, you'll have enough to convince the police it's suspicious."

"I certainly hope so." She still had her doubts. Presenting a negative – the absence of Emma – would not be an easy sell.

"I'm sure they'll listen. If she's not there, something must have happened to her."

She shrugged. What more was there to say?

"We've done everything we can," Jerry insisted, his fingers like steel bands around her wrist.

Then, as she prepared to move on, he loosened his grip. "We still have a couple of days left before we go back." His tone lightened. "How about we just take off for the weekend? We could go to one of those fancy fishing lodges where they wine and dine you after a hard day's fishing."

She looked at his strong, sun bronzed hand. "You know we can't do that. No, it's out of the question." Why did her words lack conviction even to her own ears?

He let go of her wrist reluctantly, giving it a faint squeeze as he did so. "Okay," said hesitantly. "Let's just go find Emma and then talk about it some more."

She busied herself finding the car key, avoiding his eyes.

Once they were both strapped in and ready to go, he gave a heartfelt sigh. "Just one more thing before we take off. I told you Madison is going to join me at Christmas. What I didn't tell you was that she's hesitating again. She's not sure whether she'll make it by then." He looked out through the window at a couple loading their cases into the back of a car. "And to tell you the truth, I'm not sure I want her to come. I like being with you and I don't really want it to end."

"It doesn't have to. I'd be delighted to meet Madison. You'll have to invite me to visit once she's settled in."

He gave her a quizzical look. "You know what I'm saying, and having you and Maddie be buddies isn't what I have in mind."

What's with him today? I don't want these heavy conversations. Not now. Not with Adrian hot on my heels. "Jerry." She started the car. "All I care about right now is finding out what's happened to Emma."

He frowned, bit his lip, and said nothing.

The road to Lake Taupo cut through a forest of deep satisfying green that provided shade and infinite peace. Only the hum of the car's engine broke the silence. Every once in a while, they passed a truck hauling giant denuded tree trunks to the timber mills. As they passed each truck, the delicious smell of the forest was accentuated by the sharp tang of freshly cut wood.

Wanting Jerry to enjoy the scenery, Nicole drove. After about twenty minutes, he put his arm along the back of the seat and swung around. "Wonder if that's friend Adrian hot on our heels?"

Nicole looked in the rear view mirror and shivered. A red sports car was closing fast. She put her foot down. The car, an Italian sports model by the look of it, drew close and then swept past. The woman in the passenger seat gave a condescending wave.

"Phew!" Nicole's shoulders relaxed.

Then she caught sight of Jerry grinning from ear to ear. "Thought that would get you."

"That's *not* funny. You just took ten years off my life."

"Come on now, stop being so jumpy. Just relax, we're way ahead of him."

Lulled by the hush of the forest and the heavily scented air, the sudden roar startled them both. No sooner had they absorbed the sound, when the sight of massive clouds of steam pouring out of some buildings to the right of the road caused Jerry to give a startled, "Jeez! It's the hobs of hell!"

Although she had been expecting it, she still sat awestruck for a full minute before explaining. "No, it's the geothermal plant. You're right though, all that roaring is coming from the bowels of the earth." She pulled over to give him a better view. "They harness the steam to turn turbines that produce electricity. After the steam cools, they pump the water back into the ground. So you have a perpetual energy supply."

"Wow! That's impressive."

As she moved on to the shoulder of the road, she raised her voice over the roar of the steam. "The geothermal plants supply about fifteen percent of the country's electricity."

"Fantastic. Can we go take a look?"

"Not right now. I don't want to be late for my appointment." She started the car, checked the road and pulled out.

She looked at her watch. Plenty of time, but they might be held up somewhere. She put her foot down. They drove on, eating up the miles on the straight, smooth road, until they came out of the forest and the sparkling blue expanse of Lake Taupo opened up before them. "It's way too early to call on that woman. Let's go grab a cup of coffee and then arrive at a respectable hour so we don't catch her before her morning tea. I don't want to have to deal with a grouch."

"Good thinking," Jerry said, "but she's bound to offer us a cup of tea or something. Let's go down to the lake. I'd like to stretch my legs. All this driving is for the birds."

"Okay. Look out for a spot. There should be a small park somewhere along the east side of the lake. The beaches are better here."

A few minutes later, Jerry said, "Right up ahead. There's a sign. Looks likely."

Nicole pulled into a small green area with a few picnic tables set under shady trees and parked the car close to the lake. Jerry bounced out of his seat and strode across the grass to a little rocky cove. He looked across the crystal clear waters of the lake to the backdrop of volcanic peaks. "Now according to my guide book, this lake is over two hundred square miles and full of trout. How about you continue the Emma-hunt while I see how many fish I can catch?"

"Going to be a bit awkward without a car. Shall I just drop you off in the town?"

He turned to her with a broad grin. "I'm not deserting you at this stage of the game, but it looks awful tempting." He jumped off the small bank on to the beach, picked up a piece of stone and tossed it into the air. Then ran his finger across it. "It's pumice isn't it? Just like the stuff my mother made me use to clean my dirty fingers."

"Yes, that's why the lake bottom is so white."

Jerry went down to the water's edge and tested the temperature. "Cool but not bad. Will be good for swimming later."

At that moment, a small campervan pulled in beside their car and two small boys erupted. Yelling at the top of their lungs, they ran down the bank and plunged into the water. Their mother emerged from the camper, towels and picnic basket in her hands.

Plonking them on a picnic table, she looked around. "Good morning. Gorgeous isn't it?" She began spreading a cloth across the table. "Think after I've fed the two bottomless pits, I'll have a swim too. That water looks just plain delicious."

"Morning," Jerry responded. "I'm waiting until the sun warms it up a bit more. I'm your basic wimp."

After strolling along the little beach, Nicole and Jerry sat on a grassy bank and watched the children splashing each other and shrieking with laughter. Across the lake, a few fishing boats headed for their favorite spots.

Nicole, still antsy, got to her feet. "Let's go find this place."

"Stop worrying. Adrian's probably still bumbling around in Auckland looking for her. Unless, of course," he added heavily, "Emma's called him and he's going straight to her."

With an exasperated sigh, she shook her head. "You still think I'm nuts don't you?"

"To be honest, yes. However, on the off-chance you're right, I don't want you to run into Adrian on your own. He could be dangerous."

She turned and made for the car, hopped into the driver's seat and fastened her seat belt. He got the message, rushed round to his side and jumped in. As she entered the address of the writer's retreat into the GPS system, the mother hauled two protesting children back to the camper.

They drove slowly through the little town of Taupo, stopping often to let tourists cross the road. The majority wandered along, cameras at the ready, others wore shorts, hiking shoes, small back packs and determined expressions.

A small road led away from the town and they wound their way up past scattered houses until a sign led them through a grove of trees to a clearing with a great view of the lake. Nicole drove carefully past a pen of angora goats to a long, wooden house, painted white with blue trim; sort of a reverse Wedgewood. When she stopped the car and turned off the engine, a medium-sized steer ambled over and regarded her seriously through the side window.

Feeling a little edgy, she asked Jerry, "Do you think he's tame?"

"Looks that way to me. Since I've got the car between me and him, I'll get out first."

The steer didn't move.

At that moment, the front door opened and a small woman in jeans, blue short-sleeved shirt and flip flops came out. "Don't worry about Harold. He's harmless. Just likes to greet people."

She came over to the car and gave Harold a slap on the rump. He turned toward her, then ambled away. "Okay, you can come out now." She grinned at Nicole.

"I hand fed him for the first few weeks so he thinks he's a household pet. Even let's my five-year old niece ride on his back."

Nicole climbed out of the car, stuck out her hand and said, "Hello, I'm Nicki, here to see if your resident writer is my friend." The woman's hand was strong and warm. Still feeling vaguely guilty about catching the woman this early in the morning, she added, "I hope we're not too early."

"No problem. Come on in and have a cuppa. I'm just polishing off my toast. I'm Carrie, by the way." She turned to Jerry.

He immediately came over and offered his hand. "Jerry. Pleased to meet you."

She led the way back to the house and as they entered they were immediately ambushed by two golden retrievers eager for attention. Nicole leaned over and stroked a silky coat and was immediately rewarded by a long warm tongue on her hand.

"Out of the way you two. Come in to the kitchen." It smelled comfortably of toast and tea. After ushering them to seats around a scrubbed wood table, she whisked the newspaper, folded to the crossword, off the table and picked up the teapot. "I'll make a fresh pot. Would you like some toast?"

"No thanks, we had breakfast before we left Rotorua. But a cup of tea sounds just the ticket." Jerry sounded pleased with himself for the English phrase.

Carrie's eyes crinkled. "Tea coming right up. There are mugs and cups over on the dresser. Help yourself. I find that works best. Some people drink tea in huge mugs, others like it in pretty china ones."

As the kettle boiled, she refilled the milk jug and put out a bowl of sugar.

"Have you managed to contact your husband?" Nicole asked.

"Yes, he called me last night after the fish stopped biting." She pointed to a very small house about 100 yards away. "The woman sitting over there *is* English."

Jerry let out a triumphant. "Great."

Nicole, still worried, asked, "Did he tell you her name?"

She heard the sound of a car approaching fast. It drew up close to the front door.

It wasn't Adrian.

Carrie went quickly to the door. "Hello, Bob, what do you need?

They couldn't hear his response.

"Okay then, I'll let Ryan know. Key's in the ignition."

She came back into the room and walked back to the kettle which was starting to make encouraging noises. "Bob's a neighbor. He shares some of our equipment. We couldn't really afford a tractor, neither could he, but between us we're in good shape." She warmed up the teapot and tossed in a couple of tea bags. As she added the boiling water, she continued, "God knows when that man is going to relax. He was an attorney in Wellington and came here to take life quietly. Doctor's orders. But he just doesn't know what retiring means. Keeps going flat out."

She put the lid back on the teapot, then slipped a bright orange knitted tea cozy over it.

"Did you get the writer's name?" Nicole prompted.

"No, sorry. I did ask, but he'd forgotten. Good thing we only have one daughter or he'd forget her name too."

"Could you call him again?"

"No need. He'll be here soon, or maybe she'll smell the tea and be over. Whenever I settle down with a cup of tea or coffee, someone always seems to arrive."

Jerry, obviously feeling guilty about interrupting her breakfast, said, "Sorry, we disturbed you while you were having breakfast. Nicole's just very anxious about her friend."

"No worries." She brought the teapot over to the table and settled down taking a large bite of toast.

"Can I pour the tea once it's brewed?" Nicole asked.

"Thanks."

"You've got a great property here," Jerry said. "Love your view of the lake."

"We like it. Both had hectic jobs in Auckland and decided to chuck them. Move down here and live the good life."

"Great idea, but you're still pretty busy by the looks of things with those goats out there. They are yours, aren't they? Then according to the woman at the Writers Association, you run classes as well."

"The classes are just for enjoyment. I get to meet a lot of writers that way. Anyway, I generally invite someone down for the weekend to give a class. Don't have to do much work myself." She pushed her cup in Nicole's direction.

Guess that means the tea's ready. Nicole pulled the pot toward her, lifted the lid and gave the tea bags a squish. Carefully replacing lid and cozy, she poured Carrie a cup, filled Jerry's gigantic ceramic mug and her elegant porcelain one. "Milk everyone?"

"Yes," Carrie answered and obviously deciding Nicole already knew Jerry's preference, continued, "I do a fair bit around the place between hand raising any creature that needs it and looking after the garden. But I worked ridiculous hours for years in the finance industry. I'm not interested in doing that anymore. I leave that to the neighbor!"

"You're a writer, aren't you?" Nicole asked.

"Yep. Write cookbooks and I'm planning to do one on goat breeding too. Don't know a darn thing about goat breeding but since I need to understand it better to save vet bills, I might as well kill two birds with one stone."

"Bit of a stretch from cookbooks to goats isn't it?" Jerry interjected.

"You know us girls. Good at multitasking." Her Cheshire cat grin lit up her eyes. She finished her piece of toast and pushed the plate away bringing her tea cup squarely in front of her. "Always imagined I'd have hours to spend writing once I retired, but around this place there's always something needs doing. Mark you, I think Ryan is the real problem. He's always dreaming up schemes, then delegating most of the work to me. That's the problem with being married to an ex-executive. They're used to delegating."

"So why don't you hire a handyman?" Nicole asked.

"What, and ruin all my fun giving Ryan a hard time. No way."

The phone rang. Nicole froze.

It wasn't Adrian.

"Ryan says he'll be here in about fifteen minutes. Want to take a look round the property while you wait?" She looked at their mugs. "Or do you want some more tea?"

Nicole polished off her tea with two gulps. "No, thanks." She sprang to her feet. "Can I go over and see my friend now?"

Carrie looked at her watch. "No, it's too early. You can't disturb her yet. She might have been up until two this morning writing. Whole point of being in a retreat is that you can write whenever you like. No responsibility. It's amazing how much you can get done when no one disturbs you."

Nicole felt another guilty twinge about taking up Carrie's time. "But you know if I could just pop over and see the writer – it's probably some complete stranger – we could be on our way and leave you in peace."

"You're no problem." Carrie laughed. "You're saving me from the chores. Ryan will have to help when he gets home! Come on, I'll show you around – you'll enjoy the menagerie – then you can go over to the writer's cottage."

"But . . . " Nicole protested.

"No buts. All you have to do is give her another thirty minutes peace. Thirty minutes isn't going to make much difference to you."

Oh, yes it will if Adrian turns up. She was itching to go over and peek through the cottage window. One little peek, and they could be out of here before he arrived.

As Jerry picked up the mugs and took them over to the counter by the sink, Carrie whisked her newspaper away. With a lingering look at the crossword, she straightened it out and carefully folded it back together again with the front page headlines on display. Giving it a last smooth, she set it on the kitchen table. "It bugs the hell out of Ryan having to read the paper after me. Can't stand the crumpled ruin I hand over. In the cause of familial accord – and hoping he won't notice I didn't bring him anything back from my trip – he'll be greeted by a pristine paper." Nicole cast a look at the very used-looking paper. "Well, as pristine as it gets after me." She flipped a red-gold curl that had escaped her headband.

Nicole took a peek at the headlines. She hadn't had time this morning to linger over the teapot with the paper. 'All Blacks annihilate Springboks' 'Massive hunt for Jud Jason under way' 'Dollar's unprecedented high means hard times for the dairy industry'

"What's happened to Jud Jason?" He was one of her favorites – a pop idol who could actually sing.

"His Lear jet went down – he was piloting it to a gig in Sacramento. They lost contact with him and haven't been able to find him. They think he must have crashed somewhere in the Oregon mountains."

"Some tough terrain there," Jerry interjected.

Carrie strode toward the door. "Let's get going." The two dogs leapt to their feet and stood noses to the door. She opened it and they tumbled out. "We've a duck pond on the other side of that grove of trees. I'm hoping for some eggs soon. I can add a few duck egg recipes to my book then. I like to try things out before I write about them."

Thirty minutes. Thirty whole long minutes. Nicole followed Carrie out of the door and looked anxiously down the driveway. Nothing stirred in the dappled shade.

Jerry followed them both out of the door. "Why did you decide to breed goats?"

"Just thought it would be fun. I reckoned they'd help clear the land, and we can sell their wool. There are plenty of weavers around here that love Angora wool."

They walked over to the grove of trees, the sun warm on their back, and the scent of hydrangeas wafting over from the bushes clustered near the house. The two dogs rushed around in front of them, sniffing everything in their path. One of them picked up a large piece of broken branch and laid it at Jerry's feet. "Okay, boy. I can take a hint." Jerry threw the stick over to a stretch of grass that bordered the fenced off goat area.

"You've got a job for life now Jerry." Carrie continued walking to the grove of trees, telling Nicole how she had found the property and the problems they had persuading the previous owner to sell. Nicole tried hard to look interested as she blocked out Carrie's voice and listened for the sound of a car approaching. The minutes ticked by.

They wove their way through a small stand of eucalyptus trees; the bark hanging down exposing beautifully rounded tree trunks. The sharp distinctive smell of their leaves reminded her of a trip to California. Emerging from the trees, they came upon a large round pound with muddy, grassed banks. Three ducks plunged inelegantly into the water and swam furiously for a couple of minutes leaving a widening wake behind them. Just as suddenly, they turned, realized Carrie was there and swam back hopefully. She pulled a slice of bread from her jeans pocket, broke it into pieces, and tossed it out into the water. In the ensuing squabble of ducks, Nicole scarcely heard the car engine. She froze.

Jerry, who in spite of the boisterous dogs had managed to keep up with Carrie and Nicole, turned and strode back through the trees. "Hey, Carrie, it's a Land Rover and two men. Must be your husband. One of them just pulled out a cooler."

Carrie quickly threw the remains of her largesse to the ducks and returned to the house. Nicole, sure the husband would know who the woman in the writer's cottage was, rushed along with her. Ryan petted the overjoyed dogs as he waited for Carrie, then slung his arm around her shoulder and ushered her back into the house.

"Just a minute. I want to introduce you to Nicki and Jerry. They're here to see our writer. You remembered her name yet?"

"No. Will as soon as I see her though."

Nicole offered her hand to Ryan. He was tall and rangy with hands the size of frying pans. He smelt of tea tree, crushed grass, mud and fish. "Soon as we've given Phil here a cuppa, I'll unload the car and he can take the fish and be on his way." He looked across at Jerry. "You two want a couple?"

"Take them," Carrie urged. "You can't buy trout here. Have to catch your own, but you can take these to a restaurant and they'll cook them for you. I'll pack them in ice since I don't suppose you have a chilly bin."

"Thanks, that'd be great." Jerry grinned. "Hope I'll get a chance to catch some myself before we leave."

The phone inside the house rang. Carrie ran to the door, rushed through and grabbed it before it stopped. A few minutes later she emerged. "The husband of our writer is on his way here now. Popular woman isn't she? I'm looking forward to seeing her."

"Is he far away?" Nicole asked hopefully.

"No, he's in town already. Should be here in a few minutes."

Nicole's stomach churned. Trying desperately to be casual, she asked, "Can I go talk to your writer now. Maybe she isn't my friend, and if not, I don't want to be in the way when her husband arrives." *In fact, I want to be as far away as possible before he gets here.*

"Okay then. Off you go. Just knock before you bowl in. She might still be in her jammies."

Jerry walked toward the car, turning to her as he left. "I'll wait in the car for you. If it's not Emma, we'll be on our way."

"Hang on mate. Let me get your fish first." Ryan sounded annoyed.

"Yes, sorry, didn't mean to be rude, but I'm not too keen about this husband. I think I know who he is, and somehow I have the feeling, he's not going to be pleased with us." He covered the confession with a bashful grin. "I'd love that fish. And I'd like to take you both out to dinner tonight if you're free." He shot a worried look in Nicole's direction.

Nicole heard the sound of a car approaching. She took a deep breath and hurried toward the cottage.

CHAPTER 34

Nicole's walk resembled a 100 meter sprint as she sped across the large expanse of lawn, and hurtled around the tumbling hydrangea bushes to the writers' cottage. The cottage, built of some dark wood bleached to streaked silver by the sun, had only two skimpy windows in the rear.

As she rounded the corner, she gaped at the stunning view of the sparkling lake with its mountainous backdrop. In front, set on a short stretch of grass, tucked in the shade of a large, Pohutakawa tree, was a wooden table with bench seats on two sides. She bounded up the front steps to a wide verandah that had two large wooden chairs with overstuffed cushions. An overly busy bee, on route to the masses of blue Michaelmas daisies that fronted the verandah, narrowly missed her. The idyllic spot caused a fleeting vision of writing a long sequel to War and Peace.

Ears cocked to catch the sound of approaching footsteps, heart pounding, she took a deep breath and knocked on the door. The bleached wood felt warm on her knuckles. She could hear someone moving around inside but the door remained firmly closed. After what seemed at least five minutes but was probably no more than one, it opened. A woman stood there, but eyes narrowed by the brilliant sunshine outside, Nicole had difficulty seeing into the shadowed interior.

She pulled the door open a little farther and, uninvited, stepped across the threshold. With Adrian due to arrive at any minute this was no time for social niceties. The woman, slight, suntanned, in faded blue jeans and a soft cotton shirt with rolled up sleeves, stood in stunned silence for another long moment. Just as Nicole's eyes adjusted to the light, the woman dropped her hand from the door, "NICKI!"

Nicole's knees buckled. "Emma." She swallowed, fighting tears. "Oh, Emma it's really you."

"Of course it's me. But what are you doing here?" A puzzled expression followed the delighted smile.

"Nobody has heard from you. I've been worried sick. And even Iris has started to worry."

Emma frowned. "But I called Adrian and told him I was on a retreat and didn't want to be disturbed. Didn't he let you know?" She clucked her tongue in annoyance. "Of course, he wouldn't have known that he should contact you."

Nicole heard a car door slam. Adrian.

"Do you mind if I sit down a minute? You've given me a shock. I've been hunting all over North Island for you and was really beginning to worry that something had happened to you."

"Of course, of course. Come on in and sit down. I'll get you some tea." *At least she's still the same old solicitous Emma. Let's hope Carrie keeps Adrian talking for a while.* "You are silly worrying. But never mind, bless you."

Emma ushered her into the little room, the sunshine blocked by blinds, and pointed out an old- fashioned rocking chair by the pot bellied stove. "It's really comfy."

Nicole sank into the chair grateful for the support. As her heart rate slowed, she became aware of her surroundings. The room was sparsely furnished but comfortable. The only sound the soft tick of the clock. A large open bookcase was crammed with paperback novels, a beautiful leather bound Complete Shakespeare with gold lettering, several dictionaries and a thesaurus. A wooden sideboard stood against the far wall, and scattered sheepskin rugs added comfort to the polished wood floor.

In an alcove, a large desk sported a laptop, printer, and piles of typed pages in no perceivable order. A wooden shelf adorned with carved driftwood, and a large clock made of polished kauri dominated one wall. The rest displayed several paintings of the lake in oil and pastel.

"I can't imagine why you've been so worried Nicki. What on earth did you think had happened to me?" Her sudden mischievous grin and twinkling eyes were another surprise. "Did you think I'd found a toy boy?"

Nicole hesitated, wondering what to say. At that moment, the door exploded open and Adrian rushed through, closely followed by Jerry. Emma turned pink with pleasure and Adrian came over and enveloped her in a bear hug. After a moment, Emma leaned back and said, "It's great to see you, darling, but why are you here?"

Adrian released her reluctantly. "I missed you. So I just hopped on a plane and I'm going to whisk you away for a weekend. I hear you've been working way too hard."

"That sounds delightful. But I really must finish this project. Look how much I've done since I arrived here. It's great just being able to write with no interruptions." She pointed to the piles of papers stacked on the desk.

Jerry who had been hovering close to the door came forward a few steps. "Nicki, I just popped over to tell you I'm going to spend some time with Ryan. He's promised to tell me about some good fishing spots. As soon as you've had a chat with Emma, come over and join me."

Nicole, her attention focused on Emma, gave him an abstracted, "Okay."

He grinned broadly and inclined his head toward Adrian and Emma who were deep in conversation. "See you in a bit then." He cocked one eyebrow in a sardonic 'I told you so'.

She ignored him. He left.

Emma, suddenly remembering she had another guest, said, "Let me make a cold drink and we'll go outside. It's too nice to be stuck indoors." A troubled look crossed her face. "Adrian, I don't think you've met Nicki before. She's a good friend of mine from home."

Adrian's look conveyed a wealth of comments, but he murmured a polite, "No, dear, we have met already. Iris invited us both to dinner one night while you were away."

"Oh, good." She smiled at them both. "I've a whole pitcher of freshly made lemonade – thanks to Carrie's lemon trees – I'll just toss in some ice and take it outside. We can all sit and chat for a while."

"Great idea. It's hot out." Nicole got to her feet and headed for the kitchen. "I'll get some glasses. I assume they're in the kitchen."

"No, they're in the sideboard over there under the window."

Nicole went over to a sideboard crammed with glasses of all shapes and sizes. She picked three blue tinted tumblers, took them outside and set them on the rail that lined the verandah. She then settled down to wait for Adrian and Emma who had disappeared in the direction of the kitchen.

After ten minutes longer than it would have taken to put ice in a jug, they emerged, Emma still looking very pink. She poured the chinkling ice drink into the tumblers and handed them around. She took the other chair and Adrian sat on the deck with his back to the railing facing them.

The cushions, warmed by the sun, slightly rough to the touch, sank, enveloping Nicole in a comfortable cocoon. Bees buzzed and the scent of lavender filled the air. She didn't feel remotely relaxed. Although Adrian had greeted her affably, his eyes, tinged with a slight hostility, watched her closely.

Emma, oblivious to the tension beamed at both of them.

Nicole sipped the sharp, sweet lemonade to moisten her dry mouth. "So how is your project coming along Emma? Is it very difficult?"

"It was terrible to start with, but after I'd had a talk with a writer Ryan knew, I've been writing up a storm. It's not very good but Carrie is an expert and a woman in our photography group told me that she would be able to help me turn it into a real book."

"But Carrie only arrived home yesterday."

"I know. That was a blow when I first got here, but I knew she'd turn up soon and Ryan suggested I get started on my own. He said she'd be a lot more help if she knew what I was attempting."

"Sounds like a good approach. But I tell you, you're a braver woman than I am. I wouldn't have the foggiest idea how to get started."

"Oh, you're so much cleverer than me, you'd have no trouble." With a worried glance at Adrian, she looked around, anxious to change the subject. "Where is the man that came with you Adrian? He seems to have disappeared."

"He wasn't with me, but he followed me over. I assumed he was Nicki's friend."

"Yes," Nicole laughed, "that was Jerry. He's a workmate of mine and we came on holiday together. He just popped over to say he was going somewhere with Ryan. Jerry's dead keen on fishing and Ryan's a guide."

Emma's eyebrows went up. "A very good looking friend. You've been on vacation with him?"

"Yes, when he heard I was coming here on vacation, he asked if he could come along. Said he wanted a native guide."

Adrian threw back his head and laughed. "Now there's an original line!"

Nicole suppressed a sigh of relief. Thank god they didn't know Jerry's real reason for coming.

"I've booked us in for a nice luxury weekend at Huka Lodge, Emma." Adrian said. "Just think of it. A bottle of bubbly to start, then a four course meal with all the trimmings."

"It's a beautiful spot, Emma. Those falls are spectacular," Nicole added. She looked at them both and began to feel like a spare wheel. "I should leave you two to make plans. I'm really glad you're enjoying yourself over here. We'll get together when we're back home again." She got to her feet. "Right now though I need to be on my way. I've some friends in the area I promised to look up."

Emma leapt to her feet. "Must you go so soon?"

"Yes, I'm afraid I really must. Thanks for the lemonade." She gave Emma a long hug. "I just wanted to say hello and make sure these Kiwis are treating you right." She turned to Adrian. "Goodbye, Adrian. Nice to see you again."

As she moved toward the steps, he smiled and now it was a genuine smile that started with his eyes. "Enjoy the rest of your holiday Nicki."

I will now that I don't have to worry about Emma anymore.

CHAPTER 35

The search for the pop idol, Jud Jason, was under way in Oregon's Cascade Mountains. When the plane crashed, the radio signal died, and air traffic control could not pinpoint his location. In view of his popularity, and the extreme weather conditions, a massive search had been mounted.

Ty Johansson's party had been searching for two days now. Ty covered his ears against the clatter of the helicopter as it gained altitude, swung round, and headed east across the mountains. His back ached, his thighs screamed at every step and his hands were freezing, but he kept going. He made his way along trails running with water, clambered over slippery downed trees, cold, hungry and exhausted.

It wasn't as if he was used to this. Sure, he was a member of the ski patrol – had taken first response training, tried to keep fit in the off season by running - but he was an accountant. He spent his days chained to a desk in a comfortable, air-conditioned office in Portland, Oregon. Then came the call before the first snows arrived. He hadn't completed the usual pre-season warm ups that honed him to his particular peak of fitness. No match for the macho young skiers who powered down the slopes, but pretty darn fit for a forty-year-old.

Not that he minded being called out. His fourteen-year-old daughter had screamed with delight when she heard he was going to join the search for Jud Jason. She, like most teenage girls, was in love with Jud. Now, she was sure her dad, who solved all the family problems, would bring her hero home alive and well. He'd walk a million miles for the delight on her face if he succeeded, but cringed at the thought of the look on her face if he failed. He stepped up his pace.

With the weather closing in, and the air search due to be called off, they needed as many feet on the ground as they could muster. If Jud was injured in the crash, he would die of exposure unless they found him quickly. As he slogged along in the chilly, wet conditions, taking gulping breaths of the mud-tinged evergreen air, he knew he'd go on searching whoever was lost out there. He wouldn't wish that sort of death on his worst enemy.

Mercifully, Sam – big, blonde, ruddy-faced with a long bouncing stride – shouted over his shoulder. "Let's take ten minutes. Make sure to drink plenty of water." He threw his pack down on the ground, pulled out his water bottle and an energy bar, and after a long drink continued. "They just called off the air search. There's another front coming in. Freak snowfall by the sound of it. So it's up to us. We've got to find that poor devil before he freezes to death."

Ty sank down on his pack, feeling sure he'd never be able to get up again, but he pulled off his gloves, dug in his pocket and pulled the wrapper off a MojoBar, guaranteed to keep you going. He paused before taking a bite. Okay, bar do your thing. My poor legs need you. He took a bite, swallowed painfully, pulled out his water bottle and took a long swig. That felt better. He tried the next bite. Mm, good. Not the steaming bowl of soup he craved, but it was better than nothing. He glanced across at Jackie. She'd told him she was a personal trainer. She was leaning back against a sodden tree trunk eating nuts and raisins out of a zip lock bag. Looked as relaxed as if she was at the movies. *Grrrr!*

After what seemed less than two minutes, although his watch told him it was ten, Sam yelled. "Time to move." He jumped to his feet. "We must cover as much ground as possible before the storm hits. We'll split into two groups." He glanced up at the sky where clouds were already building. "Jackie, you lead the second group.

Ty, Stu and Jack, you go with her. Everyone else with me." He pulled out his map and pointed. "We'll meet at this rocky outcrop. Should be able to make that before dark. We can shelter inside the caves there and light a fire."

Ty clambered painfully to his feet. Even they were beginning to play up. He'd go out and splurge on a better pair of boots when he got back home. Visions of walking around a nice warm mall shoe-shopping swam before his eyes. Pair of high end Bass ones. That would do him. Pricey but worth it.

Jackie's voice broke into his reverie. "Come on Ty. You're with me. Let's go find that plane and put that dumb Swede," she grinned across at Sam, "to shame."

Sam came over and thumped her playfully on the shoulder, the slap of wet glove against heavy jacket noisy in the stillness. "Go find him, Tiger. I'll buy you a beer if you find him first."

The search continued. Ty gritted his teeth and kept going although the desire to curl up somewhere and sleep was growing hour by painful hour. He'd even crawl in a hole with a bear if he found one. If it was asleep it would radiate plenty of heat, and if it wasn't, being eaten by a bear seemed preferable to this prolonged agony.

Jackie, constantly checking the terrain, clambered up every rock that appeared to the right or left hoping to get a wider view of the mountains. She'd clamber back down again shaking her head, and off they'd go again. After sliding down what must have been the fifth rock, she fell into step beside Ty. "That snow's coming in fast. I don't think we're going to make it to the rendezvous point." He looked up and saw clouds moving rapidly overhead. The wind had picked up. "We'll get lost for sure if we continue. Keep your eyes peeled. There should be some caves around here. I came up here last summer and we found some then."

As she spoke, Ty felt the first wet flakes hitting his cheeks. Small flakes, not even destined to lie on the ground for long, but doubtless the beginning of the front. The wind howled in the top branches, pushing small flurries in his face. He forced his tired limbs to pick up the pace. He didn't like the idea of being stranded out here in a snowstorm.

The four searchers walked as fast as they could as the snow thickened. It was lying on the ground now and the trail was becoming slick beneath their feet. Ty could feel a damp trickle inside his left boot. That's all he needed. Leaking boots. They pushed on for another hour, and he began to feel the first surge of panic. He'd heard stories of what happened to people stranded on the mountain during a snow storm. They needed to find shelter fast.

The light began to fade, the snow thickened. Sticking to the trail became difficult. Thank god for Jackie; she seemed to know where she was going. But she was young, and probably overconfident. He hoped she wouldn't lead them into a ravine.

"There it is," Jackie whooped in triumph. Poking out of the snow, huge boulders piled by some long ago earth movement, towered above them. "Stay here for a minute." She clambered up and after a few minutes yelled, "Come on up. I've found a cave."

Ty followed the others up the slick boulders. He tried to remember all the things he'd learned at rock climbing class. Keep your weight on the balls of your feet. Use your arms for balance not for hauling you up. Carefully plan your next move and push yourself with your legs. His feet, clumsy in hiking boots, slipped in the footholds. He lost his balance. Almost fell. Panting, scared, he pushed his face on the rough rock face and took a deep steadying breath. The rock scraped his face, but it was solid. He clung on. Tentatively, he reached up with his hand, scared to move his feet now that he was securely anchored. Slowly, carefully, he took one foot off the ledge and moved it upward. His hand shook with the effort of hanging on, he felt the cold sweat running down his back. His heart pounded loud in his ears. The snow kept falling and the wind tugged at his jacket.

At last, his foot found a hold. He moved his weight, oh so slowly, to the left. He pushed upward. Teetered again. Stopped. Held his breath. Pushed his face into the rock and felt blood trickle down his cheek.

"Come on Ty. You're almost there." The long arm of Stu, a young gangly creature, offered him a hand the size of a shovel. "Hang on to me. The others have me anchored."

Ty exhaled a heartfelt sigh and grabbed Stu's hand. Devoid of a glove, it got a firm grip on his wrist and pulled him steadily upward. As they pulled him over the lip, he collapsed on the rocky terrain. "Thanks, guys. I just decided not to attempt Everest this year."

They all laughed in relief and followed Jackie into the cave. It was wide-mouthed with an uneven rocky bottom and overhanging rocks. Outside the light was fading fast. In the cave it was pitch black. Stu pulled out a flashlight and played it around the cave illuminating the spooky corners. Ty hoped there weren't any critters living there.

"Okay, guys, let's look around and see if there's any wood. It's going to be darn chilly in here tonight."

At six foot one, Ty had to duck his head frequently as he searched the floor with the aid of Stu's reflected light; it wasn't easy avoiding all those overhead rocks. Jackie, with her efficient little flashlight, moved away from the group searching for wood and a corner where they could lie down.

Ty found some wood. It had some charred pieces; someone else must have sheltered here. Anyway it was a start. He took the pieces back to the entrance and started off in another direction.

Stu yelled "Hey, I've got a whole bush. Someone must have dragged it in to make a fire, but probably left it because it was too wet. It's good and dry now. Must have been here ages."

A loud startled 'OO -OOW!' silenced them. Horrified, they listened to an ever-diminishing scream.

Ty looked at the others. They all stood paralyzed. He moved carefully in the direction of the scream. Right behind an over-hanging boulder was a chasm. "Bring your light over here Stu. Move carefully. Mind your head."

Stu played the light down the chasm, it yawned black as pitch. Ty leaned over, dank, dry air rose, but all he could see were boulders.

"Jackie, can you hear me?" Ty strained his ears. He heard a soft moan. Thank god she was alive. "Jackie, Jackie, answer me. We can't see you. Are you okay?"

Ty held his breath. Finally, after an eternity, a shaky voice floated up from the chasm. "Yes, I'm okay. I was just checking. I'm bruised all over and my right ankle's not working but apart from that I'm functioning."

"Can you see our light?"

"I can see it sort of. There's a big ledge above me. I hit a couple of them on the way down. They broke my fall." He could hear the effort in her voice. She was in pretty bad shape.

"Don't move. Stu will come down and get you. We'll put a rope on him and secure it up here."

"No, you don't need to. Just throw a rope to me."

Ty looked across at Stu who raised dubious eyebrows and said in a low voice, "If we put a loop in the rope and she puts it under her armpits, it'll work. If I go down, I might knock her off that ledge, and by the echoes we're getting I'd say it goes a long way down."

"Okay, Jackie," Ty forced a calm, confident voice. "The rope will be down in a minute. Be darn sure you put it under your arm-pit and hold on tight."

Stu spoke quietly to Ty. "She's a tough cookie that one. She's done gymnastics since she was five. She'll be fine."

They sent down the rope and after she gave them the signal, they pulled her up very slowly, stopping every few seconds to make sure she did not hit a ledge. Jackie's voice growing louder and firmer gave them instructions.

A horrified scream rent the air. Then, "Oh my god, oh my god, oh my god."

Ty told the others to stop pulling. "Jackie, take a deep breath. Relax. You're safe."

Now she was sobbing. Gulping and sobbing.

"Jackie, stop it. You're going to be fine. We've got you. You're safe."

"But, but . . ." she sobbed and went on sobbing for a full minute. Finally, she managed a weak, "It's a body. On the ledge."

"Okay, okay. Be calm. Be brave for me and touch it. Is the body warm? Is the person still breathing?"

"Please, not Jud Jason," Stu exclaimed.

They could see Jackie's little flashlight flickering. She was near the top. "No." Her voice was horrified, terrified. "Its . . . its been dead for a long time. Get me out of here now. PLEASE."

They hauled her up, and she tried to stand, but she was shaking and unable to loosen the rope. Stu took the rope off her and Ty pulled her up to her feet gently and put his arms around her. He pulled her head into his shoulder and stroked her hair. This erstwhile confident young woman was no taller than his daughter. "It's going to be okay." He signaled over the top of her head to Stu. Get the fire going. They needed to warm her up and get her a hot drink. She was suffering badly from shock.

Stu, with crisp efficiency got a fire going, and asked Jack, a swarthy rather clueless youth to boil some water. "I'll go down and bring the body up."

"No," Ty said. "Leave it where it is. We don't want to sit here all night with a body." He gestured over Jackie's head and Stu got the message. Sitting around with a dead body wasn't going to help her recover. "We'll call the park rangers, and the police will probably want to come too. Once the weather opens up anyway."

CHAPTER 36

"**Y**ahoo!" Jerry chortled as they drove away from the writers' retreat beside the lake. "Mission accomplished. The lost Emma has been found. The happy couple reunited."

"Shut up, will you. Okay, so you were right. I was worrying about nothing."

"Come, come, now Nicki, would I say that?" He paused. "I must admit I was glad to see her safe and sound though. For a while, you had me convinced she was a goner." He swerved to avoid three hikers tramping up the small road, equipped with oversize packs and boots to match. "So, congratulations Sherlock, you solved the case."

Irritated by his banter, she still felt great knowing that Emma was alive and well. She turned to watch the hikers, all lean, fit and suntanned. "How about that for an idea?"

"What?"

"Let's go for a hike. We're overdue for some exercise. I'll stop at the visitor center and get a map."

"Yep. I like the idea of a gallop up a mountainside, sandwich at the top, and an afternoon fishing. Finally, round off the day eating a slap up dinner with Carrie and Ryan."

Sounds as if it's playtime for him at last. She found the visitor center and pulled into the parking lot. She sat a moment in the car. "I forgot to remind Emma to give Iris a call." She looked at her watch and dug out her cell phone. "I'll give her a quick call now."

"Don't know why you're bothering. Iris won't be worried. Didn't you say she's sailing in Scotland? Probably forgotten all about Emma and is busy adopting bedraggled dogs," he shuddered, "she'll probably hire a piper to stop them feeling homesick."

Nicole ignored him and called. The phone rang six times, then Martin's warm, confident voice told her they weren't home right now, but to please leave a number and they'd call back. "Hi, this is Nicki. Just wanted to let you know I found Emma and she's looking great. I'll call again tomorrow."

"Wonder why she's not answering? Hope she hasn't gone overboard." But even as Jerry laughed, she had a nasty thought. "You know Iris is hopeless in a boat. I hope Martin's taking good care of her."

"Hey, Nicki, you're not going to start worrying about Iris now are you? I'm going to have to buy you a kitten when we get back to give you something to look after. Else you're going to be on perpetual people hunts every time any of your friends take off on vacation." He shook his head in despair. "And much as I have enjoyed this very strange vacation, I draw a line at tramping over the banks and braes in a gray drizzle."

She ignored him and decided to call again in the morning.

The visitor center provided them with the name of a good lakefront motel, a trail map, and an assurance that there were no snakes, poison ivy or animals to worry about. Also a recommendation for a good sandwich shop.

They hit the sandwich shop first, then booked into the motel, rooted out a day pack and hiking boots, slapped on suntan lotion and set off.

It felt good walking up the track, stretching her calf muscles, working up a sweat in the sun. When they reached the tree line, they enjoyed cool and pleasant conditions for another hour. Finally, they broke free of the trees at the top of the trail and climbed to a lookout point. She stood transfixed, drinking in the striking blue of the lake, the three volcanic cones in the distance and puffy white clouds almost stationary in the sky. Jerry came up from behind and laid his arms around her shoulders. Relaxed, she leaned back against him and they stood there for a long time.

<><

Pleasantly tired after the hike, they went back to the motel and while Nicole made tea, Jerry called a guide and arranged for a boat in an hour's time. They flopped down in the armchairs and munched cookies washed down by three cups of tea.

Refreshed, they walked to the wharf and found the boat tied up against the dock ready to go. Their guide, a big, loose limbed character with a beaten up old hat on his head, introduced himself as Dan and told them to hop in the boat.

When he set off at speed to the other side of the lake, she relished the wind on her hot cheeks. Once there, he slowed down and anchored near the mouth of a small stream. As the guide handed them rods, Jerry asked "How many fish can we catch?"

"You can catch as many as you like." He grinned. "But you can only take home three each, and they must be at least 40 cm."

"That's 15.7 inches," Nicole added.

"I knew that, and what's more I bet I catch more than you do."

They spent a pleasant time anchored by the stream jigging for trout. After Jerry had caught several more trout than Nicole, Dan winked in her direction. "Let's move. I'll take you over to the western side and we'll do some trolling. I've got some lures that could land you a whopper."

The boat left a wide wake on the still water, and the breeze felt cooler as the sun sank toward the horizon. Trolling turned out to be a lot of fun, and even Dan got excited when Nicole landed a very impressive trout. Enough to put Jerry's to shame. Thrilled by the catch, she held it for a brief moment, and then slipped it gently back into the lake. "Off you go home, sweetie, and produce a lot more just like you."

"Heck, sakes, Nicki!"

"I couldn't have eaten that beauty. You caught us plenty for dinner."

≪≫

They returned to the motel, and took showers before going out to dinner. As the water pounded on her body, she washed away the smell of fish and the sweaty grime of the hike with a rose-scented lotion. When she left her room, Jerry was sitting glued to the television. "They had to call off the air search for Jud Jason because of bad weather."

"That's awful. Will the ground search continue?"

"I'm sure it will. Although some teams had given up because of a snow storm approaching. Can't imagine why, there are plenty of places to shelter in those mountains." His voice was reassuring but he looked worried.

Over dinner Ryan asked them if they'd like to go fly fishing in the morning, Jerry jumped at the idea. She declined. "Thanks, but we need to be on our way tomorrow. We have to be in Auckland for that early flight the day after." Noting Jerry's outraged face, she said "You can go if you get up good and early. I want to stay and pick up some presents for the folks in my office." She also wanted to phone Iris again in the morning. Surely she'd be home by then.

CHAPTER 37

After Nicole left, Adrian moved over next to Emma. He sipped his drink slowly, savoring the tart sweetness of the lemonade, and looked at the garden, the trees, and the lake. He took a deep breath of the flower-scented air. "This is a nice spot."

"Yes, it's peaceful and no one ever bothers me." Emma sighed contentedly. "Oh dear! I really must go over and say hello to Carrie." She stood up. "After all, I'm only here because I came to see her." She babbled on, her voice getting faster and faster. "Didn't expect her to be away when I arrived. She'll think me very rude if I don't go over and introduce myself."

Good old Em, always worrying about what other people think. "Don't go yet, Em. I want to talk to you for a while. I've missed you."

"I've missed you too, dear, but I really should go over and introduce myself."

"A few more minutes isn't going to make any difference. Don't forget she's been away for a while too. She probably wants to talk to her husband. And she's had Jerry and Nicki land on her before the day hardly warmed up. Give her a break."

Emma sat down reluctantly. "I suppose you're right."

"Of course I am. Now, how soon can we get away? I'm dying to do a little touring before we go to Huka Lodge. I've made reservations so we don't have to worry about what time we arrive." He grinned. "Let's eat dinner there though. We'll arrive early enough to enjoy a bottle of bubbly in our room first."

"It sounds nice, but I need to organize my stuff here before we go. It'll only take about an hour. Why don't you take a nap? Or shall I make you something to eat first? You must be very tired after running around looking for me."

"No thanks. I don't need anything to eat."

"Why on earth were you looking for me?" She looked amused. "I told you I was on a retreat. All you had to do was wait a few days and I'd have called you."

Why isn't she flattered that I've come to see her? "But Em – you don't understand – I missed you. Home just wasn't home without you." He had no intention of telling her he needed to see her before that interfering Nicole turned up and gave her some more wild ideas.

"Oh, come on Adrian! You're always traveling. You're away for weeks sometimes. You've never been bothered before."

"Yes, but I was at home. That's different. When I'm at home, you're always there."

"Oh, but really . . . "

"And, you decided to stay here rather than come back with me."

"Well, you know how worried I was about writing this book."

That's just it. You thought the book was more important than me. Aloud he said, "I'm glad you've been able to get started. After we come back from our romantic weekend, you can have a chat with Carrie and then we'll be on our way."

"On our way where?" Emma said in a very small voice.

"Why, home of course. I came down specially so that I could travel back with you. You know how you hate flying and finding your way through airports. L.A. is a real pain."

"But I don't want to go home yet, Adrian. Carrie is here now and I can get some real help with my book."

"For goodness sakes, Em. You've got all the facts you need and there are dozens of writers in England who can help you. Let's face it, we live in Hardy country; there are going to be oodles of writers around."

She still looked dubious. Obviously scared of making new contacts. "I'll make some calls. Find a writing course and an editor for you. Even a book doctor once you've put the first draft together." He felt pleased with all the research he'd done. "I can set it up so that you're helped along each step of the way."

"I don't want to go back."

"What!" His head snapped up. "Surely you don't need more time here."

"I do." She squared her shoulders and looked him straight in the eye.

He got up and sat on the arm of her chair, putting an arm around her. "Be reasonable, dear. You've had months here. It's time to go back home." He felt as if he were dealing with a petulant child. Why is she going on like this? Must have been that damned Nicole inciting her to riot. Never mind, he'd soon put a stop to that once they were home.

She turned a bright pink under her tan. "No, Adrian, you don't understand. It isn't just the writing. It's nice of you to want to help, but I don't want to go back."

Now he was totally perplexed. "What do you mean?"

"I don't want to go back to Dorset."

"You've had a good long holiday, dear. You've found a new hobby. That's great. But holiday time's over. It's time we packed up and went back. We can come again next year if you like. Make a regular thing of it just like Bermuda used to be."

"No." Her tone was definite. "I want to move here. I've some good friends and I like the lifestyle."

"That's all very well but remember," and this came out through gritted teeth, "we have to live. It takes money." These women who don't work seem to think money grows on trees.

She got up and moved over to the rail, leaned back against it and turned to face him. "Don't worry. I've thought it through. You can work here just as easily as in England. Then you can take off on your seminar tours to the States and Europe. You do all your research on line so you can write your articles and prepare your talks just as easily here as there."

Good heavens, she'd been thinking about this for weeks. Not a word to him though. There she was looking totally relaxed and confident. She was being ridiculous but she certainly looked good. That new haircut, the tan and the casual attire, he'd forgotten how attractive she was. She'd been such a mouse for so long, all he'd noticed were the home comforts she provided. For the first time in their relationship, he was caught on the back foot. Didn't know what to do.

"Em, I don't want to argue with you. I need some time to think about this."

She moved over and laid a soft, warm hand on his arm. "Of course you need time. It's a change and it will take a bit of doing. Selling the house and everything. But it'll be worth it. We can buy a lovely property here with the money we'll get from our house."

He stood up and put his arms around her. She smelled faintly of lavender. She snuggled into him barely reaching his shoulders. "You smell good enough to eat."

She broke away and gave him a push. "Go outside and sit over there." She pointed to a lounging chair set in the shade of a large pohutakawa tree overlooking the lake. "Think about it. It makes sense." She moved toward the door. "I'll just finish what I was doing and then make us a nice lunch. You must be hungry – I bet you didn't eat any breakfast."

This new, self-assured Emma was doing his head in. He really did need to sit down and think. He walked slowly over to the chair, and sat down in the shade of the pohutakawa; he felt reassured by its solid trunk and wide branches. The cool shade was a balm to his bewildered mind.

A retriever came bounding over from the main house, and after receiving the expected pat, lay down at his feet content to doze in the shade beside him. Funny how dogs always knew when you needed company. With the exception of those psychotic dogs of Iris's. Wonder how Martin's getting on with her up there in the Scottish Isles? She's probably adopted about three stray Westies by now.

He lay back and closed his eyes. Desperately tired, he wanted to sleep but his mind wouldn't let him. Memories of their last night in Kingfish Bay whirled in his mind. And the scorching memory of his plan. The perfect plan that was to change his life. So carefully plotted all those months ago. So perfectly executed right up until he reached the end . . .

He had planned ahead to make sure the later stages of his life were a shining pinnacle, not just a slow, dreary slide into old age.

Emma had been a good choice as a wife. She'd supported him all through his career. Seeing to his creature comforts, and giving him the encouragement and space to become successful. But she seemed unable to change; couldn't grow into the corporate wife. One who could entertain his clients, and move in the elevated circle of friends that came with success. Someone who could listen to his day-to-day problems at work and offer solutions. A partner who could enjoy living the good life with him.

So she had to go, but divorce was far too expensive. How could he enjoy the fruits of his success if he had to hand them over to her?

However, she had been good according to her own lights, so it was important to let her end be a happy and peaceful one.

On the Sunday before he put the last stage of his plan into action, he took her to church. He felt it was important that she should be at peace with her maker. They went to the pretty little church in Mangonui – to the regular Anglican service – not the happy/clappy one that preceded it. He had to admit he had a few qualms about his plan during the service, but once outside in the sunshine again, he pushed them to the back of his mind.

He organized a wonderful farewell party for her too. All the guests thought it was a farewell party for them both since they were leaving for England the next day. He invited everyone from the small bay where they were staying, and made sure he included her new friends from the photography club.

He gave his girlfriend, Jennifer, money to buy a debit card and promised that he would send a regular allowance if she would wait for him. He asked her to go to various towns to see if she would enjoy living there. He had made it clear they could live wherever they liked since he worked from home for several months each year. He impressed on her the importance of buying something in each town; either stay at a motel, go out for an expensive dinner or buy herself a dress or some earrings. Such a simple way of establishing the perfect alibi. The trail of expenses on the card would reassure the police Emma was alive and well. Of course, he had no intention whatsoever of settling down with that silly little tart Jennifer.

He encouraged Emma to come fishing with him. At first, he had to bait the hook, and take off the wriggling fish for her when she caught one. But gradually she became confident in the boat and looked forward to their fishing trips. She was a bit overawed the first time he took her out night fishing, but when he told her how lovely she looked by moonlight on the ocean, she twittered and began enjoying that too.

The night of the party was fun. All the guests had agreed on pot luck so that Emma and Adrian were not stuck with dirty dishes on their last night before they left the bay. The food was wonderful – crayfish, sushi, oysters, huge steaks, meat pies, Cornish pasties, casseroles, pizzas and mountains of salad and sweet corn. The desserts were out of this world.

Emma was in her element. Laughing and talking with her friends from the photography club, she looked ten years younger. And as the evening wore on, after he had carefully kept her wine glass full, she was talking to everyone; completely relaxed.

After the guests left, he'd taken her in his arms, told her she was marvelous. Tipsy as she was, she believed him. He suggested they go out for one last night of fishing. A romantic cruise by the light of the moon – that was a bit of an exaggeration, it was only a quarter moon. He didn't want it to be light enough for people to see them in the boat.

He had set the boat up earlier in the day. Slipped a small bottle of brandy on board too. Just in case she sobered up. So they were soon on their way zipping across the black water, slipping through the slim shining path of the moon. He took them way out beyond the off shore island so they were right in the Pacific current. She stood in the bow, the wind blowing through her hair, laughing and happy. Surprisingly, she looked very attractive. He couldn't even put that down to the amount he had drunk. He had nursed two beers all evening. He needed to be very sober for the last stages of the plan.

Once out past the off-shore island, and thus out of sight of the bay, he anchored and they settled down to fish. He managed to get his line tangled in hers, knowing that she would lean over the side to try and untangle them. She was always sure she was at fault. As she leaned over the side, he picked up the large hammer they kept on board in case they landed a large feisty fish that needed a tap on the head to stop it thrashing around. All he had to do was give one swift blow to the back of her head, tangle her legs in the spare anchor chain, and tip her over the side. She would sink and drown immediately, painlessly, and her body would never be found. The off-shore current would whisk it out into the ocean in no time.

He picked up the hammer. Then looked at her leaning there, worried that she was causing a problem, but still giggling from the effects of the alcohol. She looked so small, so slim, and so vulnerable. One blow and he could live the perfect life with Cindy. Gorgeous, long-limbed Cindy. Cindy his true soul mate.

He lifted the hammer. Looked at Emma. Little gullible Emma. His hand dropped. He couldn't do it.

He reached for the bottle of brandy. Took a deep swig. It burned the back of his throat but it didn't help. He thought about Cindy. The shining, self-assured Cindy with the luscious body and quick wit.

He picked up the hammer again. Looked at Emma, so sweet, so vulnerable. But she'd changed. Taking that trip with the photography *club had opened her up; made her more talkative. The new sun-tanned Emma with the wind-blown hair was attractive too. Funny how he hadn't noticed her for so many years. He tapped the hammer against his left hand. Somehow, life with Cindy didn't seem so important anymore.*

He put down the hammer, packed up his fishing gear and they headed for shore.

He got up from the chair, felt the sun scorch his back as he moved out from the shade into the sunlight, and gazed across the lake. With a heartfelt sigh, he realized how glad he was that he hadn't carried out the perfect plan.

CHAPTER 38

Totally relaxed after his morning's fishing, Jerry lounged back in the car seat. "So what are we going to do when we get to Auckland?" Before she had time to answer, he added, "I think a nice luxurious hotel overlooking the ocean and a bang up meal are basic essentials. This is our last day. We've worked hard and long and deserve a break."

"You call fishing, working?" Nicole asked.

"No. I was referring to Emma hunting."

"I was thinking of something educational like the museum," She said poker-faced. He looked wary. "But perhaps wine tasting would be a better idea." His shoulders relaxed."We'll book into a hotel, pick up some French bread, cheese and fruit, and then tootle off sipping. It's only twenty minutes out of town. One of the wineries has a great picnic spot. So lunch al fresco."

"That sounds good. Serious research into the New Zealand wine industry. But aren't all the wineries in South Island?" Jerry asked.

"No, there are plenty here, and in Hawkes Bay, and Martinborough. You'd need a week or two to do any serious research."

"Sounds good to me."

They booked into a suite with a fantastic view of Auckland harbor. Jerry wandered around the bedrooms, study and living area equipped with sofa, comfortable chairs and a media system.

"Do we really need to go back? I could settle down here quite comfortably for a month"

"Yes. Unfortunately, there's the small matter of earning our living."

"To banish the thought let's head for those vineyards."

After a short drive, with several stops at vineyards along the way, they settled down at a picnic table overlooking the valley. The shaded area was a welcome respite from the sun, and the cheese, fruit and French bread went well with the wine provided by the vineyard.

After half an hour, Jerry said, "This is delightful, but I think it's time we headed back."

"Yes. There's a coffee shop about five minutes from here – I think a very large coffee is called for."

"Don't worry. I have imbibed judiciously, taking minimal sips. I am fit to drive."

"That's good, but I'm not so impressed by your virtue. You spent ages sipping samples and getting advice. Sounds as if you're going to hit the wine stores big time when you get back home."

He sat back and sighed. "Just think about it. I'll return to my flat in London and sit, sipping and remembering the neato time we've had."

Feeling mellow after the wine tour, they returned to the hotel, sat out on the balcony watching the yachts, and lay back in the loungers. She felt delightfully relaxed, with the salt breeze caressing her cheeks, the cry of gulls, and the rattle of rigging.

"Hey, come on, wake up Nicki. It's getting late."

Startled, she opened her eyes and saw that night had fallen. The lights in the restaurants bordering the harbor gave a cozy glow, and navigation lights flickered across the seascape. Jerry, dressed in slacks and smart shirt with his hair slicked back from the shower, stood on the balcony grinning at her. "Time for us to go out and celebrate the end of our successful Emma-hunt."

Yawning, she stumbled off to the shower. Once the water hit her, she felt wide awake, wonderful. Half an hour later she was dressed and ready to go.

Jerry beamed at her when she emerged from her room. "You look great. Sleeping in the afternoon agrees with you. Let's hit the town. Tomorrow and work loom on the horizon."

"Away with the thought. There is no tomorrow. Let's go to that fancy seafood place we saw earlier. I'm hungry."

They walked to the restaurant, enjoying the evening bustle around the harborside restaurants and the balmy night air. The restaurant was almost full but the waiter ushered them to a table in a quiet corner. The lights were muted and the table covered with an impeccable white linen cloth and gleaming cutlery. A small vase of fresh flowers formed a centerpiece.

The waiter handed them two large leather-bound menus and filled their water glasses. He pointed out the wine list and asked them if they would like something to start. Jerry said "I think the occasion deserves a gin and tonic, don't you?"

"Yes, thank you." Nicole smiled at the young waiter. As he went to get their drinks, they studied the menu. After a long silence, Jerry stated, "I'm going to start with Oysters Rockefeller. And I vote we drink champagne to celebrate our successful mission."

"I'll go along with that. Order Pelorus if they have it. It's my favorite." The waiter arrived with their drinks and after a long discussion with them on the merits of the various fish dishes, took their order.

They sipped their gin and tonics and chatted about the trip, and discussed what time they needed to leave for the airport in the morning. Around them, people settled down to order, and gradually the sounds of the restaurant – the murmur of conversations, the sudden bursts of laughter, the clink of glasses and cutlery – provided a warm cocoon.

After about ten minutes, the oysters arrived and the waiter filled their champagne glasses. Jerry took a sip. "You're right. This is great. Where does it come from?"

"Mmm." The crisp, yeasty flavor tingled on her tongue. "Marlborough. It's from the same winery as Cloudy Bay."

They enjoyed the oysters and fish dishes and finished their meal with a crème brulee. Feeling pleasantly over-full they wandered back to the hotel. Nicole put on a pot of coffee, Jerry looked for a movie and they settled down on the sofa. By the time the coffee was ready, and Nicole had poured two cups, Jerry produced a bottle of brandy. At her raised eyebrows, he said, "I picked it up in Lake Taupo. You never know in mountainous areas when you might need it. I didn't see any handy St. Bernards on our hike yesterday."

He took two glasses out of a cabinet, and poured a measure for them both. He handed one to her, raised his glass and said,

"Here's to a great traveling companion. I've enjoyed my tour. Even though it was mostly Emma-hunting, we certainly had some fun along the way."

She sipped hers. It must be the effect of the champagne – it tasted better than usual. "You've been a useful co-sleuth, but I think I'm retiring now. I always fancied being a Miss Marple but I think I got a bit carried away where Emma was concerned. Bit embarrassing really."

"No. You were right to be suspicious. I'm just glad it turned out so well." He picked up the remote. "Let's get this movie rolling."

They settled back on the sofa and long before the end Jerry had her in his arms.

◈

After her shower next morning, she cleared the steam from the bathroom mirror and surveyed her face. "Nicki darling. You never seem to learn. Just steer clear of champagne in future." Her reflection grinned back at her.

She put on her well worn comfy jeans, a newly washed blue shirt and sneakers. As she packed her bag, she left out a sweater for the plane; she knew she'd freeze on board without it. With still damp hair and no makeup, she went through to the kitchen to make tea.

Jerry had beaten her to it. The table was laid, juice had been poured, and he was just filling the teapot. The toaster popped up. "Breakfast is ready madam. The special today is toast and honey. I don't know about you, but I don't feel very enthusiastic about food right now."

She caught his eye and suppressed a grin. She could see by his twinkling eyes, he was having a hard time keeping a straight face. He turned back to the toaster, placed the four slices in a toast rack and put them on the table with butter and honey.

Nicole sat down and sipped her juice. Jerry put his head outside the door, retrieved the newspaper, and came over to the table, planted a gentle kiss on her head, and gave her the front page section. He kept the sports page for himself. With a faint headache and queasy stomach, she didn't feel too much like reading, but she flipped through the headlines. "Oh, good, they found Jud Jason. He managed to crawl away from the plane. He's got a few broken bones, but he'll be okay."

"The teenagers of the world will heave a collective sigh of relief," Jerry quipped.

She drank two cups of tea and ate one piece of toast. That felt better. She pushed back her chair. "We'd better get a move on. I'm packed, so I'll go along and check us out."

Jerry gave a heavy sigh. "Oh, boy. Back to reality."

He moved toward her. With an adroit side-step she reached the door, and said over her shoulder, "Hurry up and get packed. We've a plane to catch."

His face fell but he headed for his room.

◈

They checked in and were directed to Air New Zealand's business class lounge. Jerry was annoyed they hadn't arrived earlier when he saw they could have had a free 15-minute foot, or head and shoulders, massage. Instead, they checked on their flight and had a quick cup of espresso. The concentrated caffeine did wonders.

Outside, in the shopping area, people were stocking up on duty free goods, and hitting the clothing stores and souvenir shops. "Hang on a minute, Jerry, I have to get one of these T-shirts 'We support the All Blacks and any team playing the Aussies'. There's an Aussie in my department. I'll have to go back wearing that one."

"Shame on you. Come to think of it though I'd better pick up a few things. There's an admin that always helps me out when I'm snowed under." He picked up a nice paua shell bracelet with earrings to match. "Do you think she'd like these?"

"Yes, that's nice. But come on we'd better hustle or we'll end up missing the flight."

They made their purchases and waited impatiently as the shop assistant rang up their goods. Loaded with packages, they set off along the corridor leading to the departure gate. Just before they reached it, two tall, broad-shouldered policemen in dark blue pants and short-sleeved shirts stepped in front of Jerry. "Mr. Patterson. Jerry Patterson?"

Jerry looked stunned. "Yes, but what . . . "

The senior, serious faced one, said, "Mr. Patterson we'd like you to come with us."

"Look, I've a plane to catch."

"Not today, sir." As Jerry protested and started to walk away, the other policeman grabbed his wrists and handcuffed him. They immediately walked him off to the side away from a gaping couple who were hurrying to the gate.

CHAPTER 39

Stupefied, Nicole watched Jerry, sandwiched between two large policemen, disappear through a side door. A woman, with an athletic build, dressed in quiet beige slacks and brown silk blouse, materialized at her elbow. "Detective Inspector Johnson, Auckland police. Can I have a word?" She steered Nicole over to a chair.

Nicole's weak knees sank gratefully on to the utilitarian plastic of the chair. "You're in the police?"

"Yes, plain clothes." She produced her wallet and flashed an identity card.

"So what's going on? Our flight leaves in about thirty minutes."

"I'm afraid your friend won't be going on it."

"Why not?"

The inspector's face betrayed nothing. "I'm afraid I don't really know. It's an Interpol thing. They just asked us to bring him in." She looked Nicole in the eyes, her tone sympathetic but firm. "They would like to ask you some questions. So if you come with me, I'll drive you to the station."

"Why on earth should I?" Confusion was turning to outrage.

"They just want to ask you a few questions." Then noticing Nicole's expression, she squared her shoulders and added, "This is only a request. We have no reason to hold you. As far as we are concerned, you are free to go and catch your plane."

"But what does Interpol want me for?"

"They think you might be able to help clarify some things about your friend."

Nicole looked at the last passengers hurrying to the boarding gate. She decided to join them. Then hesitated, did she really want to sit on that long flight not knowing what had happened to Jerry? If she went to the police station, she'd at least find out what was going on. And maybe she could help him. She turned back to the detective.

"Okay, let's go. I need to find out what this is all about." With a final glance at the departing passengers she added, "I need a few minutes to switch my flight until tomorrow. Hope they'll do it at this short notice."

"Don't worry about that. I'll have a word with them. When do you want to go?"

"I'll catch the same flight tomorrow. I need to get back to work." She'd call the office as soon as the flight had been re-scheduled.

They went back to the business class lounge and the policewoman had a quiet word with the woman in an attractive uniform behind the desk. Nicole could not hear what she said, but the woman turned her impeccably made up face to her and with a pleasant smile asked for her ticket and new departure date. She clicked away on her terminal and within minutes, Nicole, clutching her new ticket, followed the policewoman out to her car.

The detective, who said her name was Jill, talked as they drove into the city. She told Nicole the All Black team would be arriving at the airport shortly, asked if she had enjoyed her vacation, and pointed out some new gardens that had been opened. Nicole let the words wash over her, and politely murmured a few replies, while her mind churned endlessly. What was going on? She went over and over their vacation, but couldn't think of any reason for them to take Jerry into custody. But then it clicked, Interpol. It must be something he did in England. But what, what, what?

The car drew into the curb beside the police station. It's attractive rock wall façade, depicting solidity and safety, did nothing to lessen her confusion. She hurried along beside the detective. Jill spoke to the man at the desk then whisked her through to an office where a man in a crisp casual shirt and slacks lounged in a chair hugging a cup of coffee.

He stood up when Nicole arrived and introduced himself. "Brandon Glover, ma'am, Interpol. Can I get you a cup of coffee, or some water?" She could smell his Polo aftershave from her side of the desk.

Nicole's head swam. Why did the policeman have an American accent? "Yes, coffee would be good thank you." She paused a moment, collected herself. "But what I'd like more is an explanation. What have you done with Jerry?"

"He's talking to one of my associates right now. I'm hoping you can help me out. We know very little about him." He nodded to Jill Johnson who was hovering by the door. "Could you rustle up a coffee for Nicole."

Nicole didn't miss the amused look on Jill – the detective inspector's – face as she went to get the coffee.

Brandon settled back in his chair and asked Nicole a string of questions. How long she had known Jerry? Where had she met him? What they had been doing over the past two weeks? When he got to their relationship, he looked deeply skeptical, and in view of the past night, she had to admit it was no longer platonic.

Time dragged on. Nicole finished her coffee. Jill Johnson sat beside her and drank coffee, but did not offer a single word or suggestion. Nicole began to think she was sitting in to make sure this bully-boy American cop didn't pick on her. After all she was an innocent New Zealand citizen as far as Jill knew.

Finally, Nicole reached the end of her tether. "Okay, enough of the questions. Tell me why you're holding Jerry. What do you think he's done?" By this time, she had begun to think this irritating character, who was asking a million questions, was just handling some major bureaucratic screw up.

He sat up straight in his chair. "We're holding him as the prime suspect for the murder of his wife."

Nicole, eyes wide with shock, struggled to protest. "There must be some mistake."

"No ma'am. The body of his wife was found in a cave in Oregon. The search party looking for Jud Jason found it. Jerry Patterson was the last person to have been seen in his wife's company."

Nicole looked at the detective in blank horror.

"We're taking him back to the States tomorrow. He'll stand trial there."

"But, I can't believe it." She shook her head trying to stop the nightmare-like story running in her mind.

Jill Johnson put a reassuring hand on her arm. "They have a lawyer in there with him, and he'll have time once he's in the States to put his defense together." She looked across at the Interpol detective and at his slight nod, she said "Let's go now. I'll find you a motel. We'll call the airport and they'll deliver your bag."

CHAPTER 40

Two days later, Nicole unlocked her cottage door in England. As the door creaked open, she slipped inside and leaned back against its solid reassurance. Her gaze flickered over the brick fireplace with its massive oak mantel, the low beams and small windows that had stood there for a hundred years. The old furniture, worn rugs, gleaming copperware jugs and the comforting smell of wood. Dropping her bags, she walked over and sat in the fireside chair. Settling back, she ran her hand over the woven fabric and relished its feel.

She sat for a long while soaking up silence, solitude and permanence. Finally, she roused herself and once unpacked, checked her emails. The staggering number appalled her but she felt far too tired to care. She riffled through the stack of mail; nothing interesting, not even a postcard from her mother.

After a shower, she decided she should probably eat something, but her stomach clenched at the thought, so she settled for a pot of tea. As she raised the second cup to her lips, the phone rang.

Jan, her friend from Seattle, felt as bewildered by Jerry's arrest as she did, but said his clever ruse of pretending his wife had left him, and his move to England, all showed premeditation. The chance of proving his innocence looked slim. "I feel so cheated. Wasting my sympathy on him when she left."

Nicole heard a Cliff-type rumble in the background, and an irritated "What?" from Jan.

More rumblings, then Jan was back on the line sounding surprised and more than a little angry. "Cliff wants you to know that Jerry wanted to divorce Madison some time back and started proceedings. But he backed off when one of Madison's friends – Sonia, a very sharp attorney – made it crystal clear she would go after him. She promised to take him for every penny he had. The attorney insisted Madison had been a good wife. Cliff said the poor bloke had worked his tail off; worked eighteen hour days while Madison went to the gym and the spa. Now she was going to take all his money."

Nicole tried to grasp what Jan was telling her. Jerry had always talked about Madison with affection. Not a word about any problems. Had she ever really known him?

She realized Jan was still talking " . . . what ticks me off is that Cliff never said a word to me about this. Insists it was a guy thing. He also thinks Jerry got dead unlucky. No one would have found her body if it hadn't been for that search for the pop star. It was a chance in a million that someone would go down into such a remote chasm." She gave a snort of disgust.

Nicole's head spun and the tea churned in her stomach. But Jan was still in full flow. " . . . feel terrible now that I introduced you to him. I hope you didn't get involved. I know you mentioned you'd given him some advice on his apartment."

"No. I just helped him out." Her skin crawled at the thought of her night with a murderer. Those hands. She shuddered. But she still felt too used, raw and vulnerable to talk about it.

Convincing her he wanted to help find Emma, she thought bitterly. He was probably watching to see how she intended to track her down, so he'd know how to counter any moves to find Madison.

She felt bad, too, about lying to her best friend. Maybe she'd tell her about it later. But not now.

Instead she said brightly, "Auckland's changed a lot since I was there last. That new rail system is pretty neat, and " . . . Jan interrupted her with a string of questions and they talked for over half an hour.

⬩⟨⟩⬩

She'd only been back at work for a week but she found herself working twelve-hour days to catch up. Not that she minded. This way she had no time to think about Jerry.

She came home one Thursday evening completely exhausted. After she'd dumped her briefcase by the desk, she went to the bathroom and washed her face in the hope of giving herself the energy to get some food. She looked in the refrigerator. Nothing but some milk, butter, bread and an old lump of cheese that wouldn't appeal to a starving mouse. Well, I suppose I could make a toasted cheese sandwich. The thought wore her out. She slumped down in the fireside chair.

The doorbell rang. "Yoo hoo, it's just me."

Oh hell's teeth, not Iris. The thought of all that chatty energy made her head ache.

But Iris came in with a steaming casserole in her hands. A delicious aroma of beef and garlic wafted in almost overpowering the smell of dog. Iris put the casserole on the table and then opened the bag she had slung over her shoulder. She produced a salad, fruit and some cookies.

"Jeez, thanks, Iris, that's marvelous."

"Don't thank me. Thank Emma."

"Emma? Is she back?" Even as she said it she felt a faint thrill at the idea.

"No way. She loves it where she is. But she sent me strict instructions to feed you at least once a week. She said you never look after yourself."

Tears pricked the back of her eyes. Good old Emma. "Did you talk to her? How's she doing?"

"She loves it there. Has been house hunting for the past week and has picked out something she wants. Adrian will be over in a couple of days to sell their house here."

"How's he doing?"

"He sounds happy too." Iris looked pleased. "He's going to work there the way he used to in Bermuda. Difference is that Emma has a life too. She isn't just running around after him all the time. Mark you, it still sounds as if she's constantly cooking stuff for that photography group."

She picked up her bag. "She also told me I shouldn't stay here too long. I was just to feed you and be on my way." She gave Nicole a long appraising look. "She's right, you look whacked. What you need is more fresh air. Saturday we'll do the heath. Right now I'll leave you to your meal."

After Iris was gone, Nicole went over to the casserole, took a deep appreciative sniff, then decided a glass of wine would round the meal off nicely. She put out cutlery, dished herself a generous portion of salad and casserole, poured a glass of wine and sat back.

After she finished her meal, she took the plate to the kitchen but felt too tired to clear the table. She made a cup of coffee, carried it into the living room, and settled down in her favorite armchair with a book. After the first few pages, her eyes began to droop, she sank deeper into the chair feeling deliciously drowsy. The doorbell rang.

Irritated, she sat up and looked at her watch. Who on earth was it? She stumped over to the door which burst open the minute she undid the latch.

"Hello, Nicki, thought we'd just drop by and say hello darling. We're on our way to Paris." Her mother enveloped her in an energetic, perfumed, hug.

Before Nicole could recover from the surprise – the last postcard had come from St. Petersburg – her mother released her. To be replaced immediately by the hunk, blonde, suntanned, muscular, who gave her a light hug and kissed her on the cheek. "Good to see you Nicki." He was as young as she expected, but there was something very solid and reassuring about him. Maybe it was those rock solid muscles.

Out of the corner of her eye, Nicole could see her mother looking around, noting the one place setting at the table, the book beside the chair. She could almost hear what she was thinking.

Still standing by the door, smiling shyly, but looking awkward, was a hunk look-alike; same broad shoulders, crinkly hair and heart-stopping blue eyes.

"Nicki, say hello to Andy, Scott's cousin. He's working in London, living on his own so we swung by to pick him up. We're all going to Paris for the weekend and thought you should come along."

Unbelievable. Mother still refuses to give up her crusade to get me to marry again. This time irritation was overwhelmed by amusement at her indefatigable mother. She tried to keep a straight face but it was too much. She threw back her head and laughed. Andy – another member of the stay single brigade – after a moment's hesitation, joined in.

At the sight of her mother's astonished expression, Nicole struggled to get her laughter under control, and began to gulp an apology. As she gasped through the first words she caught Andy's eye and suddenly they were both laughing helplessly again.

Paris was going to be a lot of fun.

THE END

Acknowledgements

M any thanks to the Quixotics: Meg Hellyer, Frances Evlin, Mac McCullough, Trish Corbett and Jeanette Kiel for their excellent critiques and unfailing support. My thanks also to Carole George and Sandra Lyon for their very helpful reviews. Also to Leila Kalmbach whose copy editing went way above the call of duty, and to Dave Schlosser for his ever helpful advice.

8623823R00154

Made in the USA
San Bernardino, CA
17 February 2014